CELEBRITY FAKE DATING, BOOK ONE

FAKE DATING
Adrian Hunter

SKYLA SUMMERS

BOOKS BY SKYLA SUMMERS

Celebrity Fake Dating Series

Fake Dating Adrian Hunter

Fake Dating Zac Delavin

Fake Dating Daxton Hawk

Fake Dating Adrian Hunter
Copyright © 2022 by Eliza Luckey

All rights reserved. No part of this book may be used or reproduced in any manner whatsoever without written permission except in the case of brief quotations embodied in critical articles or reviews. This book is a work of fiction. Names, characters, businesses, organizations, places, events and incidents are either a product of the author's imagination or are used fictitiously. Any resemblance to actual persons, living or dead, events, or locales is entirely coincidental.

Contact Information: www.skylasummers.com

ISBN: 978-0-6455663-1-4 (paperback) 978-0-6455663-0-7 (ebook)

Cover Design: Okay Creations

Editor: MK Books Editing

To my husband.
None of this would be possible without you.

And to the gatekeepers who have said no to me 400+ times.
I'll make my own luck.

Chapter One

There were three reasons why graduating high school was the best day of my childhood. One: escaping my small life in Alaska where people only knew me as "Tory's sister" or "the fat girl with pink hair." Two: I was about to embark on a once in a lifetime opportunity of studying fashion in Milan. And three—the biggest reason of all: I would never see Adrian Hunter again.

Seven years later, I'm freaking out because there's no hiding from Adrian at Tory's wedding.

Why does his sister have to marry mine? And why can't they get married on one night, like every other couple does, instead of dragging the celebrations out for an entire week? As of today, I'm living in a nightmare, trapped with Adrian for the next seven days. Shoot me now, please. I would like that very much.

"You're quiet, Verena. You don't like the resort?" Tory's hands fidget behind her back as she watches me explore each room of my bungalow.

"Are you kidding? This resort is a palace. You're

mistaking my Adrian nerves for dislike." I join my sister in the living room. "I see you've put my money to good use."

Dad's heart surgeon salary too. I'm not the only one paying for this behemoth joining of families. If you look up "extravagant wedding" in the dictionary, you'll find reference to this week. It will read: *a secret destination wedding at the tropical Whitsunday Islands, Australia, to prevent paparazzi and rabid fans of Tory's sister from gate-crashing. All guests' flights and accommodation paid for by the Valentine fortune. Oh, and if you're planning on vacationing that week at the Hayman Island Resort, don't bother, because the Valentines have reserved the entire island.*

I am one hundred percent to blame for the extremities needed for this week.

"I still can't believe you gave me that money," Tory says.

I shrug. "I'll sell one of my designs and break even." Plus, I'm hoping my financial contribution makes up for all the pre-wedding events I've skipped out on, and all the other life milestones I've been absent for over the past seven years.

Tory, I'm the worst big sister, I know, but I can't attend your engagement party. My designs are in New York Fashion Week.

Tory, there's no way I can fly back to Sitka for your bridal shower. I'm so sorry, my reality show is filming during that entire month.

In truth, I am the worst big sister, and maid of honor. I could have easily rearranged my schedule. But... ugh... Adrian! Coming face to face with him before necessary was not an option. Even without the hindrance of Adrian, returning to Sitka is the equivalent of reliving the most embarrassing moments of my life all at once. If I went back to the place I grew up, I would be the awkward girl everyone remembers. The nobody. The black sheep of the family.

Correction: I'd be the black sheep of Sitka.

The life I've worked so hard for in New York, my fashion label, my reality show—none of it will erase their view of me. In their eyes, I'll always be an outcast. I can't say seeing them here in Australia will be much different, but at least this isn't anyone's home turf.

"Hey, do you know where the concierge left my luggage?" I open the double doors to my bedroom. It's all deep tones of wood in here, matched with the most beautiful hibiscus aroma. Afternoon sunlight streams through the glass walls, shining onto a canopy bed. But none of my belongings lie waiting.

"I'm sure your luggage will be delivered soon. I'll call the lobby," Tory says.

I step out into the back garden as Tory makes the call. And here I was, innocent little Verena Valentine, thinking I knew what luxury meant. Owning a penthouse in Manhattan with front row views of Central Park has nothing on this resort. This bungalow has its own infinity pool that overlooks the crystal waters surrounding Hayman Island. I can walk out onto my own private section of the beach. Sunsets will be amazing here, sipping a cocktail as I lounge on a pool float. If there's one positive thing about this week, it's that at least I'll be suffering in style.

I take a breath, filling my lungs with the salty sea breeze, and tilt my head up to the sky. The sun's warmth feels beautiful against my skin. Summer in January. I want to kidnap these deadly UV rays and bring them home to obliterate the snow.

My eyelids slide shut, stealing every sweet moment of bliss I can find before the inevitable of facing Adrian. It's a shame that this trip—intended to be a fun getaway for my sister's wedding—will be no vacation at all.

I can do this. I can face my family and all the people from my past. I'm not the girl they remember. I can be civil to Adrian.

I want to support Tory.

I want to support Tory.

"Your luggage is on its way now. You have seven suitcases?" Tory laughs as she joins me outside.

I open one eye to meet her. "You do know who you're talking to, right? Technically I only have six for my belongings. The wedding dresses are in the seventh."

Her face lights up. "Phoebe and I can't wait to see what you've designed for us."

"You'll love them. I promise."

"And your maid of honor dress?"

"Ugly. Absolutely disgusting. No one will be able to look at me."

She swats my arm. "Everyone will be in awe of you. It's been, what, seven years since you were home?"

"So? They watch me on TV."

If anyone's the slightest bit interested in me, it will be so they can find out the dirt on my life and bring gossip to their friends back home. Tory, on the other hand, is Little Miss Perfect in every aspect of life. I don't hold it against her, but there's no denying she's the golden child. The one that makes sensible decisions. My parents have never been prouder than when she announced her acceptance into medical school (in their words, a "sensible" career choice), or the day she got engaged to her high school girlfriend—who just so happens to be the daughter of my parents' closest friends. Aside from college, she's never moved away from Sitka and plans to grow old there with her soon-to-be-wife and the perfect children they'll have one day. All the women in our family are dark-haired Mediterranean beauties, but Tory has inherited superior genes, replicating a Botticelli painting.

"I'm not going to steal your thunder," I say as we lie on a daybed, its sheer curtains flapping in the wind. I'm so exhausted from the transit I could fall asleep right here. Now there's a thought—sleep through every unnecessary moment of these next seven days. "I'm more than happy to sink into the background. No one will even notice me."

"You're beginning to sound like Adrian."

Mention of his name sends me stiff. "Don't compare me to him."

Tory smiles. "You're still hung up on him?"

I scoff and gaze out at the ocean. "The guy told everyone in high school that my middle name is Vagina. It's clearly Virginia, for fuck's sake."

"I forgot about that. You have to admit, in hindsight, it's kind of funny."

"Yeah, well, how about you walk around for a year with everyone calling you *Verena the Vagina* and see how you like it?"

"Hey, you gave it back to him just as bad. I remember that time you swapped the clothes in his gym locker for a dress."

"That was payback and hardly equal," I say. "If anything, it made all the girls love Adrian more, seeing him walk half-naked through school to find clothes. What's his issue now? Doesn't sound like Adrian to be sinking into the background. He's probably annoyed this week isn't about him. I bet you it's a tactic to earn sympathy and make everyone cater to his every need."

"Jeez, listen to you. Haven't enough years passed for you to move on from your falling out?"

I scowl at her, because enough years can never pass when the love of your life breaks your heart.

And gross... I can't believe I just referred to Adrian like that.

"If you must know the issue," Tory says, "Phoebe asked Adrian to be the MC, and he said no."

"Seems kind of rude. I'm glad, though. Saves me from having to look at his face."

"Don't start. You said you would behave yourself around him."

"Relax," I tell her. "I don't even plan on speaking with him."

"You know, there was a time when you two were best friends."

"Tory, there was a time when I was in *love* with the guy. Don't remind me of how pathetic I used to be."

She gasps, sitting up tall. "You were in *love* with him?"

"Come on, you had to have known that."

"I thought there may have been a crush involved. Remind me again why you hated each other so much?"

"*Hate.*"

"What?"

"You used past tense. I still hate him. And I'm not discussing this with you any longer."

Tory's phone rings. Perfect timing. "It's the bride. I should go," she chimes, then wraps me in a tight hug. "It's so good to see you again. We need to spend lots of time together this week."

"Definitely."

Her arms are warm around me, and I realize I *have* missed

this. Us as sisters. We FaceTime occasionally but I can't remember the last time I saw Tory in person. To be honest, I'm surprised she asked me to be her maid of honor. We were close as kids but have slowly drifted apart over the years.

Tory hops off the daybed with her phone still ringing in her hand. "Verena, I'll give you some time to get settled in. Make sure you're not late for the welcome dinner tonight. Oh! I almost forgot." She pulls a folded piece of paper from her pocket and hands it to me. "Here's this week's schedule. See you tonight."

The schedule is planned down to the minute with events I'm required to attend highlighted in yellow, all leading up to the wedding at the end of the week. I don't know why I'm surprised at the attention to detail. When we were kids, Tory's favorite hobby was organization. I guess nothing has changed.

I flop back onto the daybed as soon as Tory leaves my bungalow.

Ten minutes pass.

Twenty.

My luggage still hasn't arrived.

I make a call to the lobby, but no one answers. I've got thousands of dollars of clothes in those suitcases. Are they just lying in a pile in the lobby?

Five minutes later, I make another call, and there's still no answer. I begin thumbing a text to my two bodyguards hanging out in the next bungalow over, the ones who Tory gave strict instructions are meant to be lying low this week and pretending like they don't exist unless I'm placed in a life-or-death situation. The text goes something like this: *Help! This is totally a life-or-death situation. My luggage hasn't arrived, and I can't leave the safety of my bungalow in case I run into Adrian. Please bring my bags to me and I'll give you both a pay raise.*

I delete the message before sending, hating the power Adrian already holds over me. If I cave in and hide from him, he wins by default.

A further twenty minutes pass and I'm still in my bungalow, knees bouncing as I rock back and forth on the bathtub rim, psyching myself up to leave my bungalow. I'm a despicable excuse for a woman. Months of mental preparation have all flown out the window and I'm a ball of anxiety over this man that I've spent my entire life either loving or hating.

There's only one thing that snaps me out of this funk.

My babies.

And when I say *babies*, I'm referring to my beautiful clothes that are sitting out in the open, alone and afraid, vulnerable to being kidnapped. And besides, I am Verena fucking Valentine. Who the hell is Adrian? Some nobody who peaked in high school.

I puff up my long, dark curls, refresh my makeup, and push up my breasts. After a day in transit, I'm not in my finest form. But I wore this uncomfortable yet magnificent dress in preparation for the slightest chance that Adrian would see me arriving at the resort. There's no way I'm letting him witness me in anything other than a stunning outfit—designed by me, obviously. The dress is short and floral with real-life roses adorning the bodice. Practical? Not at all. The roses will be dead within a day. But you don't get anywhere in the fashion industry by playing it safe. My stilettos are a pain in the ass too, but this situation is worth sacrificing comfort.

After a five-minute walk through the resort where I harness my best Kendall Jenner catwalk strut for Adrian precautions, I arrive at the lobby, finding a group of paramedics. I officially feel bad for complaining about my luggage. Resort staff are gathered by a stretcher, peering down at one of their colleagues.

"I'm fine," the sick staff member says, pale as anything in the stretcher. I lose count of how many times he repeats himself.

"You collapsed," a paramedic tells him. "Better to be safe than sorry."

That eases my guilt a little. No one is seriously harmed. And thank God Adrian is not here.

I scan the lobby for my luggage. As with everything else at this resort, I'm standing in pure luxury. There's a coastal theme shared among each building. It's an open lobby with no walls, only columns and a thatched roof. And there, across the lobby, are my babies. Given the current health emergency among staff, surely I can take charge and wheel my own luggage back to my bungalow? I don't want to be a burden to anyone. But seven suitcases? I'll need to make a few trips.

I attempt to position the first suitcase upright so that it's on its wheels. The suitcase is heavy, though, and I strain every muscle in my back as I try to lift it. After a series of unflattering grunts and swear words, not to mention the devastating number of petals that have fallen off my dress, I go stumbling backward, landing flat on my ass. I'm quick to my feet, hot with embarrassment as I straighten my dress and look around. Thankfully, no one notices me. It would appear everyone is still consumed with the paramedics. With more caution, I move onto the next suitcase, and crap, this one is heavier.

I'm bending over—tugging at the handles, pretty sure

my dress is about to ride up my ass and reveal my G-string—when I hear a deep voice say my name.

My eyes shoot open. I know that voice. It's ingrained in my memory and will remain there for the rest of eternity.

Fuck. Fuck. Fuck. Not like this.

Adrian Hunter is not meant to see me for the first time with my ass sticking in the air and me sweating over luggage. I'm meant to look hot in a bikini, laughing in the distance with a bunch of sexy men chatting me up by the pool. He's meant to think, *Fuck, why was I such a dick to Verena all those years ago?*

Bracing myself with a deep breath, I stand tall and turn to face Adrian.

And wow, this is bad. This is one hundred times worse than I anticipated. Coming into this week, I thought I prepared myself well for our reunion. I memorized a list of amazing comebacks to all of his rude comments that are sure to fly my way. I designed a flawless wardrobe and have been hitting the treadmill harder than usual. But I forgot to prepare myself for the "Adrian charm."

It's true what they say about men getting better with age. Adrian is so beautiful that part of me thinks he might be Satan. No one can look this good without selling their soul to the devil and then murdering the bastard to become his successor.

Adrian is taller than I remember, and his shoulders have filled out. Either he runs daily or spends serious time in the gym. I mean, look at those muscles poking through his shirt. *Hot damn.*

My fingers tingle with the urge to twist the dark lock of hair hanging over his eyes. The thought must be written all over my face because the next moment, Adrian tucks the stray hair back. Now he's smiling at me. No dark glint of malice is in his eyes. Just a pure, genuine smile. The sight of him looking at me like this is a punch in the stomach, reminding me of all the good times we shared. If it weren't for all the bad blood between us, I swear I could fall in love with Adrian all over again.

Oh, fuck.

Chapter Two

I've figured out Adrian Hunter. He's bringing his A game to this wedding by using the same tactic as me: look irresistible to piss the other one off. He's calculated the exact angle to stand in this lobby so the afternoon sun gives his skin an enviable glow. He deliberately wore navy blue because he knows the color is delicious on him. And that cologne, what is it—*Verena Kryptonite?*

"Hello, Adrian." The words snap out of my mouth with an acidic taste.

Adrian's smile eases into something smug. He knows his presence is pushing my buttons, and it pleases every bone in his body. Perhaps I should act happy? That would really set him off.

"Searching for a longer dress in your luggage?" he asks.

I bite my tongue so he doesn't see how furious that question makes me. This is how Adrian works—no blatantly rude comments, but instead, he is the master of subtle remarks that have snide undertones, designed to keep me up all night ruminating over him. The kind of comments that catch me so off guard I'm too speechless to say anything in return, and it isn't until hours later that I've developed a comeback, but my time for glory has passed.

I'm too fat to wear a dress this short is what Adrian really means. I scroll through my brain for that list of snarky comebacks I prepared, but of course, they've all abandoned me.

When I don't reply, Adrian continues, "I'm surprised to see you alone. Don't you normally have a group of minions running around after you?"

He's on a roll.

"*Assistants*," I correct. "Contrary to what you may believe, I can manage on my own."

"So, no plus-one to carry your luggage?"

"So, you're still a jerk?" There we go. Not my finest comeback, but at least it's something.

"I'm asking a friendly question."

"Well, don't. *Goodbye.*" I turn back to my luggage.

"I see you're still acting like a bitch."

My blood boils. I grab the handle on two of my suitcases and pull them after me as I exit the lobby. In a perfect world, my hips would be swaying with a sexy walk, but the suitcases are heavy, and I end up yanking them.

Adrian doesn't get the hint I want to be left alone, and he catches up, walking alongside me on the garden path.

"Why are you following me?" I hiss.

"Come on now, babe, there's no need to take that tone with me. I'm interested to know what my childhood friend has been up to."

"Read the news. Turn on the TV."

"Oh, I have. Quite some interesting stuff as of lately."

I freeze, knowing that for the past six months, all the media have been covering is my breakup with Jake. You can't look anywhere without seeing a heading that says

Fashion sensation cheated on by long-time boyfriend, or *Verena turns to alcohol to wash away the pain.* I was out drinking one time.

One time!

I keep walking, ducking my head to avoid overhanging palm leaves. "I bet you were laughing with pleasure over my failures."

"Mostly."

"What a superb human you've grown into, Adrian. Rave to me all about your success."

"You haven't asked Phoebe or Tory about me?"

"I haven't thought about you in seven years."

He chuckles, strolling beside me with hands in his pockets. "I don't believe that for one second. I know you, Verena Valentine. You would have been cursing the day that my sister proposed to Tory. Your little heart would have been beating so fast at the thought of seeing me again."

"Right, of course," I deadpan. "So, enlighten me, what has the marvelous Adrian Hunter been doing all these years?"

"Living in London. Working as an accountant."

Knew that already. "Look at you, big shot. Let me guess, married with kids?"

"I'm in the same boat as you, actually. Newly single."

"She cheated on you, too? Can't say I blame her."

"There was no cheating."

My bungalow comes into view as we turn a corner. Part of me wonders if I should walk in a different direction so Adrian doesn't know where I'm living for the next seven days. But I can't tug at these bags for much longer, and there's still five back at the lobby.

I stop for a breather, refusing to look straight at Adrian

because I'm too afraid for my ovaries. "Why are you telling me about your love life? And what makes you think I care?"

"Just trying to bond with my childhood bestie."

"I'm not interested in hearing about your sad life."

Adrian leans one shoulder against a palm tree and grins at me. He pauses for a moment, deep in thought, then licks his lips. "I've got an offer for you."

"I don't want to hear it."

"Verena..." He sighs, running a hand through his hair. That stupid lock of hair falls back out of place, hanging over his forehead. "Can't we just...put the past behind us and start fresh? After all, our sisters are getting married. We'll be as good as family. You can't escape me for another seven years."

"Don't flatter yourself. I've been living my life, not scheming ways to avoid you."

"You honestly didn't come to the engagement party because of work?"

"Yes. You had nothing to do with the decision."

He smirks, knowing me too well to believe the lie. "Regardless, I want to move on. You and I can be friends again, right?"

"You're serious? You're not trying to trick me?" I glance at the palm trees around us. "Where are the cameras? Is this some kind of prank?"

Adrian places a hand over his heart. "Honest to God. You're forgiven for switching my biology paper to a bunch of swear words and getting me suspended from school."

I scowl at him. "You're still not forgiven for all the crap you put me through, but if it makes this week slightly less miserable, I guess we can have a truce."

"That's a start. So, about this offer—"

"Being civil to each other wasn't the offer?"

"Of course not," he laughs. "I need your help."

"Adrian, you are unbelievable. This is why you want to clear the air, so you can get something from me? I should have known this was too good to be true."

I grab my luggage and make a move for my bungalow, but Adrian steps in front of me and my breasts bump into those perfect muscles in his chest. Heat rushes to my cheeks, because now all I can think about is seeing him with his shirt off. He laughs again, and I'm beginning to think he's a frickin' mind reader.

"Verena, I'm being genuine. Hear me out. I would think you of all people could sympathize with me, given the disaster of your last relationship."

The blush in my cheeks turns into hot rage. "What does *that* have to do with anything?"

"If you'll be quiet for one moment, I can explain. Here's my current dilemma. Phoebe is friends with my ex and has invited her to the wedding. So, as you might guess, this week will be awkward for me."

My face perks up. "Your week will be a nightmare? Fantastic."

"A complete nightmare. But your situation is more pathetic. You got dumped by some dude a few months ago. *And* he cheated on you."

My teeth grind together. "Adrian, I could hit you right now. What is your problem with me? I told my sister I would be civil toward you, but you're even more of a jerk than the last time I saw you."

"Calm down. All I'm saying is, won't it look pathetic for Verena Valentine to be riding solo at a wedding, especially after the cheating scandal? Everyone will pity you. I've had people offer their sympathies toward my situation, and I'm a boring nobody. I have to watch my ex be happy with her date, when all I want is for her to be here with me instead. We already had an awkward encounter at the pool where I saw her kissing her new guy. There's no way I can survive an entire week of this."

"What's your point?"

"I want us to help each other out of a sticky situation." Adrian scrunches fingers through his hair, cringing. "Look, this is painful for me to ask, but do you wanna pretend we're here together? Like, dating?"

I burst out laughing. "Okay, I must need my ears checked because I know you didn't suggest what I think I heard."

"I'm serious. You're Verena Valentine. The world loves you. It will be the perfect antidote to my dilemma. My ex will be jealous if she sees me with you. They say you always want what isn't yours, right? By the end of the week, she'll be begging me to take her back. And I'd be doing you a favor, too. No one will pity you."

"Wow. You are really something."

"Is that a *yes*?"

I continue to my bungalow, purposefully wheeling my luggage over his foot. "It's a *fuck you*, Adrian."

Chapter Three

"The dickhead asked me to be his fake girlfriend—so he can win his ex-girlfriend back—after he said I'm fat and pathetic!" I shout into FaceTime back in my bungalow. I'm perched on the bathroom counter wearing nothing but a towel as I shave my legs for tonight's welcome dinner. And okay, Adrian didn't use the words *fat* and *pathetic* to describe me, but he implied as much.

"What a jealous piece of shit," Darius's deep voice growls through my phone screen while he sits at the sewing machine in my New York office.

As my personal assistant and best friend, he's dressed in the best, sporting a pinstriped suit I designed for him. His signature slicked back, dark hair is a mess from the number of times he's raked angry fingers through it during this conversation. If I ever decide to sell menswear, Darius has the exact look I want modelling the line. The exact look when he's not fuming over Adrian, that is. Everything about Darius is sleek and suave. The bone structure in his face is strong and masculine. His dark skin adds extra depth to the shredded muscles in his torso.

Yeah, I've seen him without his shirt on multiple times. It's a nice view.

"Verena, women kill to have your curves. You want to know what Adrian's problem is? He's annoyed that you're the one who came out on top after all these years." Darius has never met Adrian. He's just heard me rant about him non-stop in the lead-up to this wedding. Regardless, his words are a comfort.

"I need you here." My voice comes out as a whine. That's how desperate I am. "There's no way I can survive the week without you."

"You're not stealing Darius from me," a second male voice says from Darius' end of the call. Though the owner of the voice is out of sight, the depressed tone tells me it's my other closest friend, Zac. "Penny and I are on the rocks again and I need Darius' support. I don't know if I can save our marriage this time."

Darius repositions his phone camera, bringing into view Zac, who's lying on the ground, staring up at the ceiling with a look of despair on his face as if he's given up on life. So, nothing out of the usual for him. "Oh, yeah, I forgot to tell you we have company," Darius says. "You see the stress I'm dealing with? Two friends in crisis and meeting business deadlines for you while you're vacationing in paradise."

I run the razor up my leg. "What happened with Penny this time?"

"We had a fight last night." Zac smooths a hand over his black hair. "A gossip site reported that I'm sleeping with my co-star for this new musical I've been cast in—which obviously isn't true. But Penny has it in her mind that I'm trying to get even for the affair she had. She never came home last night and hasn't answered any of my calls."

I so badly want to give Zac my speech of *Why are you fighting for your marriage when she cheated on you? Leave her! I left the asshole who cheated on me and I'm better off,* but he's heard those words hundreds of times and my input has never changed his mind. Despite the miserable mood the marriage always has Zac in, he's a romantic at heart and remains committed to Penny. He says he doesn't want to lose his high school sweetheart and that they'll work through their issues. He knows my opinion on that too, that all she's working through is his money. Right now, though, he needs an ally on his side. A friend to support his decisions. I'm not here to rub salt in his wounds.

"Can I do anything to help?" I ask him.

"There's nothing anyone can do."

"I don't know about that. It sounds like you and Penny need an escape from the media and a chance to reconnect with each other. What if I organize for you two to spend a weekend in Paris? You always say how much you loved your honeymoon there."

"That's nice of you, but the media can still find us in Paris."

"Ahh!" I throw my arms up, rejoicing as a brilliant idea hits me. "Why don't I fly you both to the island I'm on? I've gone to so many lengths to stop the public from knowing I'm here."

Zac sits up with a sudden look of determination. "You actually make a good point. This could work. Maybe a vacation is *exactly* what Penny and I need."

"Yes!" I squeal. "Darius, you have to come to Australia too. I'm having a mental breakdown over Adrian and need you with me for moral support."

Darius cuts a thread from the garment he's sewing. "What's the point of me being there if you have Zac?"

"Zac's focus will be on his marriage. I need you for all the times he won't be around."

"You've left me with a ton of work in the office."

"Screw the work. It can wait." I toss my razor in the sink and rummage through my perfume collection.

"Use the Dior fragrance I gave you for your birthday," Darius says. "You'll have everyone kneeling at your feet."

"I want *Adrian* kneeling at my feet. *He's* the pathetic one. I can't believe I let him walk all over me like that."

"What about all the insults we devised?"

"You guys devised insults?" Zac asks. "That kind of *is* pathetic. And yet, I feel left out."

I give Zac the finger. "Not insults. We created a list of defensive replies because that's how dire this situation is. But I can't remember a single one of them when I look at Adrian. You guys, Adrian is beautiful. He's the most gorgeous thing I've seen in my life."

Darius nods at Zac. "More gorgeous than Mr. Heartthrob over here?"

Despite the miserable side of Zac we always see, when he steps into the public eye, he knows how to turn on the charm. All the ladies and teen girls swoon for him. We met two years back on my show when my manager hired him to give me singing lessons. He'd just finished a movie adaptation of this hot new musical and I would have jumped him myself if we'd both been single.

"Adrian is a hundred times more gorgeous than Zac," I tell them. "I'm in serious trouble. Look, Darius, just say you'll come to Australia. I'm freaking out. In all the years we've known each other, when have you seen me freak out?"

"Only that time you were confined to the bathroom after mistakenly eating gluten at your fashion show in—"

"Jesus Christ. I think I've made my point. Adrian is my weakness. I'll do anything to get you here. Accommodation will be free, and you guys won't have to fly commercial. I'll send my private jet back to New York this very second."

"I'm sold," Zac says. "If I can track down Penny."

"Verena—"

"No, Darius. Don't make me be a bitch and demand it of you as your boss." I'm running a straightening iron through my hair now because what the heck is with the humidity in Australia? "Whoever suggested this wedding take place in a tropical location is a fucking idiot."

"I believe that was you," Darius says. The sewing machine hums as he glides fabric beneath the needle.

"Well, I'm a fucking idiot. Look how frizzy my hair is."

"Yeah, it's not great," Zac agrees.

I glare at Zac and he shuts up. "Okay, Darius, think of this as a business trip. Or that I'm paying you to take a vacation. How could you turn down the Whitsundays?" I pick up my phone and flash it around the bungalow, giving Darius a mini tour of the resort's luxury. "You'll be in paradise. All you have to do is come here and be moral support. I'll organize for Sarah to run the office."

Darius lets out a huff of air. "If I arrive at that resort, all the guests will think we're dating."

He has a point. Rumors spread that we're secretly dating ever since my show aired an episode of Darius and me attending our weekly Latin dance class. The dance we were learning together was steamy, I'll give them that. There was a lot of ass grabbing, hips rubbing against each other, and heated eye contact. But for us, everyone's accusations of our romance are laughable, considering Darius is gay. I suppose they assume he's straight because he doesn't fall into the typical stereotypes of a gay man. He's made the decision to conceal his sexuality from the public, and I'm happy to keep the secret with him if that's what he wants.

I've lost count of how many times someone on *TMZ* has commented on our relationship, saying, *You can't fake that kind of chemistry*. It doesn't help that the two of us are joined at the hip, on and off the show, or that we have countless fan sites dedicated to the shipping of Darena. Or as I prefer to call us: Varius. No matter how many statements we've issued to the public about only being friends, they never believe us.

But... hang on a second.

"Darius, you're a genius! All the guests *will* think we're together. Adrian won't bother me *and* he'll be annoyed that I'm succeeding in life with a new boyfriend."

"This is messed up."

Zac pats him on the shoulder. "Totally messed up, but you live for drama."

"I do," Darius agrees.

"Come on," I beg. "*Please*. Say yes."

Darius continues sewing. "My Middle Eastern hair will hate the humidity as much as yours."

"So? We'll suffer together."

I know I've won when Darius leans back in his chair and sighs. "You're doing all of this because of Adrian Hunter?"

"Yes!" The word bursts from my throat so loud I'm sure my bodyguards in the next bungalow can hear.

"Tell me again why this guy has so much power over you."

"You know why."

"Yeah, you loved him and now you hate him," he drawls, placing the garment to the side and looking straight into the camera lens with his massive brown eyes. "Listen,

Verena, if I'm traveling across the world to play up this romantic crap between us, I want to hear the whole story."

The story that I have refused to talk about in any kind of detail over the past seven years. But desperate times call for desperate measures. With a loud exhale, I launch into our history, starting all the way back at conception.

Our mothers have always been the closest of friends. They were pregnant with Adrian and me at the same time. We can practically say we've known each other since being in the womb. The two of us were best friends since day one. We went to school together. We spent every afternoon playing together in the backyard. Everyone joked about our future, saying we were destined to marry each other. Secretly, I adored when they made those comments. I'd been infatuated with him from as young as I can remember.

Our dynamic took a swift change once we entered high school. Adrian hit a growth spurt. His shoulders broadened, his voice deepened, and he shot up in height. My best friend turned gorgeous, and suddenly I wasn't the only one in awe of him. All the girls wanted to be around Adrian, and boys wanted to be his friend. Everyone liked him. He was the most popular kid in school, and anyone could see he loved it. The attention was like a drug to him.

Meanwhile, I stayed the same. Puberty hit me later. I was a child beside Adrian. I hated the way he now looked at other girls. I hated how his time was divided a hundred different ways, instead of directed all at me. He moved on with his life while I stood still—a loner girl with a sketchbook as her only friend. The difference between Adrian and me was that I didn't need a large group of friends to feel happy. I didn't need to be the center of attention. All I wanted was him.

Come junior year, we weren't on talking terms. He was

embarrassed to be seen around me, and I was plain pissed off at him. If it were somehow possible, Adrian had grown even more handsome. He was captain of the baseball team, never missed a party, and more than once I'd seen him hidden behind a school building, pressing a girl against the wall with his mouth while sliding a hand up her skirt. There was no doubt in my mind he took girls to bed. Adrian oozed sexual energy. Everything about him screamed sex, sex, SEX! I'm surprised I didn't get pregnant just by looking at him. But of course, that didn't happen, because here I was, heavier than ever, going through my emo stage of fluorescent pink hair with terrible bangs and always dressed in black. His immaculate conception sperm wouldn't go anywhere near me.

On the odd chance Adrian and I were forced into social situations together—like family gatherings—the interaction between us was stale and filled with awkward chitchat. He struggled to hold eye contact with me. He'd constantly be scrolling through his phone, giving me one-word replies. I hated him, yet that didn't stop me from being so pathetically in love with him. There wasn't one moment during each day that Adrian Hunter wasn't on my mind. When I went to sleep at night, my hand would slip between my legs with thoughts of him.

In senior year of high school, my worst nightmare came true. Word spread around school that I was in love with Adrian, making me the laughingstock. I sat in a bathroom stall that day, crying during my lunch break because I couldn't enter the cafeteria without being taunted. Through the crack in the door, I saw two girls prettying themselves up in the mirror. Becky and Tara, the school's head cheerleaders.

"Can you believe that Vera chick, or whatever her name

is?" Becky laughed. "Does she actually think she has a chance with Adrian?"

"Probably," Tara said, brushing her golden Barbie-doll hair. "She stands no chance. He already asked me to the school dance."

That made me cry harder. I didn't have the strength to leave that bathroom stall for the rest of the school day. Even when the home bell rang, I waited another hour before I braved the school grounds. But that was still too soon.

"Verena!"

Fuck. Fuck. Fuck.

With one glance over my shoulder, I spotted Adrian and a group of his friends heading my way. My pace quickened, and with it, running footsteps came up behind me.

"Hey, Verena, wait." Adrian overtook me and blocked my path.

My gaze fell to the ground so he couldn't see how bloodshot my eyes were from crying. Behind me, I could feel the approaching doom of his friends.

"Look, Adrian, whatever you've heard—"

"Will you come to the dance with me?"

What?

All of his friends started laughing—his date, Barbie-doll Tara, among them. What the hell was this? A joke between Adrian and his friends? Ask the loser to the dance just to embarrass her? Public humiliation at its worst. Adrian and I hadn't so much as spoken a proper sentence to each other in years.

"Fuck you, Adrian. I wouldn't be caught dead with you."

His lips twitched in amusement. Seconds later, he spilled into laughter, joining the rest of his friends. My pulse became deafening in my ears and my body turned red hot, threatening to burst with tears. I stalked off before Adrian could gain the satisfaction of making me cry.

"Nice one, man," Thomas Huxley said. The slap of a high five rang through the air.

"You should have seen the look on her face," Adrian laughed. "What a loser."

That was the day I stopped loving him. I never went to the school dance, but two weeks later, after the big night, photos spread around the school of Adrian kissing Tara on stage in front of the entire student body.

Call me petty, but revenge became my best friend. The bastard needed to pay for what he'd done to me. And so began the Verena versus Adrian wars.

When I finish telling Darius and Zac the story, an explosion of swear words erupts from their end of the phone call.

"Verena," Darius growls, "nobody treats my girl that way and gets away with it. Send your jet back to America immediately. We're coming to Australia."

Chapter Four

The restaurant is crowded with wedding guests when I arrive at the welcome dinner. I'm a little late, but in my defense, every moment of my afternoon was utilized wisely. After I finished telling Darius and Zac about my history with Adrian, Darius and I spent an hour on FaceTime deciding what dress I should wear tonight while Zac left in search for Penny. I changed outfits multiple times, indecisive of whether I should choose a black dress or blue. In the end, Darius convinced me to settle for a red one I designed —a short and playful number that hugs my chest and flares out like a wildflower, dancing above my knees. Couture at its finest.

Then, on my way to the dinner, I had to make a detour to the lobby to organize a bungalow for Zac and Penny. I didn't bother informing staff about Darius' arrival. He can share my bungalow, considering we'll be playing up this romantic tension the world believes we have.

The welcome dinner is at the resort's cliffside restaurant with an ocean view I'm certain would be stunning during daylight hours. Torches light the venue, flickering in the wind and offering a dim glow on everyone's skin, which I'm grateful for since it hides my frizzy hair. Thanks, Australian humidity.

The most awkward part of arriving at dinner is finding people to socialize with. All the wedding guests are scattered throughout the restaurant, standing in small groups with a champagne in their hand and chatting away busily. People do stop and stare at me, but it's not in an *oh, look, a celebrity!* kind of way. There's judgment in their eyes.

My two bodyguards are hanging out on the perimeter of the event, sharing a meal, and looking casual for once. Is it pathetic that I'm considering hiding out with them?

It totally is. I need to put on my big-girl pants and face the guests.

I did the awkward meet and greet with my family earlier in the day, so when Mom places a sloppy kiss on my cheek, it's not quite so uncomfortable as the first time. Now I can say, *Hey, how have you been since our last catch up five hours ago in your bungalow?* instead of, *Hey, how have you been since our last catch up five years ago?*

Mom pulls me over to the table where my four aunts sit, and my cheeks get attacked by four more wet kisses. I've decided it's an old person thing. Maybe an Italian thing too. They don't know how to kiss without ruining other people's makeup.

My mom and her sisters all look the same: short and stocky with rich skin and dark bob cuts. Each one of them have purple circles under their eyes like someone punched them. Love that for me, a clear-cut image of what genetics has in store. My goal in life is to defy aging. Seriously, I'm praying cosmetic surgery will keep me young forever.

"Honey, you look lovely." Mom rubs the fabric of my dress between her fingers. "Did you design this outfit?"

"I sure did. You like?"

"I *love*." She smiles at my aunts. "Isn't my daughter talented?"

Aunt Maria squeezes my hand. "We can't wait to see the wedding dresses."

"You know, Verena," Aunt Mary-Rose says, "we watch every episode of your show. It's the best part of our week."

Okay, this interaction with my family isn't so bad. Things are actually going well. Mom and her sisters are being nice. *Really* nice.

I smile back at my aunts, shocked. "You all watch my show?"

"Of course we do," Aunt Mary-Rose tells me.

"I didn't think a reality show about fashion would be your kind of thing, but I'm glad you enjoy it."

"Are you kidding?" Aunt Rose-Mary says. Yes, my grandparents thought it was a good idea to call one of their daughters Rose-Mary and the other Mary-Rose. "The fashion part is great and watching you and Darius together is hilarious. I always knew you would make it big in this world. You have too much personality not to."

I can't tell if she's teasing me, but I'll take her words as a compliment. They're the truth, anyway. Sure, my designs earned attention based off pure talent while I attended fashion school in Milan, but talent isn't always enough. My opportunities for success stemmed from my charisma, having a quirky flare, and using those traits to form friendships with people in high places. Those contacts then set me up with the right connections in New York. My label received a ton of publicity and blew up in no time. Before I knew it, I'd landed my own reality show.

"So, have you seen Adrian yet?" Mom asks me, then winks at her sisters. "These two go way back."

"Yes, Mom," I drone, knowing where this conversation is heading. Even after all the hurtful encounters between me and Adrian, she's still set on me marrying the guy.

"Isn't he a looker?"

"Why don't *you* date him, then?"

They all laugh. Mom wraps an arm around my shoulder, pulling me to her. "Do you all hear the things that come out of this one's mouth? You haven't changed a bit, sweetheart. Verena was always my problem child. Never had an issue with Victoria, but there wasn't a single week that went by where I wasn't called up to their school because of something Verena did." She rattles it off, like my aunts are only hearing this for the first time.

Aunt Gloria rubs my arm, laughing as she adds to Mom's comment. "Do you remember when the school called for the fire department because Verena climbed so high up a tree that she couldn't get down?"

The five of them throw their heads back with laughter, drowning out my explanation that I was trying to save a cat.

Mom wipes tears from her eyes. "The whole school was watching and could see up her dress."

Aunt Maria slaps her knee. "Someone even took a video of it, and the recording went viral. The camera was zoomed right in and showed your underwear wedged up your butt."

I spoke too soon. This encounter with my mom and aunts is horrendous. I swear one of their favorite pastimes is embarrassing me. They did it all throughout my adolescence, and it appears nothing has changed now that I'm an adult.

I blow a lock of hair out of my face and search the restaurant, hoping to find a more reasonable group of people to talk to. People who won't bring up embarrassing memories from my past.

"Hey, Mom, I just saw Aria. I'm going to say hi to her."

"Oh, fantastic. Have some cousin time. Make sure you come back to us. We need to hear all the details about that good-for-nothing boyfriend who broke your heart. You poor girl."

I race out of their company before any of them have the chance to say one more thing that makes me feel two inches tall. I don't plan on talking with Aria at all. She teased me about my weight when we were kids. But as luck has it, she seeks me out with lips beaming from ear to ear.

Aria's expression quickly morphs into confusion when she looks me up and down. "Verena, I hardly recognize you. I watch your show. The camera must use glamor filters because you look bigger in real life."

Hello to you too.

She'd make a good team with Adrian.

My grandparents are no better when I see them. They tell everyone who walks by that their fondest memory of me is as a five-year-old child when I sleepwalked naked through the house.

When Tory introduces me to one of her bridesmaids, I remember why I never liked her friends when we were kids. Stacy—who I've just learned classifies herself as the maid of honor because I've been absent from the wedding preparations—has been chatting to me for thirty minutes now. She's blond, tanned, married to a doctor, and is Tory's best friend from high school who spent regular time at our house growing up. So, you'd think she would know my name is Verena but apparently not.

"Vera, I'm sure being a career woman has its moments," Stacy tells me. "But I must say, there's nothing more fulfilling than running a home and greeting your husband when he returns after a long day at work. I'm not saying what that man did to you was right. Cheaters are scumbags. But men have needs. Perhaps you should find more of a work-life balance."

I snatch a flute glass off a passing waiter's tray and swallow the champagne in one go. "You want one?"

"Oh, no." Stacy waves her hand, laughing. "Mike and I are trying to get pregnant. It's going to happen any day now. Mike can't keep his hands off me. Are you thinking about having kids? I suppose not. You've got that big shiny career of yours, don't you?"

How is Tory friends with this woman?

"Stacy, do you know the other bridesmaid, Nia? I'd like to meet her if she's around." I don't know why I say that. An excuse to get away from Stacy? Nia's probably worse.

"Yes. Nia, darling," she calls, waving over a lady to join us. "This is Tory's sister."

I'm certain she introduces me this way on purpose. After all the accomplishments I've achieved, I'm still only *Tory's sister*.

"Yes, I know who you are," Nia says to me. She's a dark-haired, pretty little thing, with dark skin to match. "I've watched your reality show. I like the name. *Valentine's Day*. It's a smart play on your last name. Kind of ironic, though, considering what happened in your love life."

Okay, wow, this is actually happening. These people really don't have any filter. I grab another flute glass, because apparently alcohol is my only ally tonight.

"Darius is *so* handsome," Nia adds. "I have a crush on him. He's the best part of the show."

"I'll tell him you said so—"

Stacy speaks over me, like she's bored with this conversation. "Have you met Phoebe's side of the bridal party?"

"Not yet."

"Well, there's the best man, Josh, and a bridesmaid, Sukhi."

"Who's the third?"

"Oh, that was meant to be Nate," Stacy says. "But poor thing, his mother was rushed to the hospital this past week and he's had to remain in Sitka to care for her. Unfortunately, we've got an uneven number in the bridal party."

"I'm sure it won't impact the big day too much."

"Everything will still be great. It just means you'll be the odd one out in photos and riding solo during the first dance."

I choke on my champagne. "What? No. They always pair the maid of honor and best man."

"Traditionally, yes," Nia giggles. "But there's nothing traditional about this wedding."

"Have Tory and Phoebe approved this?"

Stacy gives me a sympathetic look that I suspect is fake. "I don't want to bother them with something so trivial. Josh and I know each other well. We'd like to pair up. Nia and Sukhi are good friends too. We thought it would be easier this way, instead of one of us dancing with you, who we don't know at all."

Great. I'll be doing a couple's dance on my own, in front of everyone. You'd think the bridal party would all raise their hand to dance with a celebrity, but not this crowd.

"So, Tory asked me to organize a bachelorette party for her," I say. "I was thinking—"

"Oh, Nia and I have taken care of that. We've hired strippers. The only thing you need to worry about are the bridal dresses."

I don't know what I did to cause this cold manner from these two women. Perhaps they saw something they didn't like about me in the media. Maybe they're annoyed that I haven't helped with the wedding planning. Whatever the reason, this is Tory's wedding, and it would be nice for us to all get along.

"I'd like to contribute something," I tell them. "At least let me dress the bridal party for the bachelorette party. I have seven suitcases full of clothes because I don't know how to travel lightly. Everyone can pick one of my designs to wear. You two ladies will look fabulous."

Stacy giggles, pressing her fingertips to her lips. "That's very kind of you, Valery, but you're a larger size than the rest of us."

Ouch. Her reply stings like a slap in the face. I have curves but I'm not that much bigger than the rest of the bridal party. And does Stacy not realize I can alter the dresses to fit everyone?

"My name is Verena," I correct when words catch up with me, but Stacy has already stepped away from me, calling after her husband. Nia leaves without a goodbye.

That about sums up how the rest of my interactions with the guests at this welcome dinner go. People are adamant to talk to me, yet not one of them exchanges back-and-forth conversation. They're all speaking at me, instead of to me, determined to prove how great their life is, like we're in some rivalry. I bet Darius and Zac would tell me to take it as a compliment, but that's hard to do when these people are supposed to be my tribe.

On my first chance of freedom, I slink past all the guests and head for the bar.

A young bartender looks up at me halfway through mixing a drink. She pauses, turning as still as a statue. When time catches up to her, she breaks out in a luminous smile. "Holy shit. Verena Valentine. The boss warned all staff that this is a top secret wedding and I now see why.

You're probably sick of people approaching you, but I can't pass up the chance to tell you how much I love your show."

I relax onto a bar stool. "Finally, a true friend at this wedding."

"You are my biggest inspiration. Watching you is my happy place. And I don't mean to sound creepy or anything, but I love you and Darius. The two of you have this perfect dynamic and are so funny. I feel like you guys are my best friends."

"Thank you so much. I love meeting fans. Can I share a secret with you?" I lean in and whisper when she nods eagerly. "I'm a total fish out of water at this wedding. Do you mind if I hide out at the bar for a while? Talk to me so no one else does?"

Her eyes widen with delight. "This is like the best thing that has ever happened to me. And secondly, major case of déjà vu. A guy just said those same words to me." She points over her shoulder.

I only notice now that the bar is circular, and that she's referring to Adrian, who's sitting far across the other side with his eyes already on me. He's alone, which is a surprise. It's so unlike him to be missing out on all the attention. He raises a wine glass and nods at me.

I glare in response and turn back to the bartender. "Can I ask your name?"

"It's Samaya."

"Beautiful name. Do you know the ingredients for Smurf Piss?"

"The shot?"

I draw cash from my purse and hand it over. "Listen, Samaya, could you be a darling and send that man a shot of Smurf Piss? Tell him it's courtesy of Verena."

She gets to work, laughing to herself. I spin around on

my chair and face the guests so Adrian doesn't catch sight of my wicked grin. And that's when I see it—the man walking toward me. The man who broke my heart six months ago by accidentally falling over and slipping his dick into a model.

The background chatter and clinking of wine glasses fades out of existence and is replaced by the blaring sound of my heartbeat hammering in my ears. Either that, or my body has picked the worst time to come down with a case of tinnitus.

How can Jake be here? This isn't happening. *How* can this be happening?

A more important question is why do all the jackasses from my past have to look so incredible? I'm convinced they do it on purpose to spite me. Jake's grown a thin layer of dark stubble along his jaw that gives him a rugged look, and his hair is now long enough for fingers to knot through it when kissing him. I love a man in a fitted suit; not once did Jake ever wear one when we were together, but now, what do you know, he looks amazing in one with it hugging his muscles. Then there's that smile on his lips that always melted me, tugging up in one corner. His dark eyes bore into me as he approaches, like he's missed me or something.

Reality still hasn't sunken in. Jake is at my sister's wedding, grinning at me even after the terrible way we ended. The real question is—do I want Jake to be happy to see me?

Sure. I've spent months thinking about the dreaded day when we would meet again. The visions played out in a similar pattern to how I imagined Adrian and I would meet —with me looking sexy AF and him drowning in misery over how much he messed up. Instead, the Adrian situation ended with me falling flat on my ass and flashing my G-string. With Jake, I'm alone at a bar with frizzy hair. I'm not sure which scenario is worse.

I thought Adrian was hard enough to deal with, but Jake? Seeing him is *way* harder when my wounds are still fresh from the cheating.

In the hundred years that pass from when I first spot Jake walking in my direction, my heart entering arrhythmia, and me cursing how gorgeous the cheater looks, he arrives at my side, leaning an elbow on the bar.

"Verena, what a nice surprise." His legs brush against my knees like they would in a crowded bar, only there's no one beside us.

All I can manage is a stutter of words as I slide back on my stool to create distance. "What are... you doing... here?"

"I'm a plus-one at the wedding. And you?"

"Maid of honor."

"Which side?"

"Tory's."

You'd think he would know that, but Jake and I are each other's best-kept secrets. Not once during our two-year relationship did I introduce him to my family. I never had the chance, considering I wasn't willing to visit Sitka. My family never came to New York, either. And considering how the media loves to twist reality—like this supposed flirtation between Darius and me, and now with Zac apparently sleeping with his co-star—I've always kept my relationships private.

Jake was in the same position. He'd never been eager to share news of us. As a child, he grew up with nothing. His sister married into money, but Jake has fought for every opportunity he's been given and has always had a hunger to prove himself. It's one of the reasons we connected so well. We're both ambitious and hard workers. It would destroy him to have people believe he only made it as a successful restaurant entrepreneur because he leeched off Verena Valentine.

So, while the media and our friends and family knew we were each in a relationship, they never knew who the other person was. Darius and Zac were my exceptions. Jake and I didn't attend events together and he wasn't on my show. In private, however, Jake was my world. We understood each other. He told me every day how much he loved me, that he was going to marry me, and that we'd start a family.

But Jake was full of lies.

I'm questioning whether the universe is punishing me for the sins of my past life. The world has over seven billion people living on it. I traveled to a different country. Yet, Jake, of all people, manages to be at the same wedding as me.

It seems my withdrawal from him brushing up against my legs wasn't obvious enough, because now Jake places a hand on my shoulder. From the tender look in his eyes, it's meant to be a comforting gesture, but all it does is make me want to puke.

"Are you all right?" he asks, and I know he's referring to us. The painful breakup and seeing him now.

"I'm fine, Jake."

"Listen, I didn't know you would be here. This won't be awkward, will it?"

"Not on my behalf."

"Good." He takes my hand, giving it an encouraging squeeze. Before I can swat him away, he leans in and kisses me on the cheek. "It's great to see you. You look amazing. We should catch up some time throughout the week."

Without giving me a chance to answer, Jake walks off,

disappearing into the sea of guests. A flood of emotions attack me all at once. I'm remembering the first kiss we shared. It was in the rain, like one of those epic movie moments. I can't stop thinking about all the times we made love, which couldn't have been love at all if it was so easy for him to be with another woman. *Girl.* That's what she was. Barely a legal adult.

"Excuse me, Verena?" the bartender, Samaya, speaks. There's humor in her voice. I spin to face her and the shot glass she's sliding toward me—midori with kahlúa on top. "Courtesy of Adrian. Shit on Grass."

My eyes dart to him in rage. I know I started this petty thing with the shots, but after the Jake incident, I'm an inch away from hurling the shot at his pretty face.

A better idea comes to mind. Why waste the alcohol? I need it to deal with Jake's presence. I shoot it back and smile.

"Samaya, let him know it was delicious and he can send more over."

Darius and Zac need to hurry up and get here.

Trapped on an island with Adrian and Jake for an entire week. How the hell am I going to survive?

Chapter Five

In the lead up to this wedding, my biggest rule (aside from resisting World War Three with Adrian) was that I would survive this week without alcohol.

That clearly isn't happening.

I'm on my fifth glass of champagne—don't forget about all the shots I drank—and am pleasantly dizzy, alone at the bar when the speeches at this welcome dinner commence. Mom and Dad are up at the front of the cliffside restaurant, running a slideshow presentation. They're clicking through photos of family events from the past seven years—none of which I'm in.

But then, the slideshow goes back in time, starting with baby photos. There I am on the screen, next to Tory. At first, everyone's *oo-ing* and *ah-ing*, until we age up in the photos and the reactions aren't so adoring. I'm five and Tory is three. We're naked in the bath together and Tory is peeing on me.

I'm staring humiliated at the photo, surrounded by a sea of laughter from all the guests.

The next slide skips forward another couple of years.

I've put on weight next to ballerina Tory. Fast forward a few more years, I'm fifteen with a face full of zits and my pink hair makes its arrival. Mom tells some joke about Tory ugly crying in the photo because she didn't win first place in her dance competition. Yet still, her ugly crying was prettier than me.

I was wrong about returning to Sitka being the equivalent of reliving my most embarrassing moments all at once. It seems that can happen in Australia too.

There's more laughter, even from Tory. Jake is the loudest of all. He's standing close enough to call out to me. "Verena, how have I never seen these photos of you?"

I shoot back my champagne and grab another one off a waiter's tray. My eyes disobediently search for Adrian across the circular bar. I bet he's having a field day, taking a walk down memory lane. But the bar is empty. I can't find him among the crowd. He has to be here somewhere, hiding at the perfect angle while recording the slideshow, planning on leaking it to the public.

Nope. That would be Jake, holding his phone up and snapping a photo of the screen. I rush up to him, realizing that I'm far more than pleasantly dizzy from alcohol now that I'm on my feet, and snatch the phone from his hand.

Jake takes his phone back. "Babe, come on. It's just some fun."

"Don't call me that."

He doesn't hear me speak. He's snorting. Tears of humor gather in his eyes at the next slide. "Verena the Vagina! That's golden."

My mouth gapes as I turn to the screen. There's a photo of Tory and Phoebe kissing in the school cafeteria. They're the focal point of the image. Leave it to Jake to find me in the background. In the photo, I'm standing behind the two girls with my back to the camera, unaware that Adrian stuck a chunk of paper to my shoulders with the words *Verena the Vagina* on it.

Now that Jake has drawn attention to me in the image, everyone else in the restaurant notices the name and laughs with him. I shoot laser vision at my parents. They know how traumatized I was coming home from school that day. How could they choose *this* photo of Tory and Phoebe?

"Oh dear." Mom seems to be the last person to realize what everyone is laughing at. Her fingers fumble over the projector remote, struggling to change the slide.

"Get that photo off the screen, Vanessa," Dad tells her.

"I'm trying. It's not working. I didn't realize Verena was in this photo."

Jake bumps his hip to mine. "Babe, I'm learning some secrets about you. I love it. Teenage Verena was so precious."

"Don't touch me."

Jake's face drops, hearing me this time. His hand slips into mine. "Verena…"

I rip my hand from his, growling through my teeth, "I *said* don't touch me. Is she here with you? Are you her plus-one?"

"Who?"

"You know who I'm talking about."

His Adam's apple rises up and down as he swallows with an apology in his eyes. "Yes."

That one word breaks everything in me. I should have known Jake would be here with Her the second I saw him approach me at the bar, but I'd been too shocked to comprehend anything other than that my worst nightmare was walking toward me. How is it She even knows Tory and Phoebe? This is all too much to deal with.

I spin around and race for the bar, ordering an entire bottle of champagne from Samaya.

Jake's on my tail. "Verena, we can talk about this like adults."

"Talking to you is the last thing I want to do. Get away from me."

With my bottle of champagne, I slip past him and escape the welcome dinner altogether. My wobbly legs lead me out onto the beach. This resort is cursed and I want nothing to do with it. Only distance will fix this disaster. And alcohol. Lots and lots of alcohol.

I abandon my shoes and head for the water. I'm stumbling over the sand with the champagne bottle in my hand, which takes talent with this much alcohol in my system. The wind blows my dress high around my thighs, flashing my ass again, but I couldn't care less. Visibility out here is poor. The moon is dim and the torches back at the resort are like little matchsticks from this distance.

"What the fuck is wrong with you?" someone groans. Probably Jake, come to drag me back to the restaurant.

"Me?" I raise my voice. "You're the dickhead!"

"Verena?"

Only now do I notice the silhouette in front of me. It takes a few seconds for my eyes to adjust in the dark and see the person's anger morph into surprise.

Shit. It's Adrian.

I begin laughing—a very sloppy and drunk laugh—because of course Adrian Hunter is here. This is the world's way of kicking me when I'm down. "Why are you following me?"

He breaks chunks off a large stick and hurls them into the ocean with rage. "I've been on this beach for an hour. Maybe you're the one following me."

I take a swig of my champagne. "How come *you* got out of the welcome dinner? And what's got you so pissed off?"

He shrugs, only addressing the first question. "Those events aren't my kind of thing. Doubt anyone noticed I was missing."

"No, they were too busy laughing at old photos of me."

Adrian's eyebrows draw together like he's not following.

"Fat me! Verena the Vagina!"

His lips press into a line, like he's attempting not to laugh.

"That's right. Go ahead and laugh too. Run along and you might see the rest of the photos."

"I'm *not* laughing. And I'm sure the photos weren't that bad."

"Believe me, they were. Everyone was laughing. My ex-boyfriend is here! What kind of luck is that!"

Adrian ceases fire of the hunk of stick he's about to throw into the ocean. "The one who cheated on you?"

"Yes, Adrian. The one who publicly humiliated me. And he's here with the girl he fucked in my bed."

"I bet my proposition is looking pretty appealing right now."

I kick the sand. "I'm telling you I'm freaking out, and all you can think of is yourself? I'm not pretending to date you so you can win your ex-girlfriend back."

"Thought I'd try my luck."

"You know, I don't get what it is with you men. You think you control everything. I wouldn't put it past you to cook up this whole fake dating scheme so that you can win the revenge between us. What's your plan—pretend to date me for a few days then break up with me in front of all the wedding guests so I get even more embarrassed? Bravo, Adrian." I clap, giving him a round of applause. "Perfect plan. Why do you hate me so much? And what was Jake's issue? Was I not pretty enough for him? Am I still too fat? You know what? I *love* my body. I'm no size zero, I've got curves, but I've worked damn hard in the gym to look this good."

I gulp down another mouthful of alcohol, then dig the bottle into the sand and unzip my dress to prove a point.

Adrian looks me up and down, fighting back a laugh. "Verena, you're drunk. Don't take your clothes off."

"Why? You wouldn't say that to some skinny girl. Am I so disgusting that you can't stand to look at me?"

"Trust me, you have a *very* nice body. I would fuck you if I didn't hate you so much." Adrian steps forward and fastens my arms by my side, his voice lowering to an amused whisper, "The embarrassment you're feeling will be one hundred times worse in the morning if you do this."

I shrug free of him and pull the dress over my head. It falls to the sand and my world spins as I take another chug of champagne.

"Oh no, not the couture in the sand," Adrian mocks, his eyes avoiding my body. "You really should put your clothes back on."

"Would you just look at me already!"

"Verena, is that you?" someone calls. "Tory sent me to check up on you." They're entering the beach from the resort. Whoever it is, they're too far away for me to identify, but it's a female's voice. There's a small group of people following them, coming to laugh at me some more.

"Fuck you!" I yell in their direction.

"Ah, sorry," Adrian calls to them. "She's had a lot to drink."

As they come closer, I realize Tory's bridesmaid, Stacy, is leading the group. There's two ladies and a man behind her. My guess is it's Nia, Sukhi, and Josh—the other members of the bridal party that I'm not good enough to dance with.

"Did you ever consider that maybe *I* want to dance with someone?" I shout.

Their eyes scan over me in my underwear, and I see the exact moment their noses turn upward with judgment. Adrian steps in front of me, shielding me from their view. The next thing I know, I'm on the ground, retching from the alcohol.

"Oh my," Stacy says. "Yes, I read that the breakup turned her into an alcoholic."

Adrian kneels beside me, sweeping my hair back from my face. "Verena, put your clothes on," he says at the first break in my heaving while pulling me up to my feet.

"Too difficult," I mutter, wobbling with shaky knees. He lets go of me for a second to grab my dress, and I land ass-first on the sand.

"Raise your arms and I'll slide the dress over your head."

"No. Go away." I swat his hands from me, squirming in the sand as he tries to dress me. "I can take care of myself."

"Adrian, is that you?" Another new voice, because apparently having the bridal party witness this moment isn't punishment enough.

"Shit. Our moms," Adrian says to me. "They're bringing a crowd with them. Verena, come on, raise your arms."

"No."

Adrian swears, then unbuttons his own shirt and wraps it around my shoulders.

"Adrian, stop! I don't want your shirt on me. I hate you."

All of that pettiness flies out the window the instant I catch sight of Jake approaching in the distance, and suddenly I'm shrieking at the top of my lungs.

47

"What has gotten into you?" Adrian wrestles my arms through the sleeves of his shirt, but I wriggle free of the fabric.

"Jake's here. I need to hide."

My safest escape option is the ocean. I break free from Adrian by kicking him in the stomach and go stumbling along the sand. My mind spins as cold water splashes high up my legs, but I keep moving deeper.

"Verena, this is dangerous. Stop!" Adrian calls.

I glance over my shoulder, finding him waist-deep in the water behind me. "I'm fine. We're in the Whitsundays. There's not a wave in sight."

I'm not sure if it's Karma, but the next moment, a speedboat zooms by, dunking me under the water as one of its manmade waves crashes into me. My body somersaults beneath the water's surface. Darkness surrounds me, providing no sense of up or down. I swallow a mouthful of salty crap, because along with the ocean water, I felt some lumpy thing go down my throat—whether it be seaweed or tiny fish or whatever the heck is hanging out in this water. I'm calling it salty crap. The uncertainty has me heaving again... underwater.

From beneath the surface, I hear Adrian shouting my name. Is that... desperation in his voice? Even panic? Or am I hallucinating as I enter a slow and painful watery death? I have no idea how long I've been down here. My arms are flailing and my lungs beg for air. I kick in any direction, hoping for it to be the right one, until I break the surface and suck in sweet oxygen, followed by another mouthful of salty crap as a second wave crashes into me.

Arms wrap around my waist before I'm swept to the depths of the ocean again. "Breathe. I've got you." It's

Adrian. I've never felt more disgusted and relieved in the same moment.

His grip remains tight, stabilizing the two of us as I cough up water. After my first full breath, Adrian readjusts my position, cradling me to his chest with one arm under my knees and the other behind my back.

"Don't try to fight me." Adrian's grip tightens as soon as I attempt to break free. Exhausted, I give up and relax into his arms. Water splashes around us as he begins carrying me back to shore.

The reality of this situation dawns on me: Adrian is shirtless and I'm in my underwear. The warmth of his body radiates into me and I can feel how firm every inch of his shredded torso is. This would have been teenage Verena's wildest fantasy—being rescued by Adrian Hunter half-naked. In this fantasy, he'd lay me on the sand and rip all our clothes off in one effortless movement, then have hot beach sex with me as the waves ripple onto shore around us.

I've lost count of the times I've imagined Adrian moving above me, breathless and thrusting hard. Coming inside of me with no condom on.

Whoa, girl, calm down.

That was teenage Verena. Adult Verena is limp and drunk with the world spinning around her, and apparently still capable of fantasizing about sex with Adrian.

"Did you really mean what you said about having sex with me?" I mumble, trying to keep myself from being sick again. I'm going to hate myself for being this open with Adrian when the alcohol wears off, but that's tomorrow's problem.

He quirks an eyebrow. "You're thinking about sex right now?"

"Obviously. Answer the question."

"I meant it."

The space between my thighs tingles from his answer. "But you hate me too much."

"Right."

"You don't know what you're missing out on. Hate sex is the best. I'm good in bed. I'd make you beg to come."

He laughs against my ear, his hot breath sending shivers all through me. "I am going to *love* using this against you when you sober up."

"Leave me out here to die," I mumble.

"You are so melodramatic."

"I'm serious. I don't want anyone to see me like this."

"Too late. You've caused quite the scene."

"Tory will be mad with me. This week is meant to be all about her and Phoebe. Let go of me. I'll stay out here till everyone leaves the beach."

"That's not an option," he says, carrying me closer to shore. "The second I let go of you, you'll drown."

"Adrian for the win. Woo! The ultimate revenge: death. Do it. Kill me."

"Who would I have left to taunt?"

"I'll come back from the grave to haunt you. I'll be a poltergeist, so technically you can taunt me too."

He thinks about this for a moment but keeps pushing through the water.

"I have a reputation to uphold." It's my only bargaining chip left. Though it's the worst case to plead; Adrian will love ruining my reputation. This is why he's rescuing me, so he can watch my demise. "Adrian, please. I can't have them see me like this. Especially not Jake."

"Pretend to be asleep. I'll carry you past them."

"That's a stupid plan."

"Do you have a better one?" he asks.

"I've already told you all my plans."

"Verena, turning into a ghost is not a plan."

We're so close to the shore that the water sits around Adrian's waist now. This is happening, whether or not I like it.

"Ugh, fine." I give in, closing my eyes and resting my head on his chest. "Don't get any ideas about touching my boobs."

"Don't disgust me."

There's a flock of people around us the instant Adrian steps onto land. All I can hear is a variation of people asking if I'm all right and if we should call a doctor. Stacy's voice is the most distinct, suggesting she research rehab facilities.

"She's fine," Adrian dismisses, walking us through the crowd. "A night swim gone wrong. I'll take her back to her room and she can sleep this off."

Pretend to be asleep.

Pretend to be asleep.

Those four words are all that pass through my mind as Adrian carries me to the resort. I should win an Oscar for these magnificent acting skills. My brain falls for the ruse and I'm asleep before we reach my bungalow.

Chapter Six

In my drunken passed-out state, nothing is clear except that I have the most erotic sex dream of my life, featuring Adrian. I've now entered that club of women who can reach orgasm in their sleep. Multiple orgasms, to be exact.

Chapter Seven

Aside from the typical hangover symptoms of a pounding head, dehydration, and nausea, I wake hot and tingling with the Adrian sex dream tattooed in my memory. I'm disgusted at myself for how much I enjoyed it, and how satisfied yet unsatisfied it left me. I'm desperate to touch myself, but the headache prevents me.

The sun wants to torment me, shining in my eyes instead of letting me sleep off this hangover. I pull the covers over my head, but beneath the blankets lies a whole lot of mortifying flashbacks from last night. Snippets of a disaster. Seeing Jake at dinner, that embarrassing slide show, and running into the ocean to escape everyone. Pieces of the night are missing from my memory, and I can't string together a coherent sequence of what actually happened.

My eyes flash open with the obvious question. How did I get into bed? I shoot to an upright position—a terrible mistake for the pounding in my head—and peer around the room. The layout is all wrong. This bedroom is smaller than the one Tory assigned me. All the furniture is positioned back to front.

A sickening feeling washes over me when I realize this isn't my bungalow. I peek beneath the sheets and, oh God, I'm in my underwear. I race for the bathroom and wrap a towel around myself, knocking men's products off the basin in the process, then run into the living room.

Adrian is asleep on the couch.

That little scumbag. I knew this had his name written all over it.

I grab the TV remote and throw it at his head. "How did I end up in your bed? And why am I half-naked?"

He takes one look at me, smirks, then closes his eyes. "Don't tell me you forgot about your little strip show, sweetheart?"

"Adrian!"

He rolls away from me, his voice groggy with sleep. "Relax, it's nothing I haven't seen on a woman before."

I jog through my memory, recapping everything I can remember from the previous night but have no clue what he's referring to.

Bile rises in my throat as a shoot-me-now thought enters my mind. The sex dream. The multiple orgasms. Last night was the first time I experienced them during sleep. What if I was loud? What if he heard me coming? I scream internally because what if I was saying his name in my sleep?

FUCK!

"Did you hear or see me do anything strange?" I ask.

"That's debatable."

"Adrian, I swear, if you don't tell me exactly what happened between us last night, I will kill you."

All that aside, I'm trying to ignore how good the lazy upturn of his mouth looks while he's half-asleep and with bed-hair. His sex-hair would look better. Crap! Why am I thinking about such things? It's a blessing he's still got a shirt on, otherwise my imagination would be a lost cause.

"We went for a swim together," he tells me. "Remember that? You propositioned me for hate sex."

"As if I would ever do that," I scoff, instantly regretting that I asked for Adrian's recount. I'll never know what's the truth or a lie. "How did I end up in your bed?"

"You fell asleep when I was carrying you back to the resort. You had no room key or clothes, so I brought you here. Didn't touch you for a second longer than necessary. I bathed in bleach to get the scent of you off me. I'll take a *thank you* anytime."

"You shouldn't have put me in your bed. Now *I'm* going to have to bathe in bleach!"

He chuckles. "Would you have preferred me to leave you passed out on your doorstep for everyone to see?"

"You could have asked reception for a key."

"Didn't cross my mind."

"Was there anything else? I mean, did I talk in my sleep at all? You can never trust a drunk tongue."

His gaze narrows on me, followed a few seconds later by a cocky grin twitching at his lips. "Wanna tell me what you were dreaming about?"

"I didn't have any dreams."

"What are you so afraid I heard?"

"Nothing. I've been known to talk in my sleep and I'm curious. Would you just answer the question?"

"I didn't hear anything."

Whether it's the truth, I'll take it. I make a mental note to research *sleeping orgasms* the moment I return to my bungalow and what they look like to an onlooker. Shit, they better look like nothing.

"I'm leaving." I turn my back on Adrian and head for the front door. "Don't talk to me again."

"I saved you from drowning. You owe me big time."

"I wasn't drowning!" I storm out of the bungalow, slamming the door behind me.

As soon as those words leave my mouth, and with the silence that now surrounds me, I remember that part of the night and how truthful his words are. Adrian *did* save my life. I *should* be thanking him, but I can't. There's no way I will ever show gratitude toward that man.

So, apparently, they're silent—the sleeping orgasms—which means I wasn't moaning and screaming Adrian's name during my sex dream. Thank God. It still doesn't clear my doubt about saying other embarrassing stuff while drunk. Could this week be off to any worse of a start?

I want to hide in my bungalow forever, but I'm in hangover mode, which translates to starving. After getting a new room key from reception, taking that bleach bath I spoke of, and burning Adrian's towel, the bags under my eyes are packed with concealer and I'm ready to brave the breakfast buffet. Guests are staring at me as I walk through the resort. I hear their whispers. They're all variations of *Typical. Has to be the center of attention, even if that means ruining her sister's time in the spotlight.*

Aunt Gloria passes me at the pool. "How are you feeling today, sweetie? That Adrian is such a gentleman for taking care of you."

I force a smile and keep walking, thankful for the distraction when my phone buzzes with a text from my group chat with Darius and Zac.

Zac: The good news is I found Penny and she's coming to Australia with us.

Verena: Great! What's the bad news?

Darius: There's a blizzard in New York. We can't fly until weather conditions clear up.

Verena: FXDSJK!! Use your teleportation skills or something. Jake is here!

Zac: You're joking, right?

Verena: What kind of joke is that?

Darius: Hang in there, baby. You can do this.

The staring from guests continues, even when I arrive at the buffet. I grab a plate and pile it high with every bit of salty food that will cure this hangover. I know it's frowned upon, but I'm considering taking the food to go and eating in my room. Wait. Why didn't I order room service in the first place?

I grab cutlery and turn to make a run for it, but my body locks up at the sight ahead of me. Jake, of all people, is heading in my direction with a girl hanging off his arm. It has to be Her. Why is she even at this wedding? Is she Tory's friend or Phoebe's? Neither of them would know she's the one my boyfriend cheated on me with. But still...

She's got her body out on display, wearing a triangle bikini to breakfast. Who does that? I'm trying to eat here, not vomit. And she's a blond. Of course she is. Her tits are huge. I bet they're implants. That tan can't be real either. And she's young. So young.

I'm still contemplating running, but all three of us have made eye contact. Six months of avoidance has narrowed down to this moment—I'm about to be introduced to the homewrecker that tore up my life.

"Verena, we should talk," Jake says with the same

sympathetic tone he used last night. I *hate* it. His pity is one thing I can't stand.

"Sure, another time, though. I'm busy."

I walk off with my food, but She calls after me in her sweet little voice. "I'm a huge fan, Verena. I love all of your designs. I'm a model."

I turn back to them, speechless that She has the nerve to say such a thing to me. Next, She'll be asking for a modeling contract.

"This is Hannah," Jake says, like I don't already know her name. "Your performance last night... I'm not blind. I understand what's happening. You're struggling to see me. I can only imagine how difficult this must be for you, especially with Hannah here."

Ugh! This is exactly what I wanted to avoid.

"You're hung up on us. I can see you're still in love with me—"

"Jake, I'm seeing someone." The words rush out of my mouth as though I can't say them fast enough. Okay, that wasn't part of the plan. Don't panic. Stay calm.

"Verena... You don't have to make up excuses."

"I'm not. Jake, I have a boyfriend."

His eyes remain on me, seeing straight through my lie. Yeah... this is awkward. "Verena, if you want to be immature about this—"

"I'm not the one being immature." Right at this very moment, I spot Adrian, sitting by himself at a table. I swear my hand rises on its own accord, and before I know it, I'm pointing in his direction. "My boyfriend is right over there."

Shit. What am I doing?

Adrian sees the three of us looking his way and his eyebrows draw together. I plaster a smile across my face.

The next thing I know, he's walking toward us. *Fuck, fuck, fuck.*

"Verena," he says, then looks at Jake and Her, waiting for an introduction.

I discard my food on the table and rest a hand on Adrian's shoulder. "Adrian, honey, this is Jake."

Adrian's gaze darts back to me. I send him silent messages with my eyes to *please* play along. Whether he receives the message or not, his face straightens, and his tone turns territorial. "Jake? As in, cheating-Jake?"

Facepalm. This can't be happening.

"This isn't going to be weird, is it?" Jake asks him. "Verena and I are on good terms."

"I'm Hannah." *S*he bats her lashes at Adrian and extends a hand for him to shake. What the fuck is this girl's game? She's trying to steal my fake boyfriend now too?

"Not weird at all." Adrian shakes her hand and pats Jake on the shoulder. "I owe you thanks, man. Your little roll in the sheets with Jannah is what brought Verena and me back together again. Childhood sweethearts reunited." He raises suggestive eyebrows at Jake and laughs. "That was one steamy make-up session."

I have to stop my jaw from hanging open. Is Adrian brilliant or what? He knows how to serve it good. I guess it's from all those years spent practicing on me.

"My name is *Hannah*," She corrects the mispronunciation of her name. Splotchy patches of red appear all over Jake's face.

I try hard to fight my own blush when Adrian's hand slips into mine, weaving our fingers. He shakes his head, laughing at Jake. "I've got to ask, though, are you blind? How did you ever let this one get away?"

Jake's eyes switch between Adrian and me, his mouth gaping. A bunch of stutters is all I can hear from him. He grabs his girlfriend by the arm and escapes back to their table.

Adrian grins at me. "Come around, have you?"

I snatch my hand back from him. "Don't get all cocky. I panicked when Jake approached me. You were the first excuse I could think of to avoid him."

He strokes my hair. I have the greatest urge to smack his hand away, but Jake is watching from afar.

"Careful, Adrian," I say with sweetness. "If you attempt to kiss me, I will bite your dick off."

He chuckles. "Is that what you were dreaming about, my dick in your mouth?" His gaze slips out to the side, then back again. "Now it's your turn to play along. Isabelle's watching."

"Isabelle?"

"Yeah, my ex."

My eyes flash to her, intrigued by what kind of creature would engage in such a putrid relationship. Poor thing, she actually looks like a nice lady. Curly red hair, clear skin and to-die-for cheekbones. I'd love to see her modeling one of my designs. Too bad her eyes are shooting daggers through me. I suppose Adrian is getting what he wants. Which is what—to make her jealous and win her back? Who knows, or cares.

Adrian turns my face back to him. "You are the worst. Now she knows we're talking about her."

Before I can defend myself, someone nearby squeals, and the next thing I know, Adrian's mom and mine are rushing toward us. "What is this?" they say in unison.

I go rigid. Adrian runs a hand through his hair. He'll

have to be the one that does all the talking; my voice has disappeared.

"Ah, we were planning to tell you soon but didn't want to steal Phoebe and Tory's thunder," he says.

"You're... together?" Mom asks, verging on the edge of exploding with excitement.

Adrian's hand slinks around my waist, pulling us together. "Appears that way."

"This is the best news," his mom says. Cece Hunter has always been gorgeous. Like mother, like son, I suppose. But now, she's like an angel from this news, radiating light from every pore on her skin and strawberry blond hair. "I've been telling Adrian to fix things with you ever since his breakup with Isabelle." She holds the side of her hand up to her mouth and whispers humorously, "Let's be honest, I was telling him this even before they broke up. I'm so glad he finally listened."

"I kept telling him the same thing," Mom adds.

"It's true," Adrian tells me with a hint of annoyance. "Your mother rings me in London at least once a month."

"What?" My nose puckers. "What do you two talk about?"

"You mostly," he says. I can't figure out if he's joking.

Mom rubs a hand on my shoulders. "Listen, sweetheart, I'm sorry about that photo last night. You know, the one with the sign on your back. Your father added the photos to the slideshow in a rush. It was a last-minute thing. We should have checked all the photos more thoroughly."

I feel like telling her it wasn't just that one photo that was the problem. *All* of them were embarrassing, but I let the issue slide, wanting to forget about last night.

"You two should have breakfast with us," Mom says. "I

need to soak up as much time with Verena as I can get during this week. And we can't wait to hear how you two got together."

"Actually," Adrian says, "Verena and I need to take care of something first. How about we catch up later and fill you in on the details of our relationship?"

"We'll be holding you to your word," Cece tells him.

As soon as our moms walk off, Adrian's hand finds mine and he leads me toward the exit. "What about my food," I argue, digging my heels into the ground. "I'm malnourished."

"We'll order room service."

"*We*? Nuh-uh. You are not stepping foot in my bungalow and contaminating it."

"We'll go back to mine, then."

The two of us leave the buffet, only to bump into Phoebe. She's a mirror image of her mom, except twenty-two years younger, and is suffering from the same glowing-angel syndrome. Phoebe's eyes flit between her phone and us, hand in hand.

"It's true?" she asks, reading a text. "*Adrian and Verena are dating.*" There's no anger from her about the way I behaved last night. I should have expected this outcome; she's always been the easygoing one between her and my sister. All the scolding will come from Tory.

I try to tear my hand from Adrian's, but he holds on tight. "Word travels fast," he answers his sister. "Who sent you that message?"

"Mom. Why didn't you tell me?" She wraps Adrian and me in her arms, bouncing with joy. "I have always shipped you guys, even when you hated each other. You were destined to be together. You know, you shouldn't be sleeping in separate bungalows. Adrian, I'll have the concierge move your belongings in with Verena's."

Her words have me choking. "Ah... no, seriously, we don't want to be a hassle."

"Believe me, this is no hassle at all."

Chapter Eight

With a laugh, Adrian falls back onto my pristine bed, contaminating it as his arms spread wide like he's making snow angels.

"Absolutely not." I push his legs in an attempt to get him off my bed, but he doesn't budge. "We are not sharing a bed."

"Verena, couples share a bed."

"No one is watching us this closely. You're sleeping on the couch. Or better yet, outside. There are plenty of daybeds by my pool."

"*Our* pool." He folds his hands behind his head, making himself comfortable. "And why don't *you* sleep there, then?"

"Because this is my room."

"*Our* room. If you want the bed, you're going to have to earn it. I'm still waiting for my *thank you* for saving your life."

"Ugh! You are so frustrating. I'm too hung-over to deal with this."

"Okay, no *thank you*. So, what's our story?"

"What are you on about now?" I ask.

"Everyone will want to know how we got together. We need a convincing lie to tell them."

"We'll say we bumped into each other on the street and a spark grew."

"We live in different countries," he points out.

"We reconnected over video chat. This is our first week being physically together."

"Physically?" Adrian laughs, raising his eyebrows up and down.

"You know what I mean. We've been talking on FaceTime for a few months and this is the first time we've seen each other in the flesh. Problem solved. We don't need an epic story."

"So boring. They'll want details. Everyone thinks we hate each other. How did we fall in love?"

"We don't give them details." I pace back and forth in the bedroom, chewing on my nails. "You know what, I'm second guessing this whole fake relationship. I don't even know how I landed in this mess. There's no way we can keep up the lie. I have no doubt Tory is pissed at me for getting drunk last night, and now *this*. She'll know we're not dating and will be even more angry with me. I need to explain the misunderstanding to everyone."

I make a beeline for the door, but Adrian races off the bed, blocking the doorway with arms outstretched.

"Get out of my way."

"Verena, do you realize how bad this will make both of us look to Isabelle and Jake? My chances of winning her back will be zero. Plus, I saw what that jerk did to you. The whole world did. You have to admit how amazing it felt to one-up him at breakfast. The look on Isabelle's face was priceless for me."

"Yes, it was amazing, but Jake will figure us out and I'll be left even more embarrassed."

"Stop panicking and have some fun. No one will figure us out, I promise. Wouldn't you love to show Jake how great your life is without him and that he doesn't mean a thing to you? Kind of like what you've been doing to me over the last seven years?"

I give Adrian the stink eye and all he does is laugh. But his proposition *does* sound tempting.

"Fine," I sigh. "There need to be ground rules. You can hold my hand in public, but that's it. No kissing."

"You flatter yourself too much. I have no intention of kissing you."

I cross my arms and scowl.

"Holding hands seems a little tame," he says. "Isabelle knows what kind of guy I am. I couldn't keep my hands off her when we were dating. She'll see right through us if I'm only allowed to touch your hand."

"All right. But if your hands go anywhere near my chest or ass, I will make sure you regret it. We don't embarrass the other person, either. You help me look good in front of Jake and I'll make sure Isabelle is jealous enough to want you back. No more revenge on each other."

"I think I proved my loyalty this morning in front of Jake and Jannah."

My lips twitch upward. I hate smiling at anything Adrian does, but that was a gold performance. And that name he's given her is genius.

"Now that everything is settled between us," he says, strolling around the bedroom, "I can't believe they gave you this bungalow. It's so much nicer than mine." He draws the curtains back, revealing the infinity pool that overlooks the tranquil ocean, then pulls his shirt over his head and drops it to the floor.

"What are you doing?" I shield my eyes. "Just because you saw me in my underwear doesn't mean I want to see you in yours."

Lies. As much as I try to deny it, there's a spark of desire in me that would very much like to see him in his underwear or even less. I *know* the view would be amazing.

He digs through his suitcase, pulling out trunks. "I'm going for a swim. You better leave our room unless you want to see me naked."

"This isn't *our* room!"

Adrian taunts me by unbuttoning his jeans. I have no clue whether he would really get naked in front of me, but I'm not risking myself being in that situation, and run into the living room.

A minute later, Adrian waltzes out of *my* bedroom in swim trunks and heads for the pool. I don't dare look at him until he's outside and I can hide behind the curtains. Every muscle in his back is chiseled to perfection. When he turns around, I get a full-frontal view of his chest which is ten times more mouthwatering. A whimper escapes my lips as the sight of his bare torso triggers the memory of my sex dreams.

Why does Adrian have to be so frustratingly hot?

He does an effortless swan dive into the pool that would be a belly flop if I attempted such a move. When he surfaces, his brown hair is slicked back and droplets of water trickle down the contours of his strong chest.

"Great, now the pool is unusable too!"

He laughs at my words and launches into a lap of freestyle.

The doorbell chimes. I didn't realize this bungalow had

a doorbell. As soon as I answer the door, Tory barges into the living room, her eyes dark.

"What has gotten into you, Verena? This week is meant to be about me and Phoebe. You haven't even been here twenty-four hours, and twice already you've made everything about *you*!"

I surrender, holding up two hands. "I know. I'm sorry. I can explain."

"What the hell was last night and what the hell was this morning? Phoebe told me you and Adrian are dating."

Adrian joins us in the living room, dried off from the water but still distractingly half-naked.

"Oh, would you put a shirt on already?" I march into the bedroom and grab the shirt he dropped on the floor, then hurl it at his face.

He obeys, surprisingly, and greets Tory with a smile. "Good morning so far?"

She looks between me and Adrian with disbelief. "Explain this now, Verena. It was only yesterday that you were ranting for hours about how much you hate him."

Adrian grins at me. "Hours? Please, you're making me blush. Verena, you hate me that much?"

"It was not *hours*," I clarify. "And you made the cheerleaders in high school add *Verena the Vagina* into one of their cheers. So, yeah, I hate you a lot."

"I only did that because you cut holes around the crotch in my baseball uniform."

Tory stamps her foot. "Shut up, both of you, and tell me what is happening! Why does everyone think you're dating?"

Adrian shrugs. "Because we told them we are."

"And why would you do that?"

"I can explain this," I say, hushing her with my hands.

"You better."

"Jake is here."

She claps a hand to her mouth. "As in, the dirtbag who cheated on you?"

"Yes. He's a plus-one."

The hatred in her eyes is more heated than a moment ago. "Which one is he? I'm gonna rip his dick off."

"Biting, ripping," Adrian laughs. "What is it with the Valentine girls being so violent with dicks?"

Tory scrunches her nose in confusion.

"Don't ask," I warn her. "I'm sorry about last night. It was a reaction to seeing Jake and everyone laughing at that photo of me. Then this morning Jake came up to me with the girl he cheated on me with—"

"Jannah," Adrian offers.

"—and was acting like I'm still in love with him. I panicked and all I could think of was saying Adrian is my boyfriend."

Tory eyes me with a glint of enjoyment. "That was your first reaction?"

"I know, it's pathetic. Please tell me Jannah is not a friend of yours."

"Hannah," Adrian explains, and it might be the kindest thing he's ever done for me—not making me say the girl's name aloud.

"Hannah Ashley is the girl Jake cheated on you with?" Tory asks.

Of course she has some slut name like that. It's no surprise. As the saying goes—never trust a person with two first names. "How do you know her?"

"She's friends with Phoebe. Oh, Hannah is going to hear some words from me."

"No!" The word rushes out of my mouth in a panic.

"Don't you dare say anything to anyone. I don't want her or Jake thinking I'm hung up on him. And no one can know about Adrian and me. Except for Phoebe. You shouldn't start a marriage with lies. But no one else. It will ruin everything."

Tory's jaw clenches tight. She doesn't look convinced. The only thing that pulls her out of her tunnel vision is a phone call.

"Pheebs?" she answers, straining to calm down. "Yes, I'm with Verena and Adrian right now." More silence, then she says, "Yes, you're correct, they're dating."

I mouth to her, *don't lie*, but all I get in response is a grin. She's up to something. I don't know if this is payback for getting blind drunk last night, or if she finds it funny to place me in more situations with a man I despise. Either way, I'm in over my head.

"Yes, honey, that's correct. Hey, you two," Tory speaks up, looking between Adrian and me, "Phoebe wants the four of us to meet for drinks tonight to celebrate your relationship."

"Tell her we're busy," I say.

Her smile broadens. "Fantastic. Six o'clock tonight. Verena says she can't wait."

Chapter Nine

It's official—Adrian has moved in. His clothes are in my closet. His man-stuff is cluttering my beauty products on the bathroom counter. He's crowding the mirror as we stand at the *his and hers* sinks, holding back laughter while I glare at his reflection.

"What kind of romantic things should we do today, sweetheart?" Adrian asks, running wax through his hair.

"*I* was planning on attending the beach yoga session," I say, applying a ton of hairspray to tame my frizz. My hangover has eased but I still look dreadful, so I reach for my makeup.

"Perfect. I'll be on the mat beside you. Or maybe I should claim the mat behind you. Got to get a front row seat of my girlfriend bending over."

I'm powdering my cheeks, my teeth grinding as I think of something to say. One of the comebacks Darius helped me devise comes to mind, but Adrian gets in before me with another asshole comment. "I got a front row view of you in your underwear last night—"

"You know what, Adrian, I think it's a perfect idea if

you come to yoga. People will see us together, but I won't have to interact with you for an entire hour."

Adrian turns to look at me, leaning sideways against the basin. He doesn't say anything, just holds me with his gaze until I'm bursting with frustration.

"What?" I snap. That sinister grin is back on his lips, and I realize I've fallen into his trap. He probably doesn't have anything to say and is only watching me to gain a rise out of me.

"We're about to exercise and you're applying makeup?" he asks. "Aren't you going to sweat it all off?"

"Maybe I want to look nice when I'm exercising."

"Exercise isn't the time to look pretty. It's about exerting yourself. Sweating. Releasing endorphins. Much like sex."

The way his eyes darken as he says that last word gives life to butterflies in my stomach. The word *sex* rolls off his tongue so casually, but with a deeper, more velvety tone. I'm having unwelcome visions of Adrian, breathless and sweaty as he moves above me. My dream from last night is flashing before my eyes and I grow hot thinking of it, wondering if Adrian is as good in real life.

And now I'm wondering how long I've spent imagining Adrian and me having sex, because he's raising a questioning eyebrow, waiting for my response.

My focus returns to the mirror. "I wear makeup during sex and have never had an issue with it sweating off."

"You must have tame sex then."

I groan, more with anger at myself that again I've fallen for Adrian's tricks and he's gotten me talking about my sex life.

Once we've finished getting ready for the day, the two of us walk with a five-foot gap between us as we navigate through the resort and find our way to the beach for yoga.

The session is held on the same beach where I embarrassed myself last night. The water is so crystal clear and motionless I can't believe I almost drowned in it.

We're right on time for the yoga class. There must be at least fifty people here, which seems like an excessive amount since there are only half that number of mats laid out.

Adrian and I come to the same realization an instant later, our bodies stiffening as we say in unison, "Oh, hell no."

"Welcome to couples' yoga." The yoga instructor pops up in front of us with a toothy grin. She's an older lady wearing a turquoise shawl and looks like she's spent too much time enjoying the hot Australian sun. "My name is Kathy. Find yourselves a mat to share. We're about to begin the session."

My mouth opens and shuts. "We thought... We didn't know..."

"Hey, you two lovebirds," Mom calls to us from a mat she's sharing with my father. "You'll love this. Your dad and I did couples yoga a few years back, and it really spiced things up for us."

I'm about to barf at that unwelcome visual of my parents.

Tory and Phoebe are here too, along with Isabelle and her date, and Jake and Jannah. I receive another death stare from Isabelle, but it's Jake and Jannah I'm hung up on. The two of them don't even see me. They're so loved up sitting in each other's laps and eating each other's face off. I want to barf at that too.

A few mats over, I notice Stacy and her husband. He's giving her a massage as they wait for the class to begin. It's such an intimate moment between them that their goals of falling pregnant could happen any moment.

Why is everyone so sexual and gross in this class? It's couples' yoga, not couples' Kama Sutra. If they think for one second that I'm doing some weird sex pose with Adrian, they've got something else coming for them.

I yelp when Adrian places a hand on my back, his hot palm prickling against my bare skin.

"Settle down," he whispers, sliding his hand around my waist. "I'm not thrilled about this either, but Isabelle is watching us. Try to be a little less disgusted by the thought of being with me."

I oblige and take a seat on a mat, distancing myself at the farthest edge from Adrian. He catches on to my waist and draws me into his lap.

"Be nice," Adrian laughs softly into my ear.

Luck takes a swift turn in my direction because a moment later, Kathy commences the class by telling everyone to sit cross-legged and face our partners. I'm the first one to leave my partner's arms.

"Oh, Verena's keen," Aunt Gloria says.

Gross.

Kathy's voice adopts a mellow, cathartic tone. "We'll begin the yoga practice with a few minutes of mindfulness."

She asks us to close our eyes and leads us through a breathing exercise that's meant to slow our heart rate and deepen our breath. It has the opposite effect on me. My pulse is skyrocketing with visuals of Adrian on top of me again, which could very well happen in this class. Kathy is telling us to enjoy being out in nature, but I'm pissed off at how hot the morning sun is in Australia, that Adrian got sand on our mat, and how he's breathing louder than the ocean.

It seems like forever until Kathy instructs everyone to open their eyes and take awareness of our partner. Adrian and I look at each other, and he must realize how hot and bothered I am, because the tiniest smile creeps over his lips.

"Slowly, from head to toe, trail your gaze along your partner's body, taking notice of every little detail about them," Kathy says.

First, I pay attention to Adrian's hair. It's a dark, ruffled mess but is styled that way as if he knows how amazing it looks on him. Next, I study his tanned face. He hasn't had a chance to shave today, and I'm rather fond of the unkept look on him. My gaze lowers to his lips that I've fantasized a million times about kissing and how they would taste. Would he be a gentle kisser, or would he kiss with urgency? Would he kiss with his whole body, wrapping me in his arms and worshipping me like a goddess? That's how he kissed in high school whenever I caught him with a girl. He never went through that awkward adolescent stage of learning how to be good with the opposite sex. Women have always come naturally to him.

My thoughts are interrupted when Adrian's mouth parts and his tongue slides out to lick his lips. My eyes dart to his, only to find his gaze fixed on my collarbone region. A realization crosses me that I'm not the only one doing the observing here. Adrian is studying me too. And suddenly, I'm wondering what's going through his mind. Does he like my shoulders? Are my collarbones up to par? I've never considered that collarbones can be attractive, but now I'm self-conscious about mine and hope I have the sexiest collarbones in existence.

Another thought crosses my mind as I move to observing the muscles in his chest: right now, Adrian has full permission to stare at my breasts. I'm slightly mortified yet have always known I've got an impressive rack. But still, this is Adrian we're talking about, staring at my breasts.

Kathy speaks before Adrian gets the chance to gaze any lower than my shoulders. "Now that we're connected with our partner's body, we'll draw our attention back to their face. Eyes are the windows to the soul. They'll tell you more than words ever can. Gaze into your partner's eyes. Hold eye contact with them. We'll maintain this for the next two minutes."

I'm hoping a meteorite flies through the ozone layer and strikes me dead this very second. How am I meant to survive two minutes of unbroken eye contact with Adrian?

Heat spreads all throughout my body as I meet his brown eyes. They've always been one of his best features, second to his smile. His *genuine* smile, not the cocky one. But all I see in his eyes right now is competition. He's determined to be the one who holds eye contact the longest without showing weakness. As much as I hate to admit it, he's winning. Even though Adrian is only focusing on my eyes, I'm certain he can see the bright red tomato I'm turning into. Knowledge of my redness only intensifies the color. I wouldn't be surprised if someone mistook my blush for third-degree sunburns.

"Sometimes eye contact can be daunting," Kathy says, and I'm positive she's directing her words at me. "Remember to breathe. Slow and steady breaths."

Two minutes seems to be turning into a million years. What makes everything worse is that Adrian isn't even breaking a sweat. There's something smug in his eyes. He's enjoying watching me struggle.

"Let's move into our first pose," Kathy finally says. Faster than lightning, I swing my body around to face her. "Sit back-to-back with your partner."

More torture but a slightly less painful request. Everyone follows, with me and Adrian the last to do so.

A chill runs over my skin as our spines press together. "Just so you know," I whisper, "those were the most torturous two minutes of my life."

"Likewise. It was like staring into the eyes of a demon."

Kathy speaks again. "Hold each other's hands and extend your arms above your head, taking a beautiful stretch as you windmill your hands slowly from right to left."

We do so with reluctance. As I'm silently cursing this day, I catch Tory a couple of mats over, closer to the water, biting back a laugh at my situation. I roll my eyes and look away.

Over the next twenty minutes, Kathy leads us through a series of poses where we have to remain interconnected with our partner as our bodies warm up for more advanced poses. The worst pose is downward dog. I'm on my hands and feet with my ass sticking up in the air. Why does this seem to be a theme for the week?

"Hey," Adrian whispers, standing behind me. I can't see him but am certain from his tone that he has a snide grin plastered to his face. "This is like when I first saw you struggling with your luggage in the lobby."

"Your perverted mind must be enjoying the view."

"Like this," Kathy says, guiding Adrian closer to me. "This is what I meant by standing behind your partner. Step between her legs and take hold of her hips."

My eyes widen with embarrassment as Adrian takes his place. Once clearing his throat, his hot hands rest on the bare skin of my hips. A shiver ripples down my spine at his touch, and I tell myself it's from revulsion. But then why is my groin suddenly aching with need?

Regardless, Adrian's hands on my hips are not what has

me all worked up down here. In this position, his dick is inches from my groin. I don't know whether my imagination is running wild, but I can feel heat radiating from his crotch.

"That's it," Kathy says. "Gently draw her body back to you. She'll feel a nice lengthening through her spine."

Phoebe laughs at us. "That's not the only thing that will be lengthening."

I expect Adrian to laugh at his sister's joke, but he coughs and releases his hands from me.

"Don't be shy," Kathy tells him, guiding his hands back to my hips. "This movement is about intimacy and love. Pull her closer to you."

"I'd rather not," he says at the same time as Kathy gives him a gentle nudge, pressing his hips into my ass, doggy style. And oh my God, his dick is against my crotch, *hard*. If it weren't for the divider of our clothes, we'd be as good as having sex right now.

A squeak exits my throat, and Adrian and I are quick to pull away from each other. Kathy tsks and tends to the couple beside us.

"Seriously?" I hiss, quiet enough for only Adrian to hear. "You're actually hard?"

"What do you expect, Verena?" His tone is even more acidic than mine. "There's an ass poking up in the air that I'm meant to press myself against. Of course I'm going to be fucking hard. I'm only male."

"Oh, so it could be anyone's ass that turns you on?"

"Wait, now you're annoyed I wasn't hard because it's *you*?"

"Don't be ridiculous," I scoff, turning away from him so he can't see how royally I've messed up.

"What's the issue, then?"

"There *is* no issue as long as you keep your dirty dick away from me."

Our bickering comes to a stop as Kathy addresses everyone. "Next, we'll move to a base and flyer pose. Have the smaller person in your pair be the flyer. Bases, lie on your back with your legs bent at a forty-five-degree angle."

All the bases move into position. I half expect Adrian to make some derogatory comment about my weight and that he needs to be the flyer, but he lies down and waits for the next instructions.

"Flyers, step up to your base and hook the soles of their feet into the groove of your hip bones. Then reach forward and grab their hands."

Cringing on the inside, I step forward and do as told, thankful that at least there's no P on V action in this pose.

"Bases, extend your legs straight up into the air and let your flyer soar to the sky," Kathy says.

Everyone complies, and within a second, I'm in a plank position above Adrian, balancing myself on his hands and feet.

"Hey," he taunts, "you look like less of a bitch from this angle."

"Too bad, you still look like a jerk. Got an erection this time?"

"You wish."

"Bases," Kathy says, "as you get comfortable with this position, experiment with lowering your arms."

Adrian and I look at the other couples for an example. The majority of bases have lowered their arms, bringing the flyer's face closer to their own. Some are even kissing. Of course Jake and Jannah are one of them.

Adrian taunts me by lowering his arms. I growl, which

only makes him laugh. "Careful. If you don't start being nice to me, I might drop you."

"You wouldn't dare."

His arms lower farther, bringing me closer to him. "Or maybe punish you with a kiss."

I wriggle, trying to push myself higher. Trying to free myself from his grip and lean back so I can slide down from his legs, but he holds tight.

"Or you can come plummeting down all on your own," he says with tension creasing his brows. "Hold still, I'm not joking. I'm losing grip of you."

His arms lower again—whether to stabilize or taunt me, I'm unsure.

"Adrian, stop!"

"You're the one wriggling—ouch!" His arm buckles beneath me and I go tumbling down, my body landing on top of his and our foreheads bumping.

I suck in a hiss of air through clenched teeth, wincing at the throbbing pain in my head. It's only when I open my eyes that I notice how close my face is to Adrian's. My lips are hovering right above his. I can feel his breath on my face, and oh, his scent is *so* intoxicating.

We share a moment of eye contact that has me growing warm for different reasons than when Kathy made us look at each other during the mindfulness exercise. The sharp-witted Adrian I've come to know has disappeared behind those warm eyes and is replaced with the Adrian I once called my best friend.

He sits up, keeping me fastened in his lap, and runs light fingers over my forehead. "You okay?" he whispers.

I'm too caught off guard by the tenderness in his eyes to form an answer. He hasn't looked at me like this since we were children, and maybe not even then. This is something entirely different.

"Verena, are you all right?" he repeats.

"Oh, dear." Kathy comes running to us, breaking the moment. "That looked like a nasty fall. Is anyone hurt?"

I cough a few times, shaking some sense back into myself as I return from my Adrian daze. He's still holding me, so I slip out of his arms and adjust my hair, turning away from him.

"I'm fine," I tell Kathy.

"I think that's enough excitement for one lesson," Kathy says to everyone. "Let's cool down with one last stretch. This one is impossible to hurt yourself with. Here we go— wide-legged forward fold. Sit on the mat, face your partner, and spread your legs wide like you're doing the straddle splits."

Without speaking a word to each other, Adrian and I get into position. I can't bring myself to meet his eyes, unsure of how to act if the tenderness is still present in them. Or worse, if he's returned to his old ways and is all snark. Words cannot describe how desperate I am for this class to end.

"The fun in this pose is that the farther apart your legs spread, the closer you and your partner can be," Kathy says. "I've had couples do the full splits and their chests end up flush against each other."

My legs are at a ninety-degree angle. At Kathy's story, I close them a little farther.

"Oh, come on, baby doll. Don't be like that," Adrian teases.

I guess that answers my question of his attitude. Something inside me aches that we've lost that brief moment of a connection.

"I've seen you dance on your show and know how flexible you are. Open up for me, won't you?" Adrian takes hold of my thighs and pulls me closer, my legs spreading wider in the process.

His strength is undeniably hot, the way he can effortlessly move my body. Again, I have flashbacks of my dream —him moving above me, sweating from how hard he is exerting himself during sex. This time, though, the visions are more intimate and have more weight to them, because he's gazing down at me with the same affection I saw in his eyes a moment ago.

Adrian's mouth tips up on one side. "It doesn't take much to make you blush, does it?"

I avert my gaze from Adrian, but Kathy walks by, tilting my head back to him. "Eye contact, remember."

Adrian grins, confident and self-assured, with a look in his eyes that says he's won this round. I don't have any fight left in me. All I know is my heart is swimming in dangerous waters.

Chapter Ten

After that scarring yoga experience, I spend the remaining daylight hours avoiding Adrian at all costs because I'm not sure how to act around him. I hang out by my private pool, sketching designs and checking my work emails, even though this is meant to be a work-free week. Come sundown, though, Adrian and I have a date with the two brides that I can't weasel my way out of.

I arrive solo at the resort's poolside cocktail lounge, wearing a pink dress with the skirt made of feathers, because I know for a fact Adrian hates the color. He made sure I knew it in high school when I dyed my hair fluorescent pink.

There aren't any set wedding events tonight, but most guests seem to be scattered throughout the cocktail lounge, their glasses clinking as they chat in small groups with the background music of a live reggae band.

"Verena, over here," Tory calls. She's sitting at the bar with Phoebe and Adrian.

A smile lights each of their faces when they notice me. After seeing that kind look in Adrian's eyes during yoga, I hate knowing this is all an act for him. It takes everything inside me to smile back.

I didn't cross paths with Adrian before he left my bungalow, seeing as I locked him out of the bathroom while I dressed myself, but he looks effortlessly handsome again, as always. That in itself annoys me, that he doesn't need to put effort into his appearance. He threw on the first thing he found in his luggage—jeans and a white button-down rolled up to his elbows—and still manages to look sexy.

Adrian stands from his bar stool as I approach. Chills run up my spine as he slips an arm around me, kissing my hair. "Hey, beautiful. No seats left. Take mine."

"Don't be silly. Verena can sit on your lap," Phoebe suggests.

Not going to happen, especially after that downward dog erection. "It's fine, I'll stand at the bar. We won't be here for long, right? Dinner's not far off."

"Speaking of which." Tory eyes me with mirth. "All of our parents want us to gather for a family dinner. They're just as desperate to hear about you two."

Kill me. Please.

"Sounds great." Adrian takes a seat, pulling me between his legs so that I'm leaning into him. His arms wrap around my waist and his face pops over my shoulder to rest beside mine.

Phoebe watches us with a massive grin. "You look amazing together."

"It's all her," Adrian says. "I love this dress on you, Verena. Glad you wore it."

Damn, he's one step ahead of me again. His words may as well be *I know exactly why you wore pink.*

Goosebumps rise over my skin as he plays with my hair, twirling a lock with his finger. "You cold?" Adrian asks with a spark of humor in his words. He rubs my arms and hugs me closer.

"Before I forget, Verena," Tory says. "Stacy mentioned you don't have a partner for the first dance. Phoebe and I have been so busy with wedding prep that the odd number in the bridal party slipped our attention. We've been thinking, maybe Adrian can dance with you? *Please*," she begs him, drawing out the word. "I know you hate dancing and you've already said you don't want to be in the spotlight, but do it for Verena?"

I scoff at Adrian. "When did you ever say you don't want to be in the spotlight?"

"Consider it done," he answers Tory. I'm unsure whether to thank or scold my sister for this "favor."

"Perfect!" Phoebe chirps. "You know, it's so nice having you around again, Verena. Maybe now that you're with my brother, we'll be seeing more of you?"

Adrian answers before I can, meeting me with an adoring smile. "Verena told me she's coming home to Sitka this year for Christmas."

Excuse me? I did *what?*

Adrian lightly jabs my ribs. "You said so after yoga this morning. Didn't you, honey?"

He wants me to play along for who knows what reason. But I can't. Not with this. Promising my family I'll return for the holidays is not fair on them. "You misunderstood me. When I said *home*, I meant your home in London."

"We could always visit you in New York throughout the year," Tory says.

"That would be nice." As long as it's just Tory and Phoebe and not my entire family. I have barriers up around my home turf for a reason. The city is my safe space where I get to be me and not the girl from my childhood. "I do feel bad that I haven't seen you two much over the years. This might not be obvious, but if you guys ever need anything, anything at all, I'm more than happy to help out."

"Bitch, please," Tory laughs. "You've already paid for the majority of this wedding. We can't keep leeching off you."

"You're not leeching. I want to help."

"Well, thank you," Phoebe says. "Anyway, we're dying to hear how you and Adrian got together."

I shrug the question off. "Ah... you know, FaceTime chats and texts."

"Details, girl!" Phoebe demands.

"There really aren't any."

Tory swats my arm. "I know you're cautious because you live in the public eye, but if you can't tell your own sisters about your life, then who can you tell?"

I glare at her, but she only laughs in return.

"I'll tell the story," Adrian says. "Let me order another drink first. Vee, what do you want?"

My chest tingles as that name leaves his lips. The name only he ever called me back when we were best friends. Coming out of his mouth now, he speaks it with such tenderness. It reminds me too much of why I once fell in love with him.

Adrian notices the delay in my response and the pink tinge on my cheeks. The slightest smile touches his face, making me wonder if he's remembering too, or if he's laughing on the inside at how pathetic I am.

"Can you order me something nonalcoholic?" I ask. "I've embarrassed myself enough for one week."

"So, how long has this been going on for?" Phoebe asks as Adrian orders drinks from the same bartender as last night, Samaya. The young girl behind the bar winks at me and nods in Adrian's direction while mouthing, *he's hot.*

I shrug in response to Phoebe's question. "Two months."

"And how serious are you guys? Are we going to be planning another wedding anytime soon?"

I choke on my saliva. All three of them watch me as I gasp for air. Even Samaya.

When I clear my throat, I say, "We're just having fun."

"Yeah, okay," Adrian snorts, wrapping me tighter in his arms before whispering into my ear. "Jake is watching and you look like a rigid horse. Do a better job of convincing everyone we're together. If we're *just having fun*, then have some fun."

My eyes search the cocktail lounge for Jake, but Adrian is quick to plant a kiss on my cheek and I lose all concentration.

"My God, I feel like I'm the only one working at this fake relationship," he whispers again. "Didn't you learn anything from this morning? Don't look in their direction when I say someone is watching us."

"You obviously didn't learn anything either, because I said no kissing."

"Verena, I would hardly call that a kiss. If I kissed you properly you'd be weak all over and begging me to fuck you." His voice is husky against my ear, the promise in his words making heat pool in my groin.

"Is Jannah with him too?" I ask to distract myself from thoughts of Adrian taking me to bed.

"Yes. My Isabelle is here as well."

My Isabelle?

"What?" he asks, as if hearing how my thoughts dwell over his claim of her.

"Nothing."

Adrian's got his agenda. I've got mine. I can't deny that I love Jake seeing me with this handsome creature. Right this very moment, I'm imagining that Jake wants me back and Jannah sees it all over his face. I don't want the cheater back in my life, I just really want him to want me. I want him to suffer. Does that make me a bad person? By the disastrous way things have been going this week, I'm past caring. If I loosen up, Adrian is right—this could be a whole lot of fun.

I lean into Adrian's chest and twine my fingers with his, smiling at the brides. "Okay, girls, you want to know the real story of how we got together? Adrian messaged me a few months ago, saying he was desperate to talk. I only responded because I thought he might have done some soul searching and was ready to apologize for our past. Well, he did, and during our first FaceTime, he told me he's been in love with me since we were kids, and that fate was drawing us back together."

Both girls squirm with excitement once I finish telling the story. I glance at Adrian and whisper, "How's that for having fun? Am I playing along to your standards?"

"Yes, you're doing perfect," he murmurs before raising his voice for the others to hear. "You forgot to add in the part where you drunk dialed me a month earlier, confessing your love. That's what truly got me thinking about you again."

"It was a pocket dial. I didn't know I had his number saved in my phone," I clarify, my heart racing as I make up details on the spot. If Adrian wants to play, then let's play. "So, we start talking and because I've had too many drinks, I embarrass myself and tell Adrian about how much the cheater hurt me. But you know what Adrian said in return?

That every girl he's ever been with, all he could think about when kissing them was me."

Phoebe raises both hands to her cheeks. "No way!"

"It's true, actually," Adrian says, and I'm stunned that he isn't adding any more details to the story to make himself look better.

"Anyway," I continue, my voice betraying me and turning into something exhilarated, "I flew to London for a weekend to be with him. When I arrived, Adrian had scattered rose petals throughout his house and, well... it was one steamy weekend. Let's leave it at that."

"No, please," Adrian teases, "I want to hear the rest."

Tory laughs. "I think we can fill in the blanks."

Unlike my sister, Phoebe sits forward on her bar stool, fascinated by the story. "But the hate between you two, what was that all about?"

Adrian's fingers tighten around me. "You know, I don't remember. It's been so long that the past has all faded away."

His tone is so genuine that I stop for a moment, wondering if it's the truth or all part of his act. Worse still is that I have no idea what I want the answer to be.

Chapter Eleven

Adrian's parents, Cece and George Hunter, have not taken their eyes off Adrian and me during this combined family dinner at the cliffside restaurant. They're obsessed with the way Adrian's arm rests over my shoulders and how he always says *us* instead of *I* or *me*. I can see a film playing in the reflection of Cece's eyes—a montage of Adrian's and my future, filled with an army of children in our Sitka home.

My mother is worse. She keeps making jokes about how the neighbors of our bungalow will need to sleep with earmuffs to block the sounds of our baby-making. Whose parents talk like this? Give me a normal family. *Please*.

"Have you two discussed the logistics of your relationship?" Mom asks us across the dining table. "Adrian, you're in London, and we all know nothing will get Verena out of New York. Long-distance can't last forever."

"Mom," I warn.

Adrian gazes back at me with a doting smile. His fingers create swirling patterns on my arm, making it difficult for me to focus. "We're taking things one step at a time," he says. "No need to rush."

"I don't mean to play devil's advocate, but yes there is," Cece counters. "You two aren't growing any younger. Fertility drops every year past the age of thirty."

"We're twenty-five," I remind everyone. "I think we'll be okay."

Mom takes a bite of her pasta and giggles. "Time can easily slip away from you, especially when you're focusing on your career. You need a plan. Adrian, I say put a baby in her and tie her down."

From the laughter in Mom's voice, it's clear she's joking. But my limits crack. This conversation isn't even the slightest bit funny to me and I can't take one more second of the Adrian and Verena sex talk. "Should we start stripping and have sex right in front of everyone?"

None of the parents realize how irritated I am and break out in laughter. Dad hits the table. "Is that what you two were doing last night in the ocean?"

With a foul taste in my mouth, I excuse myself to the restroom.

"You okay, Vee?" Adrian takes my hand as I rise from the table, but I slip out of his grip.

"Should we join you?" Tory asks me.

"I need a moment alone."

I leave the laughing group behind as I make my way to the ladies' room. The sight of our two families together annoys me. A familiarity exists between them like they're all blood related instead of friends. It's been like that for as long as I can remember. Our families are so tightly meshed. We basically lived in each other's houses when growing up, the four adults co-parenting all of us kids. But ever since the day Adrian and I parted as friends, I've always been the odd one out. I don't belong with them. I don't belong anywhere except in Manhattan, where my true family consists of Darius, Zac, my show, and my fashion label.

Just thinking about Adrian's and my friendship breakup has me slamming the restroom stall door. I thought I'd moved beyond all the hurtful emotions of losing him and replaced them with hate. I don't know if it's from seeing Adrian again after seven years, being reunited with our two families, or the tender way he looked at me after my fall during yoga, but now my chest is aching with sadness over the day he stopped talking to me. I understand he wanted more than just me as a friend, but there was nothing stopping him from bringing me into his new social circle with him. For some reason, which I've spent years trying to figure out but never will, I wasn't good enough for him. I embarrassed him or something. I don't know.

My throat grows tight as if I'm about to cry. Instead, I push the tears away and focus on hate, because how could he have left me like that? What did I do wrong for him to leave me?

But as much as I tell myself this feeling is hate, when the tears can no longer be fought off, I can't hide from how sad I am. How much I miss my childhood friend. How I've spent years hating Adrian, but that if I could somehow change the past to get my friend back, I would do it without a second of hesitation.

Ten minutes pass before I'm brave enough to leave the restroom stall. I fix my hair in the mirror and touch up my makeup, assuring no traces of my tears can be found.

When I return to the table, there's one person missing.

"Where's your brother?" I ask Phoebe.

A glimpse of panic crosses her face that I don't know how to interpret. "Ah... He stepped out for a moment. I'm sure he'll be back soon."

If Adrian isn't here, I'm not putting myself through unnecessary suffering. "You know, I think I'll take a breather too. Get some fresh air by the ocean. I won't be long."

"Verena." She grabs my arm. "I don't think that's a good idea."

"Girl, chill." I pull free and head outside.

As I search for privacy beyond the restaurant, part of me wonders if I should be honest with Adrian and tell him how I feel—that I miss him and want to rekindle a friendship. But the cautious side of my heart reminds me of the day Adrian "asked" me to the school dance then laughed at me with all of his friends. I've got too much to lose by sharing my feelings with Adrian. Until he lets his guard down around me—correction, *if* he ever lets his guard down around me and wants to be friends—that's when I'll be honest.

The evening sea breeze whips through my hair, salty and damp, as I find my own little alcove on the path overlooking the beach. Someone has placed a table and chair here from the restaurant. I'm about to take a seat and relax, but with the wind travels the sound of a heated voice, ruining all sense of peace.

"I can't believe you, Adrian. We were together for three years and now it's like I don't even know who you are."

Whoa. Okay, Phoebe's weirdness now makes sense.

The voice belongs to Isabelle. I catch sight of her standing farther down the path with Adrian, looking like a fiery goddess as nearby torches flicker amber light over her skin and red hair.

"I had the courtesy to tell you I'd be here with Conner," she continues. "Don't you think I deserve the same respect? You're dating Verena Valentine, of all people. All it takes is a simple phone call or text. *Hey, Isabelle, just giving you a heads-up that I'm dating Verena Valentine. Oh, and we were childhood sweethearts and have been destined to be together all this time. The three years you and I spent together was only a filler.*"

"Isabelle, it's not like that," he hushes, holding her shoulders. "You know it's not. I cared about you. I *still* care about you."

Welp, this is clearly a conversation I'm not meant to be hearing. I step back, making an escape, but stumble over the chair leg and knock the damn thing over. Both Adrian and Isabelle turn in my direction. Something vile sits in her expression when she sees me. Shock in Adrian's.

"Sorry," I call, smiling with an awkward wave. "I didn't hear anything. I'm leaving."

"No, I am." Isabelle storms up the path, not daring to look at me as she passes.

I cringe at Adrian. "I didn't mean to interrupt. I came here for fresh air."

Adrian steps up beside me. "Don't be ridiculous. I've got Isabelle exactly where I want her. Did you hear that conversation? By the end of this week, she'll be begging to have me back."

"Ugh, men. I'll never understand them."

Adrian rests his forearms on the railing next to me and gazes out at the ocean. "A guy will do anything to win the girl he loves."

I join him at the railing, my hair and dress flapping in the wind. "I never knew Adrian Hunter was such a romantic."

"There are many things you don't know about me."

"Tell me something, then."

"What do you want to know?"

"What's this whole quiet-guy act you've got going on?"

He laughs. "I think you're the first person to ever call me quiet."

"You know what I mean. I came into this week expecting to see you leading every event, making speeches every night, having all the old ladies swoon after your charm, and banging all the young ones. Instead, I hear you turned down being the MC. You haven't reached for the microphone once and you even slipped out of the welcome dinner last night."

He shrugs. "I learned the hard way that being the center of attention is not a good fit for me. I get too caught up in the popularity contest and lose sight of what's important to me."

"Congratulations. Didn't know you possessed the intelligence to look inward and observe your many flaws."

"That's rich, coming from you."

"What are you talking about? I'm perfect," I tease. Adrian grins and rolls his eyes. "So, tell me about Isabelle. How did you two meet?"

"She studied education at college with Phoebe. My sister brought her home one Christmas and the rest is history."

"How did you two end up living in the UK?"

"She got a teaching job in London and I followed her there."

I shove his arm. "This is so unfair. How come no one ever hassles *you* about moving away from Sitka? At least I still live in the country."

"Maybe because I go home for Christmas every year and haven't forgotten where my roots stem from," he says, losing all humor in his voice. "You've cut all ties, Verena."

I let out a loud huff. "Here we go. If it isn't obvious, my

childhood is something I want to forget. You have no concept of how difficult this week is for me."

"Poor little Verena. Let's hear your sad story. Educate me on all of your struggles."

"You are such a dick, Adrian." I step back from the railing, ready to storm off, but he grabs my wrist and spins me to face him. It's the most serious I've ever seen him look.

"I won't understand unless you tell me."

I rip my arm out from his grip, and with it, all the pent-up emotions that spilled from me in the restroom return. "It's the way everyone in this community treats me. It's the way they've *always* treated me. I'm the laughingstock and I hate it. It's seeing *you* again, Adrian. I'm never good enough for you. You were my whole world and then you abandoned me!"

I silence myself before I can let any more truths slip out of my mouth, horrified that I already let this much escape and showed Adrian a vulnerable side of me. I'm not sure why I'm so bothered by our past when I moved on from it long ago. At least, I thought I'd moved on from it.

Adrian doesn't say anything either. The night is suddenly dead silent aside from the sounds of my uneven breathing and the ocean. The two of us are staring at each other with our thoughts running a million miles per hour. There's nothing defensive in his expression, though. He's not out for blood. I can see within his eyes that he's not creating a snarky response.

Finally, he swallows hard. "I'm sorry."

It's the last thing I expect to hear him say. I'm so taken by surprise that I end up shrugging his apology off by saying, "It's in the past," which he can see is clearly not true after my outburst just now.

"I don't think anyone knows how to act around you. People get scared of shiny, pretty things."

Again, he says something unexpected. And did Adrian call me pretty? I have to remind myself how to breathe. I repeat his words in my mind to check for their meaning and that he's not secretly insulting me.

"What's *your* issue with shiny, pretty things?" I ask.

He smiles. "I don't have an issue with them. I like them very much."

Somehow, I ease into a smile too, with my heart thumping rapidly in my chest. This moment is the most real Adrian and I have been with each other since we were children. No scheming or insults. I can see it again—that rare but genuine look in his eyes and smile. My favorite one.

I have the urge to throw my arms around Adrian's neck and tell him how much I miss him, or at the very least, ask if we can attempt to be friends again, but my sister comes into view, calling out to us from the restaurant and breaking our moment.

"Hey, you two." Tory cups both hands around her mouth. "We're going back to Mom and Dad's bungalow to play a board game."

"All right, see you later," I call back, desperate for her to leave so I can keep this moment between me and Adrian alive.

"Nuh-uh, the happy couple are coming with us."

Chapter Twelve

Mom and Dad's bungalow is beautiful, but it doesn't have a pool or beachfront view like mine. The eight of us are sitting on couches in their garden as Dad sets up the board game on a coffee table in front of us. On one side of the table, it's me and Adrian. Across from us are the two brides, Mom and Dad on our left, and Cece and George to the right.

"Everyone in pairs?" Dad asks.

"Siblings against siblings?" I suggest.

"As if," Tory says. "Couples against couples."

"Stuck with me again," Adrian laughs under his breath.

I'm not sure how to respond to him after our chat right before coming here. Nor am I sure how to behave. Did we have a breakthrough and are now being civil to each other?

Nothing is clear between Adrian and me, so I settle for saying, "I bet you're enjoying torturing me."

"Loving it." He drapes an arm over my shoulder.

I scoot away, whispering, "Jake and Isabelle aren't around."

"This charade has gone far beyond fooling our exes. Our moms can't stop radiating with joy at the sight of us."

Our whispering comes to an end as Phoebe pipes up with a question for the group. "Who's looking forward to our day out at sea tomorrow?"

George nods. "Diving in the Great Barrier Reef has been on my bucket list for years."

"Day out at sea?" I repeat.

"It's in the schedule," Adrian tells me. "You up for some snorkeling?"

"Sure. What's the day's plan?"

"We've hired a luxury yacht for all of our guests," Tory explains, bouncing with excitement. "We leave first thing in the morning and sail out to the reef. After lunch on the yacht, we head to Whitehaven Beach. I'm sure you've seen photos of it. It's that magnificent beach with the pristine sand marbled through the water. They feature it in all the tourism promotions."

"Sounds amazing."

"Can't wait," Dad says, shuffling cards. "All right, everyone, listen up for the rules of this game. When it's your team's turn, one of you will pick a card from the box and describe the word on it to your partner. If your partner guesses correctly, you move onto the next card. The aim is to get as many right answers as possible before the sand timer runs out. Everyone understand?"

We all nod.

"I'll be terrible at this game, just warning you all," I say.

"I'm sure you'll do great, kid. How about we go first?" Dad says to Mom. "Tory, flip the sand timer." She does, and Dad rushes for his first card. "Hmm... It's an action. Babies do this when they're hungry."

"Eat?" Mom answers.

"No. What sound do they make?"

"Screaming?"

"No! Vanessa, it's so obvious."

"Clearly it's not!"

"Crying!" He clicks his tongue and moves to the next card. "Oh, okay, this one will be easier. Think of Shakespeare's play. *The Taming of the...*?"

"I don't know Shakespeare."

"How can you not know this title? The answer is *Shrew!*"

The rest of their turn continues in the same fashion. It's a complete disaster as everyone watches them bicker over words, until Tory announces, "Time!"

I'm dreading my turn. Mom and Dad are usually so calm and articulate. This game is a nightmare waiting to unwind, and I'm not sure if Adrian's and my fragile relationship can survive it.

"How many words did your team guess?" George asks Dad.

"One."

"Ouch. Better luck next time."

"We'll do much better," Mom says, pointedly, "because *I'll* be the caller."

Tory and Phoebe aren't much of an improvement when their turn arrives, and I'm learning a whole new side to Dad that I never knew existed. A competitive and annoying side.

"Oh, crap!" Tory studies her card with panic in her eyes. Out of the five cards she's already burned through during this round, Phoebe has only guessed one correct word. "What is the Blue Danube?"

"Ehhhh!!!" Dad makes a buzzer noise. "You're not meant to say the word. Move to the next card."

"I think it's a river?" Phoebe says.

"It's a waltz," Mom offers, "by Strauss."

"Stop having a conversation during our turn!" Tory demands.

"Times up!" Dad yells, passing the box to Adrian and me.

My palms grow sweaty as I eye Adrian. "What on earth have we walked into? You want to call or guess?"

He pushes the box to me. "You're in the driver's seat."

"You sure?" Adrian probably wants me to call so that he can blame me for not doing a good job when he can't guess the answers. "This is a disaster waiting to happen. Look at all the anger this game evokes."

Adrian rubs my leg. "Come on, baby, relax."

My gaze drops to his hand, and I go rigid. "I can't relax when you're touching me like that."

Everyone laughs, and he withdraws his hands.

Tory turns the sand timer over. "Start!"

I pick up the first card. It's a geography category, the word being *Milan*. This is an easy one for me, but how can I explain it to Adrian? My mind draws a blank. "Um... Ahh. I don't know."

"Breathe, Vee."

I glare at him for using that name, right now of all times. It takes him a moment to understand my expression, then one corner of his mouth slants up. "Verena, you've got this."

"Ah... Okay, you probably won't guess the word, but it's the country I studied fashion in—"

"Milan!" he shouts before I've finished with the clue.

"Yes!" Shocked at his answer, I take another card. "I guess um... Oh, I know. She's a famous singer. And it's the color you hate."

"You're not giving me much to work off. I don't hate any color. Try describing the word from a different angle."

"Um... The color I died my hair in high school."

"Pink!"

"Yes!" I draw another card, stunned at how well this is going. "Okay, this guy was your favorite sports star when we were kids."

"Michael Jordan."

"Yes!" I shout on the edge of my seat, then move faster through the cards, spending less time coming up with a logical clue and instead saying the first thing that comes to my mind, because that seems to be working. "Our favorite show when growing up."

"Malcolm in the Middle?"

"No, the other one."

"Seinfeld."

"Yes!" Next card. "My favorite flower."

"Tulip!"

"Yes! The place you said we'd visit together after graduating high school."

"Egypt."

"Yeah, but which place specifically."

He pauses for a moment. "Abu Simbel?"

"Yes! Next card. Your celebrity crush."

"You."

"What?" I laugh, looking at him as if he's crazy. "No, the hot one from *The Mask*."

"Cameron Diaz."

"Yes!"

There's a telepathic bond between us. It's like I'm a child all over again, playing this game with my best friend. The two of us are shouting back and forth at each other with excitement—clue, answer, clue, answer—until Tory calls, "Time!"

I take a well-earned breather. Adrian and I are looking at each other with something that feels like amazement.

Maybe even disbelief? Then we burst into laughter, the kind where I can tell we're both struggling to breathe and see through watering eyes.

"Wow." Tory is the first to interrupt us. I look around the group, finding everyone with beaming smiles directed at Adrian and me. "Who ever knew you were such experts on each other's lives?"

Even though I'm staying clear of alcohol, I'm officially drunk off laughter. It's close to midnight and the board game finished long ago. The two brides and Adrian's parents have retired to their bungalows, but Adrian and I are still here on the couch in my parents' garden, keeping the whole resort up with our snorts and high-pitched cackles as we take a walk down memory lane. Being like this with him is the strangest, nicest, most unexpected and confusing thing I've felt in my adult life.

"Do you remember how we always snuck out after midnight on Halloween and met up at the graveyard to search for zombies?" Adrian asks me as I take a sip of my drink.

Water shoots from my nose as I laugh at the memory. I cover my nose, laughing even harder. "I haven't thought about that in years. We were so certain zombies were real. What about when we were camping in my backyard and the tent collapsed on us in the middle of the night?"

"Yes! That was hilarious. We couldn't find our way out with all the bunched-up fabric and ended up falling asleep in there."

"You two never told me about either of those times," Dad calls through the kitchen window, rinsing wine glasses.

Mom is beside him with a nostalgic smile on her face, drying the dishes. "As lovely as this night has been, it's almost twelve. We've got a big day out at sea tomorrow and you two need to get some sleep."

Adrian tugs me up from the couch and leads us to the front door. I say my goodbyes to Dad and watch with raised brows as Mom pulls Adrian into a bear hug. "The two of you together are perfect," she whispers to him, though, being quiet has never been Mom's strong suit. "Try to ground her, will you? Bring her back to us."

"Can't control a free spirit," Adrian says.

She hugs me next. "Don't mess this up."

When Mom releases me, there's an aura of bliss surrounding her. Not once has she looked this pleased in regards to me. Not when I got my acceptance letter to fashion school in Milan. Not when I opened my business or got my own show. For her, the sight of me and Adrian together trumps all those accomplishments. God dammit.

"See you later," Adrian calls to my parents.

I walk ahead of him on the torch-lit path as we travel back to *my* bungalow, which is really *ours* now that every guest at this wedding thinks we're a happy couple. Yet my heart is hurting because I've had a glimpse into the past and remember what it's like to be friends with Adrian. It feels too good—whatever this is between us—and I want it back. But I can't tell him any of this because he'd love to hold this information over my head. And what if this friendly side of him isn't real? We've been parading our "relationship" around for the entire evening and acting in love with each other on purpose. Now that we're alone, I'm terrified of what's to come.

"What's up with you?" Adrian asks as I kick a rock off

the path. I wish he couldn't read me so well. "You were having fun a second ago."

"This whole fake dating thing is a disaster," I answer without slowing my pace to engage in a proper conversation. "You heard my mom back there, and you saw how happy everyone is for us. It's going to break their hearts when the truth comes out."

"The truth doesn't need to come out. We'll tell them we broke up."

"Even that will break their hearts."

"They'll survive."

We continue the rest of the way to our bungalow in silence, with me dwelling over how much I want my best friend back, and Adrian thinking about... probably how much he loves Isabelle.

I step aside as Adrian unlocks the front door of our bungalow. My pride is too obsessed with itself to speak any of these Adrian revelations aloud, so I settle for something more shaded. "By the way, you're right. I do owe you thanks for saving me from drowning. Also for preventing further embarrassment by getting me off that beach."

He pauses, laughing to himself. "Owing me thanks and actually thanking me are not the same thing."

"Okay," I sigh. "Thank you, Adrian."

"Seriously? Verena Valentine is thanking me? I never thought I'd hear you say those words to my face."

Yep, see. This is why I went in with shields. "Don't be a prick about it."

"Oh, I'm never a prick, Vee."

My breath stops short. That name again. He's been dropping that bomb all night like it's a thoughtless habit.

Once we're inside the bungalow, I close the door behind us and step out of my heels, lowering myself a good five inches. "No one's around. You don't have to keep calling me Vee or pretending to be nice."

"Hadn't realized I was doing it." He empties his pockets on the living room table. "And I'm not pretending anything. You're genuinely fun to be around when you're not acting like a bitch."

"Do you ever stop with the insults?"

"I said *acting* like a bitch, not that you're actually one. They're two very different things."

"Adrian..." I'm about to fight back with some smart comment but decide to hold my tongue, not wanting to jeopardize this state of semi-peace we've formed. Silence lingers between us, and Adrian folds his arms, waiting for me to continue, but I don't.

"Yes?" he prompts.

Something more important comes to mind. "Did you really mean—" Ugh, I don't know why I'm asking this, but I'm already halfway through the question and may as well finish it. "Did you really mean what you said at the cocktail lounge—about the past fading?"

"Yeah, I did. It's been seven years. I'm not hung up on what went down between us as kids. And let me be clear about something. I don't hate you."

My gaze narrows with confusion. "But last night... In the ocean... You said you would have sex with me if you didn't hate me so much."

"I was messing around. Playing with you."

"Wait. So... that means..." My thoughts suddenly turn filthy.

A lazy grin pulls at his lips. "Yeah, I'd fuck you if the right moment presented itself."

I lick my lips. Is *now* the right moment?

"No, Vee, this isn't the right moment," he says, amused.

Shit. I spoke my thoughts out loud.

That same serious expression from earlier in the night returns to Adrian's face—the one when we were having a moment while overlooking the ocean. "Tell me what you remember most about our past."

His question makes all the steamy thoughts disappear from my mind. "I don't want to relive those memories. For once, we're getting along reasonably well. I'd rather not reopen old wounds."

"What do you mean 'for once?' As I recall, there were years where we were attached at the hip."

"You know what I mean," I call over my shoulder, leaving him in the living room as I retire for the night.

"Hey, what was with that whole *I hate the color pink* thing?"

I'm halfway across the room when I stop to face him again. "You hated it as a kid."

"Don't all boys hate pink?"

"My point exactly. Then there was that time in high school when I dyed my hair pink and all you said to me was *Interesting hair*."

"A: what is wrong with having interesting hair? And B: people can change their mind about colors."

"It was the way you said it," I shoot back at him, and ugh, we're fighting again. "Not one word from you in weeks, then the first time we were forced into a social situation, you gave me a dirty look and grunted *Interesting hair*, then didn't speak to me again for another month."

Adrian holds his hands up, shaking his head in confusion. "How do you remember these specific details?"

"It's easy to remember moments when someone is rude to you. Maybe that's why I have so many memories of you."

Instead of biting back, he shrugs and says, "I complimented you on your pink dress earlier in the evening."

"I know you, Adrian. You were being sarcastic."

He laughs in disbelief and runs a hand through his hair. "Okay, because you have some serious self-esteem issues—"

"I don't have—"

"Let me say this loud and clear, Verena, because I can't believe we're fighting over something so stupid. I like the color pink and I like it on you. And in case you were too drunk to remember me saying it last night, I don't think you're fat. I like the way you look... very much."

I'd be flattered if I weren't so mortified that I apparently opened up to Adrian last night about my body insecurities. "Um..." My voice thins, thinking about that sex dream, "What else did I say to you last night?"

He smirks. "I told you, you propositioned me for hate sex."

There's one problem with that. I'm not sure I hate Adrian anymore. Not even a little.

"Come on, admit it, Vee, you don't seriously hate me, not after the night we've had."

Are my thoughts written all over my face or something? How does this guy keep reading me so well?

I turn toward the bedroom so he can't see the truth in my eyes. "If you'll excuse me, I'm going to sleep, in *my* bed."

"That's not fair. You got the bed last night."

I spin around in disbelief to face him. "That's because you put me in it. You could have left me to fend for myself on the floor. That's what I would have done if the roles were reversed."

He doesn't answer me straight away. There's a face-off moment where the two of us stare each other down. It's like we're reading each other's mind, because the next moment, we both run for the bedroom, knocking over anything in our path. Chairs grind against the floor as we shove them to the side. A vase smashes to the ground, but neither one of us acknowledges it, desperate for the win.

Even though I had a head start, Adrian and his athletic body catch up within a second. We both reach the bedroom door at the same time, with neither of us able to fit through it as we wedge ourselves in the door frame. We're pushing and shoving. My boobs graze against Adrian's shoulder at one point. At another point, his palm is face-hugging me and I'm about to have an alien impregnated down my throat like Sigourney Weaver. Then he pulls the dirtiest move of all and uses his caveman strength to throw me over his shoulder, carrying me kicking and screaming out to the pool.

"Adrian, no!" I laugh. "Don't you dare throw me in the water. This dress costs more than you'll see in your lifetime."

He does this miraculous feat of strength and flips me upside down so that my head is hanging inches above the water, my hair already ruined as it soaks in the pool.

"Say I can have the bed," Adrian tells me.

My lips can't form an answer. All I can think about is how the flip Adrian just performed on me would translate in sex. That, and I'm pretty sure my ass is on display again.

"Say it." He lowers me to the water.

"All right! The bed is yours. Put me on safe ground."

With another amazing sex-flip (yep, that's how I'm referring to it from now on), Adrian plants my feet on the ground.

What a sucker.

As soon as his hands are off me, I push him into the water.

Clearly, I hadn't thought that move through because the splash sprays my dress, but I'm laughing too hard to care. He surfaces, fighting a grin that I barely see because I'm hunched over in fits of giggles.

"Verena, you are dead!"

I squeal, running for the bungalow as he climbs out of the water. As with our earlier race to claim the bed, he catches me effortlessly in his soaking wet clothes and carries me back to the pool, plunging us both into the water.

I loosen myself from his arms and come up for air, pushing hair back from my face and treading water. "Oh my God, Adrian, the dress."

He splashes me in the face. "You're rich. I'm sure you can make another one."

"That's not the point. This dress is made from the finest silk. And these are huia tail feathers. Do you know how rare they are? The dress needs a funeral now. Not to mention, the weight of this thing in the water is going to have me drowning again." I do an awkward wriggle and free myself from the soaked fabric, then toss it onto the ground.

Adrian raises a brow. "Striptease again?" I splash him back. He ducks under the water, removing his jeans and shirt.

"This isn't some competition, Adrian. Just because I took my clothes off doesn't mean you need to do the same."

"They were weighing me down too. I don't have the luxury of your rescue services if I go under."

"True."

"So, about this bed situation..." he prompts.

"We're not sharing it, if that's what you're hinting at."

"We've shared a bed many times before. Surely a sturdy pillow wall down the center will stop you from throwing yourself at me."

"You are so full of yourself."

Adrian climbs out of the pool. He grabs a towel, rubs it through his hair and wraps it around his waist, then reclines on a daybed. "Because I'm *not* full of myself, I'll be a gentleman and let you have the bed. Goodnight, Verena."

"Wait a minute!" I follow him out of the pool, covering myself with a towel. I see what he's doing—stepping back from a childish game and being the adult. No way am I letting him hold that over my head. I march up to the daybed, hands on hips, and look down at him. "I'm not letting you win this one. You take the bed."

His eyes remain closed, and he doesn't move a muscle.

"Adrian, I know you're not asleep." When there's still no response, I crawl onto the bed with him and push at his chest. "Stop being so annoying."

He laughs, pushing me back. "I'm serious, Vee, you take the bed. It's nice out here. I don't mind sleeping under the stars."

For the first time this evening, I look up, met by a velvety sheen of starlight. I flop back onto the mattress, marveling over the view. "You never see it like this in New York. It's beautiful."

The mattress shifts, and only now do I realize the position I've put myself in. Adrian and I are lying in bed together, gazing at the stars. Okay, this isn't technically a real bed, but it's still a bed.

"The stars are like this in Sitka," he says.

"I remember."

"How many times do you think we did this?"

I don't need to clarify his meaning—the two of us, lying on the grass, counting the stars as kids. "Not enough times."

My words kill all conversation. I'm regretting them the moment they slip out of my mouth. The nostalgia I'm reliving, the lightheartedness between Adrian and me, it's too much to deal with. Yet at the same time, it's not enough. I don't want this moment to end.

When Adrian speaks again, it's only a whisper. "Wanna count the stars again?"

I nod ever so slightly, not sure if he sees the movement. But I notice every tiny movement he makes, and wonder if he has the same awareness of me. All I can focus on is the way his chest rises up and down with quiet breaths. The way his lips move as he murmurs his counting. I close my eyes and listen to his soft words. One hundred... Two hundred... They're the only thing anchoring me to this world as I drift off to sleep.

Chapter Thirteen

A cold breeze stirs me from sleep. Night is still upon us and I'm in my underwear on the day bed, shivering beneath the wet towel I fell asleep in. Disoriented in my half-awake state, I push the towel away and snuggle into the warmth in front of me.

The warmth shifts at my touch, its voice groggy from sleep. "Vee?"

Adrian. I'm not alert enough to respond with words, and answer with a *mm-hmm?*

His hand snakes around my bare midsection, pulling me close to his chest like I'm his. My half-conscious mind enjoys this too much and lets me believe that I *am* his. I slink my leg between his, intertwining our bodies. My chills disappear as I relax into his warm embrace. He feels like home, so blissfully perfect that it's only moments before I drift back to sleep.

I'm alone when I wake, still outside on the daybed with the morning breeze rolling in from the ocean. A frown finds my face as I question whether the memory of Adrian and me cuddling up to each other was real. I want it to have been real, but why would he have left me then? What did the hug even mean? We were half-asleep, not thinking straight. But that's what makes this situation more painful. Adrian and I were acting from our subconscious, hugging each other because we felt close. At least, that's how it felt for me. Adrian... I don't know. I can never tell with him. I feel like I'm waking up after a one-night stand and the guy has snuck out of my home, leaving me high and dry.

I wrap a towel around myself, calling out Adrian's name as I enter our bungalow via the bedroom's French doors. There's no answer, just the sound of the shower faucet as steam escapes through a crack in the adjoining bathroom's door. It dawns on me that my fake boyfriend is naked in there, lathering himself up in soap. I don't know why that's the first thought to enter my mind. The water stops, and suddenly I'm frozen in my spot, afraid of whatever is about to happen between us next.

The bathroom door swings open and out steps Adrian in all his half-naked glory. Damp hair, a bare torso that looks so flipping fantastic this close up, there's a towel around his waist, and a surprised look on his face when he sees me.

I spin away from him and shield my eyes, flustered and acting like a teenage girl who doesn't know how to interact with her crush. "Ah... I didn't see anything."

"Good morning, Vee." I can hear the smile in his voice, which I guess means we're still on good terms.

"I'm just... I'll go wait outside until you're decent."

I bolt into the walk-in closet to organize my outfit for the day, which is a stupid idea because Adrian follows me, searching through his own belongings. The tiny closet is filled with his scent. It smells of masculine cologne and sexiness and everything that is Adrian Hunter. I'm considering hiring a scientist to capture this scent and bottle it into my own personal fragrance that I can take back to America with me. I love it that much.

He leans back against the wall, watching me.

"What?" I pretend to be busy organizing my clothes.

From the corner of my eyes, I catch him grinning. "How did you sleep?"

There's a hidden meaning within those words. I can hear it in his voice. Unable to stop myself, I look up at Adrian, feeling myself grow hot beneath his gaze. So, the cuddling was real? I didn't make it all up? I want to tell Adrian the truth, that it was the best sleep of my life until I woke alone, but the words won't leave my mouth out of fear of him hurting me again.

He bites his bottom lip and smiles at my silence. "You're cute when you're nervous."

"You don't make me nervous, Adrian."

His smile widens. The look in his eyes is so... happy. And not in the arrogant, jerk-like way that I know him for. "Well, *I* enjoyed keeping you warm. That is, until Phoebe woke me up with a phone call and I had to sneak inside not to disturb you."

Phoebe called him? A weight suddenly lifts off my shoulders knowing Adrian didn't wake in a panic and bolt to escape me. And he liked keeping me warm? As a friend, or is the intimacy from our pretend relationship messing with his sense of reality? Whatever is going on inside Adrian's mind, I smile back at him, liking this new closeness we've formed.

"Phoebe told me the yacht leaves in an hour. Think you can doll yourself up in that time?" he asks, grabbing an outfit for the day.

"I'm always a doll, thank you very much."

"True. By the way, I ordered us room service. Didn't

think we'd have time to stop by the buffet before boarding the yacht. It's on the dining table."

Adrian ordered *us* breakfast because he didn't think *we'd* have time to eat. I'm starting to like everything that leaves this guy's mouth.

"That was nice of you to think of me," I say.

"I hope you'll be happy with the selection. When I mentioned my girlfriend is Verena Valentine and she trashes kitchens and gets chefs fired if the food isn't up to par, the staff seemed very intent on keeping you satisfied."

"Please tell me you're joking."

"You'll never know."

Eager to escape Adrian's naked proximity so I can think straight again, I rush out to the dining room, finding the table filled with an array of fruits, cereals, and a continental breakfast. My eyes freeze on one plate in particular, my mouth watering at the neatly rolled crepes bathed in what has to be caramelized orange juice.

"No way!" I call out when the familiar childhood scent of Cece Hunter's famous crepes wafts up to my nose. I waste no time grabbing cutlery and let the gooey crepes melt over my tastebuds.

Adrian hurries into the dining room. "What's wrong?"

"I'm in heaven! These taste exactly how I remember. How did you get them?"

He folds his arms, leaning one shoulder against the door frame. I try to convince myself that it's a good thing he's now wearing clothes, but don't believe the lie for one-second. "Already told you, I had strict words with the kitchen staff. Gave them Mom's recipe and hounded them not to stuff it up."

I take another bite, growling at how much I've missed the caramelized orange juice sauce. "Adrian, you are the best!" I gasp at that statement, realizing what I've admitted.

"It's okay. We can pretend you never said that."

Before the embarrassment sinks in, a bout of panic rushes over me, because how could I have been so stupid, eating food without checking if it's safe for me? "Please tell me this food is gluten-free. I'm celiac."

"Of course it is. I'm not so evil that I would poison you."

My vision narrows on him. "How did you know I'm celiac? I wasn't diagnosed until my early twenties."

"I saw the episode of your show where you were confined to the bathroom the entire time."

"Adrian, that did *not* happen. I've never spoken about the disease on camera."

He's laughing again. "Your mom told me during one of our many phone conversations. It's quite interesting what will come out of that woman's mouth when she's talking about you."

"Oh, yes, these monthly chats you have with her. I still can't believe she calls you. I'm so sorry."

"What are you apologizing for? Your mom and I are *best* friends. I look forward to her phone calls every month."

I smile at his joke. "So, you know I'm celiac. Tell me something about you so we can level the playing field."

"I'm not celiac."

"Oh, that's real smart. How do you spend your free time?"

Adrian buries his hands in his pockets. "I guess I've thrown myself into work since becoming single. My life is pretty boring. I stare at numbers all day as an accountant, then hit the gym in the evenings."

"That sounds depressing. What do you do for fun?" I pop another forkful of crepes into my mouth.

"There's a lake near my apartment I run laps around."

"How is running fun?"

His gaze rests upon me with warmth, and I'm dying to know what he's thinking. "To tell you the truth, Vee, I haven't enjoyed myself in a long time. This vacation is a nice change for me."

"Seven years. We haven't seen each other in seven years, Adrian, and this is all the information I get? There has to be something else you can tell me."

He runs a hand through his hair, contemplating what to say. "I... got a girl pregnant once."

The crepe loses all taste. My gaze pins to him, and I hope the look in my eyes isn't as vicious as I feel inside. Whoever this girl is, I officially hate her. I hate myself for even thinking that.

"Only once?" I ask.

"What's that supposed to mean?"

"Come on, I saw the way you acted around girls in high school. And with all of this... perfection," I do some weird hand gesture toward his body, "I'm sure you could get a girl pregnant just by looking at her."

He bites the corner of his lip again, grinning at me. "Guess you're having our unborn love child."

"Ew, gross. Stop looking at me." I laugh, dropping my eyes back to the crepes. I'm certain my cheeks are turning red, and that I've never heard anything so hot.

Once my temperature is under control, I clear my throat and meet his gaze. "So... what happened with the girl?"

"She lost the baby early on. Maybe it was for the best. We were only twenty," he says matter-of-factly, like it was no big deal. He's hiding it well, but there's a trace of sadness in his tone.

A strange pang of guilt hits my chest, that I wasn't

there to console Adrian through the loss. The feeling is ridiculous because we weren't on speaking terms at the time. But I can't deny wishing I'd been there for him as a friend.

"Do you want kids?" I ask.

"Definitely."

With Isabelle.

There's a pain in the pit of my stomach from that realization. My body is set on betraying me this morning. "I'm not sure I'll be a good mom," I say, my eyes ballooning a second later, realizing I've said those words in a response to Adrian's answer. "That sounded bad. I didn't mean you and I would... Ugh, I need to shut up."

"Of course you and I will have a baby," Adrian says. "I've looked at you way too many times since we arrived at the resort. You're probably carrying triplets."

My embarrassment lifts into a smile. He has a way with words that I'm grateful for in this very moment. A silver tongue that is coated in snark but also knows how to ease sticky situations.

Adrian leaves me to my breakfast and continues preparing himself for the day. It's eight o'clock when we arrive at the jetty. Tory was not kidding when she said *luxury yacht*. This boat is massive and has multiple levels. All the guests are lining up, waiting to climb aboard. From memory, Tory said the wedding is close to two hundred guests, so I guess they're all here with us today.

"Looks like the six of us will be spending the day in even closer proximities," Adrian says as we take our place in line.

I follow his gaze, finding Jake and Jannah arm in arm on the ship's deck. Isabelle and her date are a few places ahead of us in the line.

"Good thing I'm wearing my sexiest bikini beneath this dress," I say.

"Good thing you can't keep your hands off me." Adrian pulls me to his side, planting a kiss on my forehead.

When I notice Isabelle's spiteful eyes on us, I nuzzle into Adrian's chest, breathing in the scent of him and exhaling a dizzy smile. I could really get used to being in Adrian's arms. Being confined on a yacht with our exes might be the best thing that's ever happened to me.

Chapter Fourteen

All guests are huddled on the back deck of the yacht as we sail through the open waters of the Whitsundays. The hot sun glistens down on us while we listen to our tour guide, Ernie, prepare us for the day ahead. He's one of those stereotypical Aussies with a thick twang to his accent and speaks in slang that I can barely understand. The guy is middle-aged and a little rough around the edges, dressed in khaki adventure gear, and speaks as if he's been our best mate for years. Even if he didn't have a thick Australian accent, I'd be struggling to understand a word that comes out of his mouth because all I can focus on is Adrian cradling me in his arms as he stands behind me.

"Hands up all o' yous who're comin' with me for a dip in the reef," Ernie calls.

The majority of hands go up while I try to figure out what Ernie said. Adrian takes the initiative by raising our arms together.

Ernie holds up the most hideous wetsuit I've ever seen. "You'll wanna load up in one o' these lil beauties."

I make a retching sound which is supposed to be for

only Adrian's ears, but everyone turns to look at me, Ernie included.

"The wetsuits might not be flattering, darl, but you'll be thankin' me, considerin' all the lil nasties swimmin' around out there. I say it on all o' my tours, that everything in Australia is designed to kill you. Stingrays, coral, and our array of jellyfish. Chances are, if you see a box jellyfish three meters in the distance, their tentacles are right beside you. The Irukandji jellyfish is the real dangerous one. The lil fucker is about the size of your fingernail and translucent. Real hard to spot. You're in trouble if you get stung by one of these. The last type of jellyfish I'm gonna warn yous about is the bluebottle. They're easier to see and look like the name implies. They'll sting like a real dickhead but won't cause serious harm. I'm not sayin' all o' this to keep yous from the water. Yous probably won't see any stingers. But just in case, wear the wetsuit and yous'll be fine. My speech is to benefit the beauty queens who think they're too good for wetsuits." He winks at me. "Trust me, love, you'll be thankin' me for it in the long run."

Everyone looks at me again. Adrian squeezes me tight, planting a kiss on my cheek before he says to all the staring faces, "Don't worry, if that speech hasn't persuaded her, I'm sure I can think of something that will."

I laugh along with everyone else. Well... almost everyone. From the corner of my eyes, I notice Isabelle death staring me again. When my gaze lands on Jake, he isn't too happy either. That only makes me smile wider.

As soon as Ernie's speech is over, guests flock to the changing rooms.

I lean back in Adrian's arms, looking up at him. "You know, I'm suddenly not so sure about swimming in the Whitsundays. It doesn't seem safe at all."

Dad peers at the sun as he passes us by and puts on his best Australian accent. "It's a scorcher today. Go enjoy the water. You heard Ernie, swimming is safe if you wear the wetsuit."

"Yeah, but our hands, feet, and face won't be protected," I say as he heads for a changing room.

"You're being pedantic," Adrian tells me. "Ernie wouldn't let us swim in the ocean if safety is such an issue. You're getting in the water with me, end of story."

"But the wetsuit... It's so gross. There's no chance of you wanting to hate fuck me after seeing me in it."

He grins in a devilishly handsome way, forming a crooked, yet perfect shape with his lips that I want to capture in a photo and stare at forever. "We already established that I don't hate you. Go get changed, Verena."

I've only just managed to squeeze my ass into the wetsuit and slide my arms into its tight sleeves. With a twisted face, I stare at my reflection in the changing room mirror.

Gross.

Adrian knocks on my door. "You almost done in there?"

"I might stay in here forever," I answer, rubbing sunscreen over my cheeks.

"Most people are in the water. No one will see you."

You will see me, I feel like saying.

"I'll give you to the count of three before I jimmy the lock."

"Ugh, fine. Let's get this over with." I rush out of the changing room and race for the water. If I jump into the ocean fast enough, Adrian won't get a good look at me in this wetsuit.

He was right. When I arrive at the back deck, barely anyone is left on board. People are scattered all throughout the water. Some are close by, swimming among a gazillion fish while Ernie throws fish food overboard. Others have already become little dots in the distance, snorkeling out by the reef. Now's my chance to jump into the ocean before Adrian catches up to me, but I can't make myself do it, not with all the potential stingers.

Adrian runs by me in a blur and bomb-dives straight into a school of fish. They're not tiny fish either, and block out the view of his body as they swim around him to gobble up food. All that's visible of Adrian is his head poking out of the sea, grinning up at me.

"Come on, Vee. The water is beautiful. Get in here with me."

"No way." I project my voice. "Those fish are freakishly big."

"The fish are too concerned about food to notice us."

"Maybe, but they still scare me. I'm fine staying on this boat."

"*Verena.*"

"You said it yourself—I'm a shiny, pretty thing. I don't belong in the water with all these slimy and deadly animals. What if a jellyfish stings my face?"

"Shiny, pretty things belong with me, and I'm in the water."

When I don't smile at Adrian's joke, he swims up to the yacht, resting his elbows on the ledge. All humor disappears from his voice. "Vee, you're seriously afraid of getting in the water?"

"Yes."

"Come closer so we don't have to speak as loud."

"No, you'll pull me in."

"I promise I won't."

I sigh and step up to the ledge, kneeling beside Adrian.

"Let's take this in baby steps. Will you sit down and dangle your legs in the water?"

I consider all the risks involved with Adrian's suggestion, but give into him, knowing that with my wetsuit on, my feet will be the only vulnerable part of my body—a fair sacrifice. I shiver as the cool water seeps through the wetsuit, dampening high up my thighs.

"Well done," Adrian says. "We can stay at this stage for as long as you need."

"I'm still not getting into the water."

He takes my right leg in one hand and a flipper in the other. Before I can ask what he's doing, he places the flipper on my foot like I'm Cinderella, then does the same to my other foot. Something about the delicate way he holds my legs, even after both flippers are on, seems so intimate. He doesn't let go of me. I don't want him to either.

"Now most of your feet are protected," he says.

"I'm still not getting in."

Adrian takes my hand in his, weaving our fingers. I almost forget how to breathe, staring down at our hands. I'm not sure what his touch means. We've been touching like this all day, on show for Jake, Isabelle, and our families. But now, everyone around us is preoccupied with the water. Not a single pair of eyes remain focused on us. This between us right now is real. He's not being nice to me for show. The only issue is I can't figure out if his touch is a gesture of friendship or something more.

It can't be more. Adrian wants Isabelle, not me.

"Vee," he whispers my name, "what if I promise to hold your hand the entire time and never let you out of my sight? I'll protect you from all of these slimy fish."

It's almost enough to make me say yes.

"What about the stingers?" I ask.

"The risk is so slim."

"But not zero."

"I'll swim in front of you and be your personal shield. Any nearby jellyfish will have to get through me first." He grins, and after that kind of sacrifice, all I can do is smile back.

"You'd do that for me?"

"I really want this shiny, pretty thing in the water with me."

My feet splash him with water. "*Never* let go."

He tugs on my hand, and I slide into the ocean with him. My first reaction isn't to shiver from the cold water or to push the hair back from my face. Instead, I scream at the sensation of hundreds of fish swimming past my body in search for food. Ernie does the cruelest thing of all and throws another handful of fish food directly over me. It sends me screaming again as more hungry fish bump into me. Beside me, Adrian laughs, then takes me by the waist and pulls my body tight to his.

"Tell me, Vee, are you honestly focusing on the fish right now instead of the repulsion of being in my arms?"

I take a breath and realize he's right—minus the repulsion part. My body is flush against his firm and perfect torso. Our faces are the closest they've ever been, aside from maybe last night when we cuddled up to each other.

"You're supposed to be holding my hand," I whisper.

"You're clinging onto me, Vee. Let go and I'll hold your hand."

Letting go is the last thing I want to do. *Because of the fish*, I tell myself. Why, then, does my gaze disobediently lower to Adrian's lips? Why can't I think about anything other than closing the distance between us?

"I can kiss you if you'd like," Adrian says.

I have to check my hearing. Yes, he definitely said that. There's a teasing spark in his eyes and nothing genuine about the comment. I'm annoyed at myself for being disappointed. My earlier question of whether his intensions are romantic or not is answered.

"The revulsion of a kiss would distract you from the ocean," he adds.

"Good idea, but then I'd have PTSD."

He chuckles, swimming away from the yacht with me still in his arms. "Come on, let's go out to the reef. You ready to put your head under the water yet?"

I lower my goggles and place the snorkel in my mouth, speaking with it between my teeth. "Now I'm kiss proof."

"Only your lips." He raises my hand to his mouth and kisses it. Damn him and his suave ways. It's too early for me to be hyperventilating in this snorkel.

Without saying anything else, he places his own snorkel on, and we both duck our faces under the water.

As promised, Adrian never releases my hand from his *and* he always swims in front, protecting me from any jellyfish that might be lurking. We reach the reef after a few minutes of paddling, and it is truly the most magnificent sight of nature I've ever seen. The Great Barrier Reef is an underwater paradise with the most vivid colors and intricate shapes. There's every color fish I could ever imagine, sparkling like a rainbow. It takes me only a second to forget all of my anxieties of being in the ocean. I abandon my secure position behind Adrian and swim beside him, gazing at the wondrous beauty beneath us and being filled with inspiration for my next collection of couture.

A surface level view of the reef isn't enough. I tug free of Adrian's hand and dive deeper to get a closer look, holding my breath as the snorkel submerges with water. Something jabs at my sides and I turn to see Adrian right behind me, smiling around his mouthpiece. He removes it from his lips and mouths the words, *I made a promise*, then holds out his hand to me.

I smile back and take his hand in mine, never letting go for the remainder of our swim, regardless that my nerves have long faded.

Chapter Fifteen

It's lunchtime when Ernie calls everyone back onto the yacht over a loudspeaker. With my hideous wetsuit slung over one arm and me now dressed in my cute beach-throw, I step out of a changing room and head for the seafood buffet.

After throwing my wetsuit into the *used* bucket, then piling up a plate of gourmet fish and chips for me and Adrian to share, I venture out onto the back deck in search of him. Even among the herd of guests, Adrian is easy to find. He's by himself with his forearms on the railing, watching the water pass by while we sail to our next destination, Whitehaven Beach. Seeing him solo is a sight my eyes are still adjusting to. He's great with conversation whenever anyone approaches him. He still exudes the charm I remember so well from our childhood, but there's something different about him as an adult. He doesn't seek out the attention anymore. He's content without being the center of everyone's focus, and I like this version of him so much more. Maybe I'm selfish, but too many years of us being separated have passed and I want him all to myself.

As if sensing my eyes on him, Adrian looks over his

shoulder and eases into a grin when he finds me approaching.

"I hope you're hungry," I say, resting the food on the railing between us.

"Starving."

The yacht bounces over the water, and Adrian catches the plate before it becomes fish food. He looks around, searching for something, then holds my hand and draws me to the only empty seat at a crowded table. Without asking, he claims the seat for himself and pulls me onto his lap.

"Eat," he says, taking a bite of fish.

I reach for the cutlery, realizing that I only grabbed one pair for myself and now Adrian is using it. He sees the dilemma on my face and passes me the fork... that was just in his mouth. If I use the same fork, is that on par with kissing Adrian? Of course it's not, but still... Adrian's germs will be in my mouth. Is it weird that I want all of his germs? I want to smother myself in Adrian essence until his molecules bond with mine and we are inseparably one. I want him to kiss me so hard that we're forced to breathe in the same air until there's only carbon dioxide left between us and we pass out from all our intense kissing.

Wow. I'm weird.

"You got an issue with boy germs?" he asks, noticing my silence.

If only he knew the obsessive thoughts that were traveling through my mind. I spear a piece of fish with the fork and place it in my mouth. All the little Verena molecules in my mouth are in a screaming frenzy, having multiple orgasms right now. Much like my dream at the start of this week.

"Hey," Adrian whispers, nodding at something in the distance. Two people are grabbing a set of stand up paddle boards. Jake and Jannah. "Let's go paddle boarding too so they can see us together."

"Not really my kind of thing. In case you've forgotten, I'm not coordinated with sports. I won't be able to stand up on that thing. It will be like yoga again with me falling."

"I'll teach you how to balance on the board," he says. "You'll be a natural in no time. It will be fun. And we'll be far enough away from the two Js that you won't notice them."

"What's the point if they can't see us?"

"Of course they'll see *us*. But we'll have no recognition of them because we'll be so consumed with each other, laughing and making out in the water. Happily in love."

"Oh my gosh." I shove him, secretly loving his joke. "Are you this much of a flirt when you have a girlfriend?"

"You are my girlfriend."

"A *real* girlfriend," I whisper.

He shrugs. "Go ask Isabelle. While you're at it, ask her if I'm good in bed. I'm sure you're dying to find out."

I roll my eyes and laugh.

"Seriously, what do you say to paddle boarding?"

"My parents want us to join them on the hiking track."

Adrian takes another mouthful of fish and swallows. "Hiking is way worse than paddle boarding. You'll get all hot and sweaty. I'll tell your parents we want some alone time."

"I've taken my wetsuit off. The material will be all cold and wet now. I don't want to squeeze back into that thing."

"So, don't wear it," he suggests. "Ernie said stingers don't enter shallow water."

"He did?"

"Were you not listening to anything he said?"

"It was kind of difficult to concentrate when you were holding me like that."

He grins. "Come on, Vee. It will be fun."

That damn grin. It wins every time.

As soon as the yacht anchors at Whitehaven Beach, Adrian and I follow everyone to shore with our board and paddle. I'm lost for words at how beautiful this beach is. My toes wiggle in the purest white sand I've ever seen. The water is as clear as glass with sand marbling through it, creating magnificent patterns.

Aside from the few of us who intend on swimming, everyone else disperses into the hiking track, set on seeing wildlife and gaining a higher view of the artwork of the water.

Adrian tosses a sunscreen bottle at me. "Lather up, baby doll. Don't want you getting burned for the wedding."

"I don't need sunscreen. I'm wearing some already."

"Hey, Verena!" an unfamiliar voice calls my name.

"Don't turn around," Adrian warns, looking over my shoulder.

Too late. I glance behind myself, finding Jannah running up to me with her fake tits bouncing in a skimpy bikini and a massive smile on her face. Jake is not far behind her. Why didn't I listen to Adrian?

"Hey, Verena, do you mind if we use some of your sunscreen?" Jannah asks as they arrive at our side.

Jake's gaze lingers on me for a long moment before he clarifies, "We forgot ours on the yacht."

I'm about to say *yes*, because how can I turn them away without sounding petty, when I catch Jannah checking out Adrian's bare torso.

"Hi, Adrian. Are you enjoying your day?" Jannah asks, pushing her chest out.

"Verena just asked me to apply her sunscreen," Adrian answers, taking the lotion from my hands. "So, yes. It's a good day. Ready, beautiful?"

Holy shit, I love the fabricated crap that Adrian can pull out of thin air. It's a skill that can't be taught. But is he serious? Adrian wants to rub sunscreen into *my* body? He's either a genius and I swear I'll be in debt to him forever for feeling me up in front of Jake, or he hasn't thought this through, and our day is about to get super awkward.

The other part of me can't believe this is about to happen. I've fantasized about this moment since I was a teen—having Adrian's hands all over me. But never did I imagine it would be for show instead of a real intimate moment. If I'm being sensible, I should tell Adrian *no*. But nothing about my time in Australia has been a sensible decision, so why start now? There's too much satisfaction to be gained from having Adrian touch me *and* for him to do it in front of Jake.

In one swift movement, I pull my beach-throw over my head and drop it to the sand, revealing my diamond encrusted bikini that's worth a fortune and makes me look like the sexiest mermaid anyone's ever seen. That plan I mentioned earlier, the one where Adrian sees me for the first time in seven years and I look hot in a bikini with men chatting me up by the pool—this is the bikini I intended for that scene to take place in. My plans may not have gone accordingly, but this scenario may be even better.

The bikini scores me the exact look I was aiming for from Adrian—a primal caveman desperate to claim what is his. I steal a glance at Jake. His eyes upon me are just as urgent, and he looks miserable that I'm with someone else. A double win for me.

I smile at Adrian, struggling to keep myself from

laughing as I adopt a sultry voice. "Yeah, baby, I'm ready for you."

He pumps sunscreen onto his palm then spreads it down my arms in one sensual stroke before massaging it in. To the left of me, Jake and Jannah are staring at us, speechless like they've walked in on a scene they shouldn't have witnessed but are too startled to look away.

I tilt my head back and moan for extra effect. "Mmm, that feels so good. Don't forget to do my chest."

Adrian pauses, and I wonder if I've pushed this show too far, but that same primal look remains in his eyes. "You didn't do your chest before?" His gaze sends me a different question, asking if I really want him to travel to those regions with his hands.

"I applied sunscreen a few hours ago. It will have worn off by now."

The tiniest growl escapes Adrian's throat as he pumps another dose of sunscreen. His hands start at my shoulders and slowly work their way down until he's rubbing the lotion over my breasts. Every inch of my body tingles as Adrian touches my most intimate parts. I'm confident my core temperature has risen and I'm about to burst into flames if Adrian doesn't rip all our clothes off and take me this very minute. Surely he has to know how much I'm loving this right now, and that this is no longer an act. I'd give anything to feel him inside me.

"Ahem..." Jake clears his throat. With the distraction of Adrian's hands on me, I totally forgot we had an audience.

"Oh, yeah, sure, help yourself to the sunscreen," I say, unable to look away from Adrian. "Baby, make sure you get my ass too. Don't miss a single spot of my body."

Adrian turns me around, his hot breath whispering into

my ear and sending shivers all over my body as he rubs my behind. "You are pure evil. You know that?"

"I'm having fun. Isn't that what you told me to do?"

He places a hand over my stomach and presses my body to his. I gulp at the sensation of him hard against my ass. "Where did you honestly think this would lead when you asked me to touch your chest?"

I spin around to face him, out of my game now that I know this isn't an act for Adrian either. I suppose we *are* attracted to each other, but is that all this is on his side—a physical need rather than emotional? Is he hard because he's touching *me*, or because he's touching a woman's body —like with the downward dog scenario?

"I hated the way Jannah was looking at you," I whisper, realizing I'm alone with Adrian, the other two already halfway down the beach.

"I didn't notice her."

With Adrian this close to me, I can feel his breath on my lips and taste his scent on my tongue. If I want to, I know I can close the distance between us and kiss him. I know he won't turn me away. He'll indulge in the kiss, and the two of us will spend the rest of the day making out. We'll probably end up sleeping together when we return to the resort.

Instead, I take the deflating option and step back, not wanting our relationship to progress like that. We'd be a one-time fling and leave this wedding never talking to each other again. As much as my body is begging me to cave and indulge in Adrian, I want the return of our friendship more. I want a meaningful relationship with him instead of complicating everything with sex, especially when he's in love with another girl.

I dip my toes in the water. "Thanks for playing along

with that whole sunscreen scene. It felt amazing to do that in front of Jake. Did you see the look on his face?"

"I was kind of preoccupied." Adrian carries the board into the water, giving me a playful splash with the paddle as he passes by. I follow him in, thankful that he's not making a big deal over what just happened between us. "And can I just say, you're wearing the most ridiculous bikini possible for this lesson."

"You weren't complaining about my bikini a minute ago."

"I'm not complaining about it now. How long did the design take?" he asks, shoulder deep in the water.

"How do you know I designed it?"

"Oh, please. It's the most over-the-top piece of swimwear I've ever seen. You're probably encrusted in twenty K of jewels right now."

I laugh. "So... you like it?"

"Hate it."

I shove his chest, grinning. He answers with his own teasing grin and taps the paddle board. "You ready for this epic lesson?"

"Only if you're ready to see me embarrass myself."

"You should know by now that watching you embarrass yourself is my favorite pastime."

The embarrassment is even worse than I anticipated as Adrian guides me through stand up paddle boarding 101. He does an effortless pushup from the water onto the board that I'm meant to copy. I can't get myself one inch out of the water without first struggling like a walrus and then proceeding to capsize. This happens at least ten times before Adrian scoops me up in his arms and lifts me onto the board.

"Now try standing," he tells me.

A cycle repeats nonstop with me either falling flat on my ass or bombing into the water. It becomes an unspoken rule that each time I fall off the board, Adrian places me right back on.

"Bend your legs," Adrian says while I attempt to stand for the millionth time. "Lower your center of gravity."

"I'm trying!" My body wobbles as I struggle to balance. No doubt, it's the most unflattering sight to exist in this world.

"Yes!" Adrian cheers, fist-pumping the paddle in the air with victory. "You're doing it."

I'm squealing with joy, barely managing to maintain balance as I shake. But I'm up! I'm standing!

My win lasts only a moment. Sensing my stability slip away, I leap off the board with a star jump. "Ahhh, did you see that?"

"You were fantastic!"

"The impossible has become possible!"

We take a breather, and it's only now things have slowed down and I've achieved standing on the board that I realize this lesson probably wasn't a good idea. I'm exhausted from all the physical activity. No doubt I'll have bruises on my body by the time evening falls. Tomorrow, I'll have muscles aching that I didn't know existed. But it's worth it. Every moment with Adrian is turning out to be one I don't want to forget.

Catching my breath, I rest my forearms on the board and let my body float. My eyes latch onto something in the distance, and the victory is kicked out of me when I notice it's Jake and Jannah kissing in the water. With a groan, I turn away, but the image is still in my mind, so I do the one thing that will get rid of it.

"Get me up on this board again," I say, determined to succeed at another round of standing.

"Hey, let's not push our luck."

Adrian is teasing, but I'm too annoyed at Jake and Jannah to respond. With all my force, I shoot up out of the water and hurl myself onto the board. There's a spark of pride within me; it's the first time I've made it this far, even though my legs are kicking and I'm pretty sure I'm about to capsize again. Adrian gives a push to help me all the way onboard. I sit up panting, too exhausted to launch straight into standing. Too pissed to do anything. My beautiful day out at sea is ruined with putrid memories of Jake cheating on me. I still don't know, and never *will* know why he cheated on me. Am I too caught up in my career? Is Jannah a better lay than me? Maybe I'm bad in bed.

Adrian catches onto my energy shift and glances at Jake and Jannah, no doubt seeing them kissing. Without thinking it through, I look back in their direction and find the two of them laughing and splashing each other.

"Screw them and their cute play fighting," I say.

"Don't worry about them. We're way cuter."

"We are?"

"Oh, yes. Definitely." His teasing grin returns. Despite all my hard work of climbing onto the board, Adrian splashes my face and capsizes me.

I go under, fully submerged, but instead of surfacing straight away, I swim for Adrian and jab his ribs.

He jerks back and I hear his muffled voice from beneath the water, "Oh, you'll pay for that, Vee."

When I surface, he wears the most sinister grin matched by dark eyes. He's out for blood. An exhilarated shriek leaves my mouth as I paddle away from him, but Adrian is faster and grabs me from behind. He effortlessly lifts me over his head and tosses me through the air, sending me plunging into the water. I'm pretty sure a nip pops out of my bikini in the process. I fix myself before surfacing and shake with laughter.

Adrian launches for me again. I hold my hands up in surrender, knowing I can't out-swim him. "Stop! I nearly lost my top."

That only makes him advance faster, but I'm not going down without a fight. Once he's caught up to me, we battle it out. I'm tugging at his swim trunks, attempting to pull them down (it's my only defense). He's trying to get a sturdy grip on me so he can throw me into the air again, probably hoping I'll lose my bikini top for good this time. And dammit, he's winning. He's got an arm around my waist. All he needs now is to bend down and grab my legs.

But suddenly I'm howling and not with laughter. The smile is ripped from my face as a blinding pain strikes my leg. "Cease fire! Ow!"

Adrian instantly lets go of me. "What happened?"

"Something stung my leg. A jellyfish, maybe? Am I going to die?"

He searches the water around us. "I don't see anything. I'm half-expecting you to start laughing any second. You'd really regret that— Oh, FUCK!" Adrian clutches his stomach. "It got me too."

"It heard you calling my bluff and had to restore justice."

"How are you able to make a joke right now? Fuck, this hurts. We need to get out of the water." He grabs my hand and starts swimming toward the shore.

"What about the board?"

"Leave it."

"I thought you said we didn't need to wear wetsuits in shallow water."

"I made that up."

"You *what*?" I yell. "I trusted you, Adrian, and now we're going to die."

Chapter Sixteen

As it turns out, being stung by a jellyfish is all the rage among the passengers aboard the yacht, until Ernie laughs at everyone's concern and informs us bluebottles aren't dangerous.

The sky is all tones of pinks and oranges as we sail back to the resort. Everyone is mingling on the back deck of the yacht with a cocktail in their hand, enjoying the music and wind in their hair while they discuss their day's adventures. I, on the other hand, have an icepack strapped to the sting site on my leg and am dosed up on painkillers, stuck in a boring conversation with my parents about their afternoon hike on Whitehaven Beach. Don't get me started on how furious I am with Adrian.

"Honey, the view from our hike was magnificent. You and Adrian really missed out by staying in the water," Mom says. "Seriously, what were you two thinking by not wearing wetsuits?"

"Adrian said we would be safe in shallow water."

Dad laughs. "He probably wanted to see you in your

bikini. Speaking of Adrian, where has that man of yours gone?"

"The restroom," I say, but it was well over ten minutes ago that he left. I scan through the crowd of passengers for Adrian. When I find him with Isabelle, my anger only increases.

They're sitting on a couch together. She's close to him. Closer than an ex-girlfriend would dare go. I have to remind myself that this was the plan all along, for Adrian to reignite his love with Isabelle. But the sight of them together makes me sick. I don't want him anywhere near her. I don't want them to be happy together. I want Adrian to myself. After all these years, I just got him back, even if it is only as a friend. I'm not ready to lose his attention all over again. At least give me this week with him.

When I take a closer look at them sharing the couch, all the anger inside me morphs into concern. Adrian is pale and miserable, clutching an icepack to his stomach. Isabelle's tending to him, resting a palm on his forehead to gauge his temperature.

Adrian gives an apologetic smile the moment he sees me looking his way, as if hoping I'll forgive him for lying to me about the wetsuit. It's done already. I couldn't ever be mad with this guy again. Not when he looks like death. I don't even excuse myself from the conversation with my parents before pushing through the crowd to join Adrian at his couch.

"How are you feeling?" I kneel in front of him.

"He's not well," Isabelle answers.

"I'm fine, Vee. Go enjoy yourself. Don't worry about me."

"You're not fine. You look terrible." I poke his arm in jest. "Who knew bluebottle stings turn men so soft."

Adrian doesn't laugh like I want him to. Instead, he closes his eyes and mutters, "That's funny."

It's this response that makes me realize the brave face he's wearing. I place a hand on his forehead and gasp. "You're really warm. Show me the sting again."

"Vee—" he protests, but he's so limp he barely has the energy to stop me. I remove the ice pack and lift his shirt, swearing when I see the increased swelling.

"Adrian, I think you're having an allergic reaction. Let me get help—"

He holds my wrist. "I've been researching bluebottle stings on my phone. There's nothing anyone can do. I have to wait this out."

"At least let me take you inside where it's quiet and you can relax properly. There are plenty of bedrooms downstairs."

"I can do that," Isabelle offers. "I've been meaning to talk to Adrian about some stuff. This will give us a good chance."

"I hardly think that's appropriate," I say, perhaps a little too sharp. "You're here with your date. How will it look if you're entering a bedroom with *mine*?"

I help Adrian to his feet before either he or Isabelle can rebut, and take his hand, clearing a path through the guests as I lead him below deck to the bedrooms. The first door is locked. The next one is too, and it's not until we approach a third door that we secure an empty room. I take Adrian inside and close the door behind us, then lay him down and sit beside him at the head of the bed.

"Much calmer down here," I say, knowing I made the right decision to draw Adrian away from all the noise on deck. He already appears more relaxed, lying on his back with his eyes closed.

A continuous banging sound picks up from one of the adjacent rooms, contradicting my words. It's followed by a moan, then someone cries out *yes!* over and over again.

Adrian and I unravel with laughter.

"Yeah, real nice down here," he says.

"You want me to pound on their door? I'll scare them enough so they shut up."

"Yeah, right." He closes his eyes again, his voice growing heavy with drowsiness. "If whoever is in there saw you in that bikini today, they'll ask you to join in on their fun."

"And you assume I'll say yes?"

"Maybe. I hope you wouldn't." His words are slower and further between. "Vee... will you stay with me?"

"Adrian, I'm not a threesome kind of girl."

"I meant... instead of returning upstairs."

My back slides down the headboard and I lie beside him. "Of course I will. Just... don't go to sleep on me, all right? Isn't that what they say—you're meant to keep people awake when they're having a reaction to something?"

There's no reply.

"Adrian?" I give him a gentle shake.

He answers with a smile. "I can't relax if I'm talking." His hand finds mine and his fingers trace slow circles around my palm. "If my fingers stop, that means I've fallen asleep."

I gulp at his touch. "Okay."

"By the way... I'm sorry about the wetsuit. Ernie said the chances of stingers are low. I just wanted to enjoy the afternoon with you."

"I'm not mad, only concerned about you."

"One last thing..."

"Yeah?"

"I didn't abandon you. And you are good enough for me. More than enough."

"What are you talking about?"

"I'm sorry." His fingers move slower, his breathing heavier. He's so zoned out that I question whether he knows what he's saying.

I watch Adrian for the remaining hour's journey back to the resort. His eyes are closed and his breath smooth, but not once do his fingers cease to trace delicate patterns over my hand.

Chapter Seventeen

Once we're back at the resort, I skip dinner at the restaurant and order room service for myself, wanting to monitor Adrian as he sleeps off his pain on the couch in our bungalow. My muscles are already starting to ache from stand up paddle boarding. I curl up at the end of Adrian's couch with a bowl of Coco Pops and skim through this week's schedule to prepare myself for tomorrow. I'll be busy with the dress fittings for most of the day. There's also the wedding ceremony rehearsal I need to attend. Tomorrow won't be anywhere near as enjoyable as today, and Adrian won't be around as much, but perhaps that's a good thing, giving him time to recover from the bluebottle sting.

I'm about to take a shower when I realize there's still one item listed on the agenda for today. The bachelorette party, which is scheduled for nine p.m.

I glance at the clock. It's nine fifteen. I'm ready for sleep, but now I have to psych myself up to be in party mode and watch strippers. I consider texting Tory and apologizing for not making it to the party, with the excuse that I need to watch over Adrian. But I don't want to let my sister down.

I leave a note beside Adrian, alerting him of where I am if he wakes. After a quick shower, I change into a short dress with long sleeves adorned in emerald gemstones, slip on some heels, and sneak out the front door.

Five minutes later, I arrive at a function room. Unlike the rest of the resort with its coastal themed interior, this place is lit by a dim red glow and the walls are covered in pink streamers, naked blow-up dolls, and boob balloons.

"Oh good, Tory's sister has decided to arrive." I don't need to see the person's face to know the voice belongs to Stacy.

When I look in her direction, I find all the young women at this wedding, plus a few game older ones, sitting in a group on the floor. Jannah is among the crowd, and I try my best not to let her presence ruin my mood. A blond, twenty-something-year-old girl stands in front of everyone, wearing a black corset and stockings. I guess she's the stripper.

The moment she notices me, her eyes almost pop out of her head and she jumps up and down. "I was told there would be a celebrity at this bachelorette party, but I didn't know it would be Verena Valentine! Wait until I tell all of my friends about this." Out of nowhere, her excitement vanishes, and her shoulders rise in panic. "Sorry, I mean after the wedding, of course. I know I can't say anything until the big day is over. Do you think I can get a photo with you?"

"Sure. I take photos with all my fans. Stacy, will you do the honors?"

Stacy rises from the group of girls with a glare, but keeps her mouth shut and takes the stripper's phone.

"I'm Jessica, by the way." The girl wraps an excited arm around me, and we smile for the camera. Once Stacy hands the phone back, Jessica addresses everyone. "All right, ladies, let's get this burlesque dance class started."

"Dance class?" I mutter to Stacy. "I thought you organized strippers for the bachelorette party?"

She swats my arm and looks at me like I'm a child who has stepped out of line. "Shush. Don't spoil the surprise. We're having two bachelorette parties. The strippers are tomorrow night."

I swear under my breath. "You know, I could have helped out if you'd let me in on all the details."

"Oh, don't be silly, Vera. You're a big celebrity with stressful deadlines and chaotic filming schedules. If you couldn't take time off to come to your own sister's engagement party, what makes you think you'd be able to organize a bachelorette party?"

It's times like this when I wish I was gifted with Adrian's quick-witted tongue, but Stacy takes her place among the women before I have a chance to say anything in return. Her words hit hard. Deep inside, I know the reason they hurt so much is because she's right. I *should* have gone to the engagement party. I *should* have worked through my insecurities and pushed myself to attend. Instead, I was too scared and only thinking about myself.

Before I have a chance to seek Tory out and apologize for my ways, Jessica turns on a sultry tune and the dance class begins. The apology can wait. My sister looks happy, smiling with her friends. This isn't the right moment to bring up a heavy topic.

Over the next hour, we're led through a list of different poses and dance moves, taught the seductive art of a striptease, and shown how to use props like feather scarfs and paper fans. Jessica even gives us tips on how to look good naked—which I make a mental note to practice later in front of the bathroom mirror. When it's time for us to split into pairs for the chair dance segment, of course I'm the odd one out, and am forced to pair up with Jessica.

"This is a *bachelorette* party." Phoebe's voice projects over everyone's noise. "Adrian, what are you doing here? No men allowed."

Part of me wonders if I just have Adrian on the brain and am hearing his name everywhere, even when it's not spoken. Regardless, my eyes whip in the direction that Phoebe is looking, and there he is. My first reaction is to smile, but reality hits when remembering the bluebottle sting, and I rush over to Adrian, placing a hand on his forehead to check his temperature.

"Why aren't you sleeping?" I ask. "Is everything all right?"

"I'm fine, Vee. Feeling much better. I woke up and you were gone, so I came looking for you. What are you all doing?"

"Secret girl stuff. I'm not sure when we'll be done. You should go back to the bungalow and rest."

"Don't be ridiculous," Tory says, having snuck up behind me. "Adrian, stay. No one picked Verena to be their partner, so she has to pair up with the teacher."

Adrian laughs. "It's like high school all over again."

I fold my arms. "Don't be a dick."

"Why don't you be her partner?" Tory suggests, and from the humor in her voice, I can tell she's taunting me.

"Tory, he's not well."

"You sound like a broken record," Adrian says. "How many times do I have to tell you I'm fine. Anyway, I'm happy to stay and be your partner."

"Oh, you'll be perfect!" Jessica joins the conversation, guiding Adrian to a chair. "Are you Verena's boyfriend?"

"Yeah." He takes a seat. "So, what are we doing?"

I place both hands on my hips. "Jessica is teaching us how to give a lap dance. I think you should leave."

"Oh, right." Adrian gives an awkward laugh. "Yeah, maybe it's weird that I'm the only guy here."

"Nonsense." Jessica pushes him back down by the shoulders when he attempts to stand up and leave. "It's normal to feel embarrassed about these kinds of things, but we're here to loosen up and have fun."

Adrian and I are left alone when Jessica steps away to fiddle with music on her phone. "This has been one heck of a day," he says. "First the sunscreen. Now a lap dance."

"This won't be half as exciting. I'll be terrible."

"Let me be the judge of that."

"Okay, ladies," Jessica says to the class, "one of you will sit on the chair as the other learns the dance. Then we'll switch."

She demonstrates the first dance move with a blowup doll positioned on the chair beside us. Jessica places her hands on its shoulders and slides her fingers down its chest. On her cue, everyone copies, while Adrian and I meet each other's gaze, trying hard not to laugh.

"Come on, have some fun with each other," Jessica tells us. "I bet you've got some moves. I've seen you and Darius dance on *Valentine's Day*. You're a natural."

"That was Latin dancing. I can do that all day with ease, but this..."

"They're the same thing. Both dances are about passion and sex."

"Adrian will laugh at me," I protest.

He raises both hands by his chest, battling another laugh. "Promise I won't."

"See," Jessica says. "Give the dance a try."

I contemplate it for a moment, barely believing what I'm about to do. This occasion doesn't share the same thrilling energy as the sunscreen one did, perhaps because *I'll* be the one doing all the work instead of Adrian feeling me up. Then there's the issue of me having no clue how to be sexy on demand. And besides, Jake isn't watching us, which detracts from the fun.

But Isabelle is.

I glance at her in the back left corner of the room. We share a moment of heated eye contact before she looks away and talks to her partner.

The whole plan of this week is to make Isabelle jealous enough to want Adrian back. The only thing is... somehow *I've* become the jealous one. It makes me all bitter and twisted inside to imagine Adrian smiling at Isabelle. Kissing her. Taking her to his bed.

A new plan needs to be put into action. The scare-Isabelle-away plan. Let her believe Adrian is so in love with me that she doesn't stand a chance of winning him back.

"Hands on his chest," Jessica instructs me, and I follow, biting my lip as I touch Adrian. "That's it. Not so scary, right? Now slide your fingers down his torso."

I keep my gaze fixed on my hands as they trail down Adrian's chest, knowing I'll lose all nerve if I look up at his face. Either that, or I'll see that same dark look in his eyes from when he applied my sunscreen, and I don't know if I'll be able to control my need for him this time.

"Next move," Jessica calls to the class. "Walk in a circle around your partner, letting your fingers snake across their shoulders."

She demonstrates with Adrian this time, and Tory cheers, "Woo! Watch out, Verena!"

Everyone laughs. Everyone except Isabelle, which pleases me greatly.

Jessica stays by our side while the other class members proceed with the instructions, as if we're the struggling kids at school who need the teacher's attention. "Okay, Verena, you're up."

I do my best to look sexy as I complete the circle, but it doesn't have the same effect I was hoping for when my ankle rolls and I almost face-plant the ground. Adrian catches me by the waist before I land, pressing his lips together to conceal a laugh.

"Don't say a word," I warn, unsure if my growing temperature is due to humiliation or the fact that Adrian has an arm around my waist.

"It wasn't as bad as you think," Jessica tells me. "Let's try again, but this time, hold Adrian's gaze as you move behind him. Let him see all of your secrets. Seduce him with your eyes."

All of my secrets? Like that my feelings in this fake relationship are no longer pretend? That I think I'm falling hard for this guy all over again?

No thank you, Jessica. Sharing my secrets is a terrible idea.

But it's too late. I dare to take a peek at Adrian's eyes, and gulp at the heat I see in them. All of my secrets are rushing out of me. All I can think about is how amazing it felt when Adrian lathered me in sunscreen today. How he didn't shy away from letting me feel how hard he was. I can't stop thinking about how much I want to feel that hardness again, *inside* of me, every day for the rest of my life. My mind is like porn when it comes to Adrian.

With these thoughts, all embarrassment vanishes from me, and I'm left with the desire to try my best with this lap dance. I want to enjoy myself and get lost in this faux relationship. We can be real for the next hour. Adrian never needs to know the truth. He can believe we're acting.

I trail a finger across his chest, our gaze interlocked as I take a slow step behind him. As I come out the other side, Adrian's gaze dips to my body for a second.

"Yes, that's it, babe!" Jessica cheers. "You're great once you allow yourself to ease up. Okay, everyone, next step. Seduction takes place when we engage all five senses. So far, we've used touch and sight. Next, we'll play with auditory. Let's get that dirty talk flowing. Come close to your partner and whisper something naughty in their ear."

I take a sharp inhale, my cheeks blossoming with heat all over again. Giggles spread among the class members, but unlike me, they all proceed with the task.

"Come on, Vee." Adrian leans back in his chair—a sight which looks hot in itself and is enough to distract me without the added burden of dirty talk. "Let me hear the best you've got. Make it up. Be ridiculous."

"Shut up. I'm thinking."

"No thinking."

"Maybe I want to put some effort into this. Maybe I want to make you sweat."

His mouth tilts into a crooked grin. Just by looking at those lips, my mind runs off on a tangent of all the things they could do to me. Suddenly, it's the easiest thing in the world to think up dirty talk. I place my hands on each of his shoulders and lean forward, feeling him shiver as I breathe heat over his ear.

"Adrian, I had the biggest crush on you in high school. Sometimes, when I went to bed at night, I would imagine you on top of me. *Inside* of me. Then, when the fantasy became too intense, I would touch myself."

I know I've done more than my job when Adrian goes still, his chest not even rising to breathe. "Fuck," he growls, "are you serious?"

"Score my dirty talk out of ten."

"You're a tease." The heated look in his eyes tells me he hasn't moved past my words.

Before I can say anything else, Jessica calls everyone's attention, demonstrating the next move with another couple. "Poke your ass out as you sit on their lap. Let them enjoy your sights. Then lean back into their lap and rub up against them."

"Vee, I would strongly advise against that."

"Okay, Verena, let me watch," Jessica says, bouncing over to us with a bubbly smile.

Adrian races out of the chair, snatching my hand in his and tugging me toward the exit. "Ah... great lesson," he calls over his shoulder at Jessica. "Maybe too good. Got to whisk this one away."

We both run out the door, snorting with laughter the moment we're alone on the dark walkway, nothing but torches and moonlight lighting our faces.

"What on earth were you thinking, whispering that in my ear?" Adrian says once he calms down, leaning against a palm tree. The flickering torchlight reveals a devastatingly handsome grin on his face.

"I was testing what you're made of."

"Not much, clearly. Now I've got to know if it's true."

"I hated you in high school. Of course it's not true."

"Says the girl who propositioned me for hate sex. Come on, you've totally thought about me in that way before."

"You'll never know the truth—"

My words are cut short by a group of men laughing, passing by in the distance. "Verena, is that you?" one of them calls out.

"Shit, it's your dad," Adrian hisses.

"What's the big deal?" I ask.

He takes my hand and places it over his dick. His *hard* dick. And oh my gosh, this is the second time in one day that I've felt his package, and I'm secretly in heaven.

"That's the problem. Get rid of them while I calm myself down." He runs back inside the building.

"Darling, are you alone?" Dad calls. "Everything all right?"

"Ah... yeah, getting some fresh air. I'm about to head back into the bachelorette party. I'll see you tomorrow."

"All right. Have fun." He continues down the pathway, taking the group of men with him.

I turn back to the party, about to call out to Adrian that the coast is clear, when someone takes hold of my hand from behind. "Verena, hey."

I give a frightened yelp and look down at our hands, then up at Jake's face. He's smiling at me. Like, genuinely smiling, as if he's happy to see me and this isn't awkward for him like it is for me. He's sun-kissed from our day on the yacht and his dark hair is ruffled with sea salt, which I'd ordinarily love, but the sight of this guy doesn't do it for me anymore. I retract my hand and brush his cheater germs against a nearby tree, not willing to taint the emeralds on my dress.

"I'm glad I caught you alone," he says. "Can we chat for a bit?"

"I'm needed back inside."

"Come on, Verena, five minutes. We haven't seen each other in six months. We have so much to catch up on. It's like there's this whole new version of you standing before me."

"*We* don't catch up, Jake. That's not the way it works when you cheat on someone and break their heart." I look up to the stars and swear, realizing I've made myself appear vulnerable to Jake and like I'm still in love with him.

He takes my jaw in his hand, tilting my head to face him. I have the greatest urge to whack his hand away but am caught off guard by the pained look that lives in his eyes. "That's actually something I want to talk to you about. It kills me to know what I did to you. Sometimes we hurt the people we love."

Holy hell. I'm not sure if Jake is about to apologize for cheating or bend forward and kiss me. Either way, I'm not equipped to deal with those scenarios.

"Ready to go, Vee?"

Jake's hand drops by his side as a door swings shut and Adrian's footsteps approach. Adrian wraps me in a hug from behind and kisses my cheek. Impeccable timing.

"Actually..." Jake begins, and from the tone of that one word, I know he wants to get me alone for a moment longer.

A higher power comes over me. I don't think my actions through, and instead do the one thing that can free me from Jake. My head turns to Adrian, and I replace my cheek with my lips, kissing him on the mouth.

Chapter Eighteen

Fuck! What am I doing?

Here I am, standing in front of Jake, breaking all of my rules and giving Adrian an open mouth kiss. Countless times I've fantasized about my first kiss with Adrian, the two of us swept up in passion and desire, our breaths tangling as one and his hands weaving through my hair. I'm supposed to feel an explosion of fireworks inside me. Instead, I'm jittery and panicked.

Adrian pauses, shocked for good reasons—I hope—and not because he's thinking about Isabelle and that this kiss is wrong. He'll play along when his mind catches up to him, I know he will, but I pray I haven't ruined things between us like I was afraid of earlier in the day at Whitehaven Beach.

I'm mortified when Adrian pulls back. Not only am I about to die of embarrassment from Adrian's reaction, but now I've made myself look like a complete fool in front of Jake—rejected for a kiss from my own boyfriend.

Adrian meets my gaze, studying my intentions. I don't see any of the heat in his eyes that was present a moment ago when I whispered dirty talk into his ear. Just plain confusion, and I pray Jake can't see it too.

After what feels like an eternity, the corners of Adrian's lips tug upward into a smile. "Let's get out of here." He threads his fingers with mine and leads us toward our bungalow.

I'm too scared to look at Jake on my way past him. As soon as I'm out of Jake's sight, I pull free of Adrian's hand and walk faster than him so I can avoid all conversation and get to my destination quicker, which is floating face-down in our pool with a bullet in my heart.

When I arrive at the front door of our bungalow, my key card won't work, no matter how hard I try to unlock the door. Adrian waltzes up behind me and takes the card from my hand, buzzing us in on the first attempt.

Smug bastard.

I dart inside, but Adrian snatches my hand before I get far.

"What?" I turn to face him, and he's right there. Right in front of me, my vision blocked by broad shoulders and his gorgeous face.

I take one step back, but Adrian closes the distance with a step forward, the same dark and hungry look from the dance class returning to his eyes. He's like a predator hunting his prey. As much as I try to command myself, I can't look away. I can't seem to calm my erratic breathing.

Adrian's gaze flicks down my body and back up. When he speaks, it's slow and in a velvety deep tone I've never heard from him before, sending my pulse faster. "You're upset with me. I'm sorry. You caught me off guard, Verena. No kissing allowed, remember? That was your rule."

"I panicked. Jake was... being weird."

Adrian steps even closer, leaving hardly any distance

between us. His gaze drops to my lips and unapologetically stays there. I can almost see a movie playing in his eyes of all the things he wants to do to me, and it's a movie I want to watch on repeat forever. R rated. Heat ripples throughout my body, pooling at my groin.

"Are you changing the rule?" he asks.

"Yes," I murmur, barely believing that I have the nerve to say the word.

The next thing I know, Adrian's mouth is on mine. My lips open with need and his tongue slides inside, claiming me. When I kiss him back, brushing my tongue along his, a growl escapes Adrian's throat that sends a new wave of heat throughout my body and makes my breasts tingle. His lips are urgent and his hands even more so as they wrap around my waist.

This isn't how my teenage self envisioned our kisses, either. They're hotter. Out of my entire romantic history, never have I been kissed so desperately. Never have I understood the appeal of being held so tight that it nearly hurts. But with Adrian, I think it might be a physical impossibility for him to hold me tight enough. My arms cling around his neck, drawing him closer, as close as he can possibly get. I need to feel Adrian all over me, and it must be obvious, because his hands travel down to my ass and press my hips against the hardness in his trousers.

It's that sensation which has my mind dizzying beyond comprehension. Earlier in the day, I was convinced kissing Adrian was a dangerous idea because it would ruin the fragile relationship we've rekindled. But now, nothing feels more right. This between us is meant to be. Whatever *this* is. I'm not sure if he's equally attracted to me or if we're engaging in a friends with benefits thing. The details aren't important right now. All I know is I've waited my entire life to kiss this man and take him to bed.

Without breaking the kiss, Adrian lifts me off the ground and wraps my legs around his waist, then carries me to the living room couch and lies me beneath him. His lips worship me, trailing down my jaw, my neck, and ravishing my chest. The muscles between my legs ache with pulsing heat as his hand slides up my thigh, slipping below the hem of my dress. I gasp, lifting my hips to show him I want this. That I'm more than ready to sleep with him. My body *craves* Adrian.

Before he takes this any further, he leans back breathless and soaks in the sight of me. "Fuck, you're beautiful," he says in a deep, guttural tone. I swear I could almost come from Adrian's sex voice, it's that amazing.

I reach up with my lips and kiss him again, pulling him back down to the couch with me. My fingers slide beneath his shirt, feeling the rock-hard muscles of his torso. A thrill rushes through me, knowing any moment now I'll see those muscles flex with exertion as he thrusts into me. I unbutton his shirt and slide it off his shoulders, in love with the sight of his bare chest. He doesn't have the same patience with my clothes and rips my dress to get it off me. Emeralds scatter across the ground. Thousands of dollars wasted, as with the dress he threw me in the pool with, but I'm too deep in this moment to care.

My legs wrap tight around his waist, and I let out a high-pitched moan when his cock rubs against my clit through the material of our clothes. I squeeze my thighs tighter around Adrian, sending the message that I'm desperate for him to keep thrusting.

A husky groan leaves his throat. "Are you trying to drive me insane?"

"You've been driving me insane all week. You have no idea how much I've been thinking about this."

"About what? Let me hear you say it."

"Fucking you."

Adrian purrs at those words and unclips my bra, bringing my nipple into his mouth. His tongue flicks over the peaked flesh, sending sparks low in my core and making my groin throb with need. Being naked for the first time in front of a guy always brings forward a sense of self-consciousness within me. With Adrian and the desperate way he looks at me, I've never been more confident in my life.

"I want to fuck you so badly, Verena. I *need* to have you." Adrian's hand slips beneath my lace panties and yanks them off, the urgency of his movements ripping them too. His lips travel down my chest, to my navel and even lower. "But first, I need to taste you. I need to feel you come on my lips."

My body swells with desire as he kisses between my legs, his tongue gliding over my entrance before pushing inside. I see stars when he licks my clit. The sensation of his tongue is so intense, making me buck my hips.

"Fuck, you're wet," he says. "You taste amazing."

His fingers slide into me, making me cry out his name as they stroke my walls.

He groans again, his fingers working faster. "The way you say my name..."

Christ. Is that my... G-spot? Whatever Adrian is doing with his fingers, no guy has ever done before, and I think it might be my new favorite thing. I've never understood the appeal of this move until now. Clearly, every guy I've been with before Adrian has had no clue about the female body. The muscles in my lower core tighten as I feel the build of an orgasm creeping up on me already. My breath comes faster and my sounds louder.

"Mmm... Yeah, let me hear you," Adrian rasps, his fingers picking up speed. "Tell me what you like and I'll do it."

"You, Adrian." I can barely speak, his hand feels so intense. "Anything you do."

His mouth returns between my legs, sucking on me while his fingers continue to tease.

"I'm going to come. I can't hold off."

Adrian climbs back over me, resting on one forearm as his other hand keeps working me. "I changed my mind. I need to see your face when you come. I want to see you enjoy this. *Me*, making you come. You don't know how much that turns me on."

The muscles in his arm flex as he works harder, his hand moving faster and faster. I gaze up at him. The sight of Adrian above me is enough to make me come undone.

"You're mine, Verena," he says, rough and with dominance. Those words push me over the edge, my spine arching as my inner muscles spasm in climax. "That's a good girl. Come for me. You look so hot when you're coming."

You're mine, Verena.

His words repeat in my mind, turning my orgasm into the longest, most intense one I've ever experienced.

When I'm finally lying still beneath Adrian, his fingers slip out of me and into his back pocket, retrieving a condom. Usually, I wouldn't be up for another round this quickly, but this is sex with Adrian we're talking about. I've had an entire life of foreplay with him. I could honestly go all night.

I slide out from beneath Adrian and straddle him on the couch, kissing him while my greedy fingers unzip his fly.

"I'm so hard for you, Verena."

His trousers come off, and I'm speechless, staring at the delicious image of Adrian's naked body and how big his dick is. He tears the packet with his teeth then rolls the condom over his shaft and pushes me onto my back.

Every inch of my body tingles with anticipation. His hand felt amazing, but it's the fullness of him inside me that I'm desperate for. I've waited too long for this moment.

Adrian pauses, his chest rising with heavy breaths as he gazes down at me. "I can't believe we're doing this."

"Neither can I."

He guides my legs around his waist and hovers over me on his forearms. The tip of his length presses against my opening as his lips brush over mine, then he pushes into me, the two of us gasping as he thrusts deep inside. The size of him has me stretched tight around his cock. I squeeze my core tighter, realizing the action is a mistake because I could honestly come from the sensation of my muscles clamping onto his erection.

"Don't move." Adrian's eyes shut tight. His face is almost pained as he says the words. "I need a moment to focus. You feel too good, and I don't want to lose control."

The amount of satisfaction I get from having this effect over Adrian is insane. He wants me. I turn him on. I raise my hips, needing friction, but he hisses at my sudden movement and presses a hand to my waist, keeping me still.

"Verena." My name comes out in a long, deep sigh, like he's begging me. "I want to take my time fucking you and enjoy every part of your body."

Holy shit. The way he talks during sex has me blushing. Though my body is aching for release, I don't dare move, wanting to keep him in me for as long as possible. After a deep breath, Adrian opens his eyes and gazes down at me with hunger. Slowly, he pulls out, then thrusts back inside me, the two of us loud with pleasure as his cock hits my back wall.

"Fuck, Verena." He pushes into me again, finding a slow rhythm.

I press up on my elbows to feel his lips on mine. Adrian's arms slink around me, one on my upper back, the other one lower, gaining leverage as he jerks his dick faster into me. We're both panting. He's working so hard I can feel the hammering of his heart against my chest.

"You feel so good," Adrian says, breathless through kisses. "If you only knew of all the things I want to do to you."

"Do them to me. Please."

"When you beg like that..." He growls, pushing into me harder.

Sweet bliss bursts through me when Adrian takes my nipple in his mouth, flicking it with his tongue and rubbing the other one with his hand. Without any warning, Adrian lifts me from the couch and carries me to a nearby table, remaining inside me every step of the way. He lays me out and fucks me from the edge of the table where he stands, watching his dick move in and out.

I flinch at the cool glass on my back, the temperature a shock to how hot sex with Adrian has made me. The two of us are working up a sweat. His forehead glistens from how hard he is exerting himself.

Adrian's thumb rubs over my clit, and I cry out his name again, clenching my thighs. "I can't last long if you do that."

He climbs onto the table, resting his forearms on either

side of my head. A look lies in his eyes like he's barely hanging on himself. "Come for me, then."

As his hand slips back between us, circling my clit, my most common teenage fantasy enters my mind, the one that would always make me orgasm the hardest when touching myself: Adrian coming inside me without a condom on. The thought of it pushes me beyond control and I'm unravelling beneath him, my body shaking from my orgasm. I want his come in me *so* badly. I want to be marked by Adrian.

He thrusts harder, groaning as my sex tightens around his dick. "Fuck, Verena. You're gonna make me come." I'm still riding my orgasm when his face tightens with that same painful look as before. But I know pain is the last thing he's feeling. His hips buck into me, then slow down. "So good. I need you. You're all mine."

We go still together. I can't move, I'm overcome with such a high. Adrian's face buries in my neck as we both catch our breath.

"That was incredible," he murmurs.

"I know."

"Can you go for another round?"

I laugh. He's read my thoughts. "Give me a minute to recover and I'll be ready—" My words are interrupted by a knock on the front door.

Adrian looks up at the sound. "Who's that?"

"No idea. Ignore them."

The knocking turns into banging. "Verena," a man calls through the door. I recognize his voice immediately. "It's me, Darius."

Chapter Nineteen

I roll out from beneath Adrian's body, muttering a curse. Could Darius have picked a worse time to show up? To be honest, I forgot all about inviting him to Australia. How is he even here? I thought there was a blizzard grounding all flights. Are Zac and Penny with him too? Please, no.

"Darius is here?" Adrian asks with a tone of suspicion in his voice. "As in, that guy from your show?"

"Um... yeah. I didn't realize he was arriving tonight. Let me get rid of him." Only now that I go to get dressed do I remember Adrian ripped my outfit and I can't greet Darius wearing it. I race to the closet and pull on the first thing I find, being my workout wear from yesterday's yoga class. When I return to the living room, Adrian is fully clothed. Dammit. I was hoping he would remain naked so we can pick things up right where we left them as soon as Darius is gone.

I peek around the front door, half opening it to give Adrian privacy. In the tropical backdrop of the resort, it's a strange sight to see Darius in a three-piece fitted suit and his dark hair gelled back without a strand out of place. But then again, this *is* Darius, and I should never expect less from him. He looks like a Hugo Boss model wherever he goes. Sleek and handsome.

"Oh, good." He folds his arms, the suit hugging the contours of his broad shoulders and muscular arms. "Reception told me this is your bungalow."

"Ah, you haven't caught me at a good time."

"Ha ha, very funny. Look, there was some mix up and reception only have one room ready, which I told Zac and Penny to take since they're all marriage-in-crisis. It won't be until midday that another room is set up for me. I need to crash here for the night."

"Oh, uh, I only mentioned one room to reception." I take caution to whisper this next part, making sure Adrian can't overhear. "I kind of assumed you'd stay with me." *Until I forgot all about your arrival because I've been too preoccupied with my fake boyfriend.*

"What happened to the blizzard?" I ask.

"The weather cleared up. Thought we'd surprise you with our arrival. So, I'm staying with you? That's fine with me, beautiful." Darius answers in a deep voice at full volume as he invites himself through the front door. I wince at the way he calls me *beautiful* and what this must sound like to Adrian.

"Darius, wait." I catch his wrist. "I'm being serious. This isn't a good time. Can you give me a minute to sort things out?"

His eyebrows rise with disbelief. "You're serious? I fly halfway around the world because you so desperately need me to be with you, and now you're telling me this isn't a good time?"

Shut up, Darius!

"It's okay, he can come in," Adrian says, leaning against

the table we just had sex on. He's smoothed out his hair and unwrinkled his clothes, giving off no trace that we slept together. "Hi, I'm Adrian." He extends a hand for Darius to shake.

Darius takes one look at him and eyes me like I need to explain everything right this second. But I can't, not in front of Adrian. After a long pause of what can only be perceived as rudeness from Darius, he shakes Adrian's hand all while dropping his voice to a territorial tone. "Do you mind if I have a moment alone with my girl? It's been a long flight. I'm tired and achy and could do with some private Verena time."

What. The. Actual. Fuck?

This can't be happening. What is Darius doing?

"Ah..." Adrian looks back and forth between me and Darius, confused. "Verena... You two are... together?"

"No," I say at the same time as Darius says, "Yes."

Adrian rubs a hand over his jaw. I can't read anything behind his brown eyes. He's a blank canvas. There's no sign of hurt that we just slept together and now another guy is telling him we're a couple. Oh shit, does he think I cheated on Darius with him? Or that I sleep with lots of people and have meaningless sex? What if he's not angry with me because the sex we just had was a friends with benefits thing for him and I'm the only one who thought it meant more?

"I'll... go catch up with the men for a bit," Adrian says.

"You don't have to. I don't want you to," I tell him, hoping he can see in my eyes how desperate I am for him to stay. "This isn't what it looks like. Darius and I are not together. He can sleep in my parents' bungalow tonight."

Darius scoffs a laugh. "Not happening, baby." He plants a kiss on my cheek and lowers a hand to my ass, then sends a wink to Adrian. "We're not together in the public eye. But behind closed doors, we're hot n' heavy, if you know what I mean."

I slide out of Darius' embrace, glaring at him. "What are you doing?"

Adrian studies Darius and me again, calculating our relationship, before saying, "It's fine, Verena. There's something I need to take care of, anyway. We'll talk later," and heads out the front door.

I have the urge to pull Adrian back and reassure him we're all good. That this guy who traveled halfway across the world because I "so desperately need him" is a platonic relationship. Not even that, Darius is gay. I'm like a sister to him. The sex can continue once I've settled Darius.

But a voice of reason stops me because I have no idea where I stand with Adrian. One moment we were kissing, then the next it turned into sex without ever discussing our intentions for each other. Was sex a one-off thing? Something casual with no strings attached and just some fun? Only now am I realizing that that's exactly what it was for Adrian, considering Isabelle is the one he wants. We were all turned on from the dance class and sex was a spur-of-the-moment thing. Now that we've had a chance to cool down, maybe Adrian is taking this opportunity to escape and get his priorities straight with Isabelle?

The worst indicator is that if Adrian is so into me, why didn't he stake his claim in front of Darius? Or be furious with me for sleeping with him when I'm allegedly involved with someone else?

Suddenly, I'm the most miserable I've felt all week.

Darius wolf whistles, giving himself a tour of the bungalow. "You've got yourself a palace here."

I shut the front door and hit Darius over the back of the

head, then drag him to the back garden by his arm. "You really screwed me over this time. What was that back there —*I could do with some private Verena time*—acting like we're about to rip each other's clothes off the moment we're alone?"

"Excuse me? I'm here saving your ass because you were having a meltdown over Adrian. And it was *your* idea for us to give off the vibe that we're romantic."

My mouth opens to deny everything, but I remain quiet, remembering it *was* my idea to have people at the wedding believe there's something romantic between Darius and me. I've just been so sidetracked with how things have been progressing with Adrian that I forgot all about the Darius plan. "Okay, you have a point."

"A *thank you* for playing along would be nice." He hits *me* over the back of the head this time. "What was Adrian even doing in here with you?"

I stop by the pool and stare at Darius with intention, hoping he's not going to make me say it out loud. At my prolonged silence, Darius takes a closer look at me, only now noticing my swollen lips and what has to be sex hair.

He claps a hand to his mouth but explodes with laughter anyway. "Oh no, this is too good. You slept with the devil?"

I wince and cover my face, peeking through fingers to gauge Darius' reaction. "We're kind of dating."

"*What?*" he spits.

"Technically, it's fake dating."

"Oh no, Verena, please tell me you didn't end up agreeing to that bullshit of his?"

I launch into a giant explanation of everything that's gone down since the FaceTime chat we had during my first night here—how this faux relationship came about, that

Adrian wants Isabelle back and is playing the jealousy game with her, and how I'm gaining so much satisfaction by parading Adrian around in front of Jake. Then I start rattling on about how Adrian and I aren't enemies anymore, that it feels amazing to have him back in my life and I hadn't realized until this week how much I miss him.

"I saw Jake tonight," I continue. "I think he was trying to apologize for hurting me, but I can't be sure because he started touching my face and it was gross, so I did the one thing I could think of to shut him up and kissed Adrian. It was only a small kiss, but the next thing I know, we're having sex on the living room table. Then you showed up and ruined everything."

"First of all," Darius starts ticking off a list with his fingers, "that's hot and I need details. Like, explicit details about what kind of kisser he is, if you were on top or him, how big his dick is—don't leave out any crucial information. Secondly, remind me never to touch that table. And thirdly, what you're saying is I came all this way for nothing and may have ruined things between you and Adrian because I made it sound like we're involved."

"Yes. I might have overreacted by asking you to come to Australia. If it makes you feel better, think of this as a business trip. The dress fittings are tomorrow. You can be in charge."

His eyelids lower halfway, unimpressed. "You told me this would be a vacation."

"Okay, sure, it can be. Whatever works for you."

Darius takes his suit jacket and vest off, drapes them over a pool chair, then unbuttons the top of his shirt and rolls up his sleeves. "You weren't exaggerating about the humidity in Australia. How long till my hair turns to shit?"

"I've got you covered. Lots and lots of hair spray."

"So, what's your plan with this guy, anyway? I don't want to pick up the pieces of your broken heart only six months after the last jerk. Especially not when I have Zac's relationship issues to deal with. Adrian is in love with another woman. He's *using* you to get her back, and also for a quick fuck on the side."

When Darius puts it like that, man, do I feel terrible.

I kick the pool water in my rage. A jolt of panic hits my chest when I topple off balance, my arms flailing as I sway toward the water.

Darius grabs my shirt to steady me. "You are a mess."

"Thank you for stating the obvious." I snatch my shirt from him. "I don't have a plan. Just... hope that Adrian starts to like me more than Isabelle."

"You *hope*? Verena, you are in deep trouble."

"I know! You're not helping!"

Darius gazes out at the ocean, sucking in a surprised breath like he's seen something scandalous. Instead of sharing the details, he enters a violent coughing fit.

"What happened? Are you all right?" I ask, never having seen him look so unflattering in my life.

After more choking and convulsing, he straightens up with the foulest look on his face. "I think I swallowed a fly."

I bend over laughing, clutching my stomach.

"It's not funny. There's an insect inside of me."

"Gross."

He whacks my arm and points out to the beach. "If you stop laughing, you'll see what I was about to show you before my body became tainted."

I take a calming breath and stand up, squinting through the darkness at two silhouettes walking alongside each other on the strip of beach my bungalow overlooks.

"Fuckwit alert," Darius says. "Is that Isabelle with him?"

Like a scared child, I duck behind Darius the moment my eyes adjust to the dark beach and I realize he's right. That *is* Adrian and Isabelle. Something inside of me stings —more than that bastard of a bluebottle jellyfish and Jake's cheating combined—to know that Adrian and I just had amazing sex and now he's moved on to Isabelle. What am I, some cheap hooker Adrian uses to get rid of all his pent-up sexual tension, then it's straight to the girl who actually matters? In his defense, it probably appears that exact way with me and Darius. But still, I can't deal.

"What are you doing?" Darius laughs over his shoulder at me. "They can't see you."

"You don't know that," I whisper, rushing to shut the lights off. "Can they hear us?"

"They're too far away to hear anything," Darius says, the two of us in complete darkness as we watch them. They come to a stop right by a beach lantern with flames illuminating their faces. "I hate to break it to you, Verena, but you've got some competition. Isabelle is beautiful."

"Don't make me hit you over the back of the head again."

We fall into silence, watching in anticipation as we try to figure out their dynamic. I stop breathing when Adrian reaches for Isabelle's hand. It's like a knife to the heart, paying credit to my hooker theory. I lose track of how long he touches her for and how many breaths of fresh oxygen I've missed out on. I'm about to suffocate here. I'll drop to the ground and die. It's actually a nice alternative, rather than witnessing Adrian kiss Isabelle. Considering the amount of times I saw Adrian making out with girls during my teen years, you'd think I'd be desensitized to the sight of him locking lips with someone other than me. But no, I can't do it. It's unbearable.

I bury my face in Darius' chest. "Tell me when it's over."

He hugs me tight, commentating their interactions. "They're hugging."

"Who initiated it?"

"I dunno."

"How can you not know?"

"Him, I think."

Another stab to my heart. "That's not good. What are they doing now?"

"Still hugging."

"What! How can they still be hugging? Is it intimate?"

"Have you ever seen a long hug that isn't intimate?"

"Crap."

"They're leaving now."

"Where are they going?" I ask. "Please tell me it's not back to her room."

"How would I know where they're going?"

"Because you're Darius and your superpower is to know all the answers to my problems."

"That's true. You're a mess without me."

"Was there a kiss?" I ask, dreading the answer.

"No kiss. Damn, you've got it bad."

"Don't say that. I can't be in love with Adrian."

Darius pulls back from me, quirking an eyebrow. "Hey, I didn't say anything about love."

My skin prickles with heat. "Neither did I. I was only saying what you were implying."

"Right."

"Shut up."

He studies my face, my *frowning* face, then takes me by the shoulders and guides me back inside the bungalow.

"What are you doing?" I ask.

"Where's the bathroom?"

"Through there." I point to the bedroom and adjoining bathroom. He sits me on the bed and locks us inside the room. "It's Robe Time."

Say no more, I understand. *Robe Time* is an official phrase that can be cited in the *Verena and Darius Dictionary (Second Edition)*. What started out as a rabid fan creating a website dedicated to the wacky list of terms coined by me and Darius actually got published into our very own dictionary that can be purchased in stores.

Robe Time: *A procedure that takes place in bath robes every time your best friend (or lover, as fans like to believe of Verena and Darius) needs an intervention. Robe Time activities can involve pampering sessions, binge eating, or watching* Titanic *and debating whether Jack could have fit on that floating door. In extreme cases where the activities are effective and both parties have forgotten the original crisis, Robe Time is relocated to the pool where the* Titanic *door theory is tested in person.*

That is the official definition of Robe Time. I'm not even kidding. I initiated Robe Time a few years back when Darius was considering bleaching his hair after a breakup. The most recent time was when I found out about the cheating scandal and Darius had to talk me out of being "that crazy bitch" and keying Jake's Ferrari.

Darius disappears into the bathroom, reemerging in a bathrobe and throws a second one at me. I strip down to my underwear and throw on the robe.

"What color?" He holds up two bottles of nail polish. One black, the other red.

I love how Darius can make me laugh during such a dire time. "*You're* going to paint my nails?"

"I didn't say I was going to be any good at it. In case you haven't noticed, we don't have access to watching *Titanic* or testing the door theory, and there's no food to binge. So, I'm attempting to pamper you."

A smile peeks through my terrible mood. "You're amazing. Let's go for black—the color of my heart."

"I like sexy red better."

We both take a seat on the ground, resting against the foot of the bed.

"Okay, here's your plan," Darius says, focusing hard to be neat while painting my first nail. "Adrian is using you to pull the jealousy card on Isabelle. Let's shove it right back in his face. Use *me* to make *him* jealous. I already made it seem like there's something romantic between us when I arrived. If he's ever listened to celebrity gossip, I'm sure he's heard about the Darena rumors. If this jealousy plan works, you'll know he has feelings for you. If not, you'll know it's Isabelle he's after."

"Darius, you're either a genius or an idiot."

"I'll take the first option."

"Let me get this straight. I'm double crossing my fake boyfriend to have another fake relationship with you?"

"Exactly."

I switch hands for Darius to paint the other one. "I'll think about it."

"Your other option is to act like an adult and talk about your feelings with Adrian."

"That's not an option. I don't want to get all emotional and messy with him. He's broken my heart once before and I can't allow that to happen again."

I check the time on Darius' Rolex. It's one in the

morning and Adrian hasn't returned from his meeting with Isabelle. What if he's not returning? My stomach sinks at the thought.

I try to rationalize the situation by telling myself Adrian hasn't been gone for *that* long. Maybe he thinks *I* need more time with Darius? Perhaps he's trying to be considerate? Whatever the answer is, I can't wrap my head around how one moment Adrian and I were having the most amazing sex of my life, then *this*.

I close my eyes, resting my head on Darius' shoulder as I try to avoid negative thoughts. But they're too hard to ignore. Come morning, there might not be any need for fake relationships.

Chapter Twenty

It's morning when I wake next to Darius on the hard bedroom floor. My neck is cramped from using his thigh as a pillow, and I'm sore all over from stand up paddle boarding. Along with the body aches, I have this cloud of doom hanging over my head because of Adrian. I don't remember what time I fell asleep last night, but I never heard him return to the bungalow.

With Darius still asleep, I fasten the belt of my robe and sneak out of the bedroom. I brew a jug of coffee in the kitchenette, miserable as I wait for the kettle to boil because there's still no sign of Adrian's return. Nothing is out of place from the way I left it last night.

I stare at the couch Adrian and I had sex on, reminiscing about how he touched me, how his lips adorned me in kisses, and the way his raspy voice said, *Fuck, you're beautiful*, and, *Are you trying to drive me insane?* Some childish part of me hopes that if I continue staring at the couch and focus on the heated memory, I'll turn into an X-Men character with the ability to turn back time and prevent Darius from arriving at the moment he did. Or at the very least, I'll get some mutant power that allows me to manifest my heart's deepest desire and bring Adrian back to my side.

A distant cough interrupts the thoughts. I glance around the living room for the source of the sound, expecting Darius to have joined me, but he's still asleep on the floor of the bedroom. I step out to the back garden, and wow, maybe all that wishing and hoping *did* turn me into an X-Men, because there Adrian is, *alone* on a daybed.

I rush back inside and grab two cups of coffee, then return to Adrian with the biggest smile on my face. I should have known to look out by the pool before getting my hopes dashed over the empty living room. His presence has to be a good sign. Why would Adrian return to the bungalow if things went so well with Isabelle? Perhaps she turned him down when they were on the beach last night. Better yet, maybe Adrian realized *I'm* the one he wants, and he ended all ties with Isabelle.

When I sit beside him, Adrian stirs from the change of weight on the mattress and blinks a few times before looking up at me. He clears his throat and wipes a hand over his face, rising to one elbow. "Hey, Vee. What time is it?"

I bite my bottom lip, caught off guard by how deep and crackly and amazing his sleep voice is. "Eight o'clock." I pass him a coffee, trying not to appear too desperate as I ask, "What time did you get in last night?"

"I dunno. It was late."

"What did you get up to?"

"Walk on the beach."

Well, at least he's not flat-out lying to my face.

"Yeah, I saw you with Isabelle. How did things go between you guys?"

He shrugs and takes a sip of his coffee, giving no elaboration. "I've heard the rumors about you and Darius but didn't realize you two were actually a thing."

"Oh, um... we're—" I'm about to tell him Darius and I aren't together but remember Darius' plan to find out if Adrian and I are more than a one-time hookup. "We're not together. We're just... It's complicated."

"I didn't take you to be the type for casual sex."

My cheeks grow heated. Man, this conversation is awkward. Can we please return to how good we were together without our clothes on? And... hang on a minute. Is he using the term *casual sex* to describe our hookup last night, or his perception of me and Darius? For goodness sake. Can nothing be straightforward with Adrian? I'm not fit to keep up with the intricacies of this conversation.

"Were you and I casual last night?" I ask.

He looks at me for a long moment, trying to figure something out in my eyes, then gazes out to the ocean and drinks his coffee. "I'm not sure what last night was. Whatever came over us, I had fun."

"So did I."

That eases the tension from Adrian's face, and I earn the tiniest smile when he looks back at me. "It probably shouldn't have happened, though. You have Darius and I..."

"Have Isabelle?"

His brows pinch together. "Right. Isabelle..."

I wrap my robe tighter around my midsection, hating every second of this stale interaction.

"I'm glad we're friends again," Adrian adds. "I've missed you."

Friends? I mean, friends is better than nothing. It's what I originally wanted for us. But now... Friends is not enough. How can we be friends after all the dirty things he did to me last night? This answers my question about our status, though. I fight back the tears, feeling like an idiot for letting myself grow attached to Adrian again after all these years.

"I don't know any friends that kiss," I mutter. "Or sleep together."

He chuckles and reclines against the daybed backrest, but the tone of his laugh is off kilter. Regardless, how can we be on polar opposites of the emotional scale right now, with him laughing and me trying hard to not let my voice crack?

"Does Darius know we slept together?" Adrian asks.

"Yes. And also about the fake relationship."

He raises a skeptical eyebrow. "And he's okay with both?"

"Not really, but he won't be an issue."

Adrian takes another sip of coffee before turning to sarcasm. "This won't be awkward at all."

The lump in my throat grows heavier. I stand from the daybed, unable to face Adrian right now. "I should... get dressed for the day."

"Vee." My name races out of Adrian's mouth. He grabs my hand and pulls me back down beside him. Our gaze meets, making my stomach flip with nerves. He waits in silence, but for what, I'm not sure. When Adrian finally speaks, it's with a soft voice. "What happened between us last night?"

"It was just some fun, right?"

He examines my face, and I pray he can't see through the shield I have up to protect my heart. Both of his hands find mine and he gives them a gentle squeeze before clearing his throat. "I'm not sure how to navigate this situation between us, Verena. We have such a complicated past and it feels like we're finally back on track as friends." He gives an awkward laugh. "Friends really isn't the right word, but I don't know what is. The point I'm trying to make is I'm realistic about where I stand with you. I know I don't have any say in your life when it's been years since we've spoken. I'm afraid of scaring you off by coming on too strong, but I have to say this. I don't like Darius. He's not right for you."

Wait, what? That whole speech was about Darius? My throat clenches to ward off another onslaught of tears because some stupid part of me believed Adrian was about to confess his feelings for me.

"Why don't you like Darius?"

"Come on, Verena," he sighs, letting a hint of frustration slip through his voice. "We had sex last night and he's okay with that? Darius is wasting your time and you're going to end up heartbroken again."

"I told you, it's complicated."

"Well, it shouldn't be. You should be with someone who can't stand the thought of anyone else having you."

I wish you felt that way about me, I feel like saying.

"Adrian... I don't want to fight. Darius is my best friend. He's not going to hurt me."

Something about my words makes Adrian flinch. "I used to be your closest friend. Look how that ended."

Oh, come on, you've got to be kidding me! It's my *friendship* with Darius that Adrian is jealous of? I retract my hands from his, creating distance between us. "Darius won't hurt me like that, okay?"

"How do you know?"

My temper snaps and I'm suddenly raising my voice. "Because no one can hurt me the way you did! Not Darius. Not Jake when he cheated on me. No one!"

We both fall quiet, staring at each other in shock. I don't know how we found our way to this place, but the tension between us has grown one hundred times deeper now that we've dug up the dangerous territory of our past.

Adrian is the first one to break the silence, his eyes pleading with me. "We should talk about our childhood. I'm so sorry, Verena. I wish I could undo all of the bad parts and never have hurt you."

I try to keep a level head by lowering my voice. "I don't want to talk about what happened between us. It's too painful. We've had such a good time together these last few days. Let's move on from the past and enjoy the rest of the week."

He slides closer, taking my hands in his again. "I *have* moved on. It's you that's holding onto pain. You're never going to give me a chance to fix what happened between us, are you?"

"Adrian..."

"I want what we used to have. Verena, I want..." He exhales loudly.

I'm holding my breath, waiting for him to finish that sentence and say that he wants me. But he never does.

I pick up the two coffee cups, desperate to return inside and be on my own. "Darius and I have a long day ahead of us with dress fittings. I have the ceremony rehearsal too." Not wanting to leave the conversation in an awkward place, I say, "Maybe we can have lunch together?"

"Sure." It's the most lifeless answer he could give.

Darius steps into the doorway, folding his arms like I'm in trouble, paired with a mischievous look in his eyes. "I've run us a shower, baby. Get inside now. Don't make me carry your sweet ass into the water with me."

Darius and I are still in our robes, and I have no doubt from the new crease between Adrian's brows that he's noticed. It probably looks like Darius and I had sex last night. How did I wind up in a mess this deep?

"Coming," I call.

Adrian swears under his breath.

Once Darius disappears inside, I turn back to Adrian. "You and I are good, okay? I'll meet you at the restaurant at midday."

"Ah... actually... I'm not sure about lunch. Isabelle said she wants to see me today. I think we're having lunch together."

"Oh?"

"Yeah, sorry, I forgot until now."

My fingernails dig into my palms, and I swear I'm about to burst into a swarm of angry flames.

But...

Hang on a second...

Adrian's jaw ticks and a flicker of bitterness crosses his eyes. The irritation in his features lasts for five seconds at most, long enough for me to catch onto its meaning. *Adrian* is pissed at *me*. The only question is why?

"Baby," Darius calls from inside the bungalow, "you have one minute before I throw you over my shoulder and carry you into the shower."

Adrian pulls out his phone. "I should call Isabelle and ask if she'll spend the morning with me too." He almost says it as a countermove to Darius' words.

All the cogs in my mind suddenly click into place and, finally, I can see things clearly. Adrian only mentioned lunch with Isabelle after Darius made that whole scene about having a shower with me. Now Adrian is announcing that he'll call Isabelle, right after Darius threatened to carry me inside.

Is Adrian... trying to make *me* jealous?

There *is* no lunch date planned with Isabelle, is there? Who forgets about a lunch date with the woman they're desperately in love with and trying to win back?

I want what we used to have. I want...

Adrian was going to finish that sentence by saying he wants *me*, only he didn't have the nerve to be honest. Winning back Isabelle isn't on his agenda at all. At least, not anymore. How can it be after the connection we shared last night?

But then what was that interaction Darius pointed out between Adrian and Isabelle on the beach? Adrian never shared any of the details; I just assumed it was romantic. For all I know, he could have gone to Isabelle to break any remaining ties between them, like I'd originally hoped. After all, we had just slept together, and it was good. *So* good. The most intense sex of my life. I know he felt the connection too.

An explosion goes off inside my head. I'm mind-blown at the intricacy of this situation we're in. Let me see if I've got this straight: Adrian and I are using each other to make our exes jealous, all while I'm using Darius to make Adrian jealous; at the same time, Adrian is using Isabelle to make *me* jealous.

My mind takes a minute to process that logic.

There's some serious next-level scheming and double-crossing going down in this bungalow. I can't be making this up. I can't be. It's laughable what he's doing. What we're *both* doing. I'm glowing with a smug kind of pride that I've figured him out. For someone else, this might seem like a far-fetched conclusion to make, but I know Adrian's ways.

He wants to make me jealous? All right, fine. We'll do this his way. I can play that game.

I know I should be the mature one and share my feelings, but there's too much trauma from the past for me to be vulnerable with Adrian. The past isn't all that's holding me back. What if, on the odd chance, I confess how much I like him, and it turns out that I'm wrong about everything and he really does love Isabelle? I mean, I don't think I'm wrong, but that little voice in my head that says *what if?* has me in a chokehold. I can't tell Adrian how I feel.

Instead, I laugh to myself, preparing to return inside the bungalow. If Adrian *is* trying to make me jealous, this could be quite the show. I want to see how badly he wants me and what lengths he'll go to get me undressed and moaning beneath him again. My groin tightens at the thought. This could be... fuck... really damn hot.

"Well," I play along, "I hope your morning and lunch date with Isabelle go well. I guess Darius and I will have some more alone time."

When I'm back in the bedroom, I close the door behind me and race to the bed, working up a sweat as I throw pillows to the ground and rip pristine sheets from the mattress that haven't been slept in once since the start of this vacation.

Darius exits the bathroom. "Whoa, calm down. What are you doing?"

"Making the bed look sex-worn and like I had the wildest night of my life with you. I'm going full steam ahead with your plan. Make yourself look irresistible today. No suit and tie. Get your muscles out and make Adrian jealous."

Chapter Twenty-One

"You had sex with Adrian?" Zac asks, lounging in his bungalow's hot tub with a cocktail. It's nine a.m. and he's already drinking alcohol. This can't be good. "I thought you hated the guy?"

"Oh, no," Darius answers for me with a cocky grin, arms spread wide over the backrest of a couch on the deck. "Quite the opposite. Verena likes Adrian so much that she's using me to make him jealous and confess his feelings. I am going to have so much fun with this."

"And I thought *I* needed therapy."

"Okay, just shut up, both of you." I take a seat on the ledge of the hot tub, dangling my legs in the water. "Zac, how are you and Penny settling into the resort?"

"It's beautiful here," he says. "Thank you for bringing us to this island. I owe you one."

"No, you don't. I'm happy to help. Speaking of Penny, where is she?"

"Right here." Penny steps out of the bungalow in a yellow bikini, her blond hair piled high on her head, and with a foul look on her face that always seems to be present.

"I'm so glad you came to Australia." I smile at Penny even though all I get from her is bad vibes. "You're about to join Zac in the hot tub? Darius and I should give you two some privacy."

"No, I'm heading to the beach," Penny says.

Zac stands from the tub. Water trickles down his firm abs as he wraps a towel around his waist. "That sounds nice. I'll join you, sweetheart." He places a hand on Penny's lower back and leans down to kiss her lips, but her head turns away from him at the last moment. Poor guy. You can't say he isn't trying.

"Don't bother coming to the beach," she tells him. "Your friends are here."

"They're about to leave for the bridal fittings."

"Yeah, I know. I overheard your whole conversation from inside. Ugh, Verena, you are living every girl's dream right now. Fake dating your enemy. Incredible sex. Can we please trade places?"

"Wow." Zac's voice drops. "Really, Penny?"

"It was a joke. Mostly. Stop taking everything to heart."

I can detect a hundred retorts brewing on Zac's lips, but he buries them deep down and smiles at her—a smile that sends every girl lightheaded when they see him sing on Broadway or the big screen. Every girl except Penny. "I was thinking we could go to the day spa and get a couples massage."

"That sounds amazing," I say, trying to help Zac out. "So romantic. I'm sure you two will love it."

"Actually," Penny says, "I want to go snorkeling."

"Very romantic, too," I add. "Adrian and I had such a nice time together out on the reef. We were hugging in the water and held hands while swimming. I'm sure you two will love it."

Penny sends me a sly look. "This Adrian guy sounds hot."

"Jesus Christ, Penny," Zac scoffs.

"What?" That one word out of Penny's mouth is all tones of vicious. "You're the only man I'm allowed to find attractive? I'm sure you think tons of women are beautiful. What about Verena, I'm meant to believe you think she is ugly?"

Whoa. How did I end up in the middle of this? "Uh... I'm really not comfortable with getting involved—"

"You're missing the point," Zac tells Penny. "Look, can we please not do this in front of an audience."

She throws her hands up in the air. "Oh, so now you don't want to talk about our issues. *I* am making an effort to discuss our marriage. What are *you* doing other than throwing rose-colored glasses on and bringing us to Australia for some happy little vacation when we're not happy at all?"

Darius and I swap awkward looks, uncertain of whether we should sneak out of the bungalow or stay to support Zac.

"We're here because we need an escape from the media," Zac tells her, and even though he is clearly frustrated, he somehow manages to keep a level tone while being yelled at.

"Yeah, well *I* need an escape from *you*." Penny grabs a towel and heads for the front door.

Zac follows after her. "Where are you going?"

"Don't follow me." The door slams shut behind her, and Zac curses.

I join Darius, sitting on the armrest of his couch. "Please tell me I didn't start that fight."

"Are you kidding?" Darius whispers. "Of course you did, but don't feel bad. During the flight here, Penny was picking fights with Zac over everything. At one point, she blamed him because my nose whistled when I breathed. I was wearing noise canceling headphones and could still hear her nagging him."

Zac paces back and forth by the front door, raking both hands through his hair. "I should go after her."

"Give her a chance to calm down," Darius tells him.

"That's an abusive relationship if I've ever seen one," I say. "I don't know how much longer I can be supportive—"

"Verena, please," Zac grumbles, returning to us on the deck. "Not now. I messed up and need to go after her."

"You did *not* mess up." I have never seen anyone more committed to fixing something that should remain broken. Zac is, like, the perfect husband. "She's gaslighting you."

"She's not. She's just... upset about that gossip article."

"*She* had an affair, and yet you're the one in trouble?"

Darius stands from the chair and pats a firm hand on Zac's shoulder. "I hate to say it, but Verena is right."

Zac pinches between his eyes like he has a headache. "I can't lose her."

"Give her some time to cool down. Come with me and Verena to the dress fittings. It will help clear your mind."

Darius and Zac's arrival at the resort has everyone running around in excited flutters. During our walk to Tory's bungalow for the dress fittings, the three of us have to stop several times for them to sign autographs. All throughout Tory's fitting, the only thing I hear are the bridesmaids, Stacy and Nia, asking Darius to take selfies with them and for Zac to perform a serenade from his latest Broadway show. The girls get a rude shock when Zac turns them down, realizing what a grump he is when out of the spotlight.

If I had any concerns about Adrian falling for this fake romance with Darius—because to me, Darius is so totally gay—those doubts are all eliminated by the way Nia hasn't stopped licking her lips at the sight of Darius. And that Stacy, a married woman, flushes when questioning him if he's single. Those who aren't close with Darius never suspect he is gay. He doesn't fit the flamboyant stereotypes that many people associate with gays. His voice is deep. He dresses well and has a passion for style, but it's in a rugged male model way. There's a masculinity about him and his mannerisms.

"You want to know if I'm single?" Darius peers up at Stacy, kneeling at her feet as he pins the hem of her dress. "Why?"

"I thought maybe you and Verena were... you know..."

Darius peeks over his shoulder at me, winking. I laugh and look away.

"That!" Stacy pounces, pointing between Darius and me. "I see it on camera too. You have this chemistry. You're even wearing matching outfits. What do you guys call that again—*DICKotomy* or something? That dictionary you have is so bizarre."

DICKotomy: *Any instance where Verena and Darius unintentionally dress in similar outfits, flaunting their telepathic bond. The phrase "DICKotomy" was coined in season one, episode three, of* Valentine's Day, *when Darius tried to teach Verena the meaning of dichotomy by using an example of their matching outfits, and how they are not dichotomous. Verena repeated the word out loud but mispronounced it as* dickotomy. *The two friends (lovers) thought her mistake was hilarious and decided "dickotomy" needed to become an official word between them with its own meaning.*

It's true, Darius and I are wearing matching outfits today, which wasn't planned, but makes us look like a cute couple. We're both dressed from head to toe in white. I'm in a summery playsuit that has slits from ankle to thigh, allowing the fabric to ripple in the wind when I walk. Darius is in full-length trousers and a button-down shirt rolled to his biceps—that also ripples in the wind when he walks. Together, we're like Beyoncé with a constant fan on us. #BestFriendGoals.

Stacy continues with her questioning of Darius and me. "Verena flew you all the way to Australia. What does Adrian have to say about this?"

Beside her, Nia's face falls flat at Stacy's implications. She tries to disguise her disappointment by helping Tory choose earrings for the big day.

Zac pours himself a glass of wine, making a mockery of my situation with sarcasm. "I don't appreciate being left out of the drama. Verena flew me and my wife out too. Maybe she's romantic with us as well. We're all in one big polyamorous relationship."

"Really?" Stacy latches on to the suggestion, taking him seriously.

I whip Zac with a tape measure, warning him to shut up. "He's joking."

Stacy gives me a sharp smile. "Say what you want, but I think I've caught onto something between you and Darius. You better be careful, Verena." Of course she pronounces my name correctly in front of other people so they can't call her out.

It's midday when Darius and I finish the dress alterations of everyone on Tory's side of the bridal party. We all head to the cliffside restaurant to grab a bite to eat, with me forced to walk behind the group while the girls drown Darius and Zac in squealing fangirl conversation.

"I love that Halloween episode where you pranked Verena by using onions to make candy apples," Stacy says to Darius, which doesn't surprise me at all that she enjoyed my suffering. "The look on her face when she bit into that onion was priceless."

For someone who doesn't like me, Stacy sure seems to know a lot about my life.

"Oh!" Tory grasps Zac's arm. "Remember that episode where the three of you learned viral TikTok dances?"

"Yes!" Nia jumps up and down. "That episode is my favorite. You *have* to do those dances for us again, Darius, *please*. Zac, too."

"Maybe another time." Darius drapes an arm over my shoulder, pulling me forward so I'm not the loser hanging out at the back.

"Thanks," I whisper as we arrive at the restaurant.

"All right, I'm out of here," Zac says to the two of us. "I need to find Penny and make this right."

"You sure?" Darius asks.

"Yeah. Plus, I don't think I can handle a minute more of... *that*." He nods to the bridesmaids.

"Call us if you need anything," I tell him.

Tory enters the conversation with a frown. "Zac, you're not joining us for lunch?"

My sister and the bridesmaids smother him in goodbye hugs. His eyes widen, sending me a help signal to pull the girls off him. I sit tight and smile back at him. *Hate you*, he mouths in return.

"Oh no." Nia cringes when Zac stalks off. "Did we come on too strong?"

Darius waves a dismissive hand. "That's just Zac. He's constantly in a bad mood."

My sister leads us through the lunchtime crowd for the bar, speaking over the clutter of voices. "We should order drinks first. What do you all want?"

"Sex on the Beach." Darius undresses me with his eyes. He pulls out his phone and takes a photo of the two of us while kissing my cheek.

"Adrian's watching?" I mutter.

"He sure is." Darius speaks louder, assuring Adrian hears. "You want a Quick Fuck?"

"I suppose you didn't hear," Stacy says as we step up to the bar, "but Verena is banned from alcohol for the rest of this week. Tory's orders."

My gaze whips to my sister, demanding she explain herself immediately.

"I didn't say it like that," Tory says. "I asked Stacy to keep an eye on you after the first night here when you got upset on the beach."

"Adrian!" Stacy's face lights up as she peers behind me. Her gaze shifts between Darius and me like she's waiting for a volcanic eruption now that Adrian has joined us.

I face Adrian, gulping down my nervous jitters when I find him grinning. His mood is a surprise. After the tense way we left things this morning at our bungalow, he's now standing here smiling at me?

"Did you see Isabelle this morning?" I test him.

"For a little bit."

Right. Sure.

Adrian sits at a bar stool and slips an arm around my waist, drawing me flush against his body. My breasts are pressed to his firm pecs and our lips are only inches apart. Oh, I like this. I like this *so* much.

"What are you doing?" I whisper.

His lips brush over my ear, his hot breath sending thrills between my thighs. "You're still my fake girlfriend, aren't you?"

"I... yes." The only issue is, I can't tell what's real or not anymore.

"Perfect." Adrian grins, but is he fuming inside? Did he see the messy bedsheets I left for him? I want him to want me so badly that he can't stand it. I want him to pine after me and spend every second of every day craving my kisses.

If I keep playing along like Adrian and I are in some blissful relationship, it will earn me no jealousy points. So, I release myself from his arms and step closer to Darius. As with last night, Adrian looks between Darius and me, studying us. Either he hates that I'm choosing to be in closer proximity to Darius, or he's noticed our DICKotomy. I'm hoping for both.

Before I have a chance to say anything, Stacy curls a hand through her blond ponytail, snickering at the sight of us. "Darius and Verena look cute in their matching outfits, don't you think, Adrian?"

Ordinarily, a comment like that from Stacy would piss me off, but for once, her snark is doing me a favor. What *does* piss me off is Adrian's lack of annoyance.

He smiles at me again and stretches a hand forward to weave our fingers. "Verena looks beautiful."

"I thought you were having lunch with Isabelle," I say when he draws me away from Darius and back into his arms.

"Your ex-girlfriend?" Stacy asks.

"Yeah, but that's a bit later," Adrian explains. He's still playing up that lie. I really *hope* lunch with Isabelle is a lie.

"Thought I might steal Verena away for a moment. I've got something important to discuss with her."

My spirits perk up. Something important to discuss? Is Adrian coming to his senses about us and ready to confess his feelings?

"We're about to have lunch," Darius tells him, blunt as anything.

Adrian's tone is just as harsh. "You haven't even ordered drinks yet. I'm sure there's plenty of time before your meal arrives. Excuse us." He stands from the stool, leading me toward the exit.

"What are you doing?" I ask, following him. "I was in the middle of something with Darius."

"Ordering drinks with sex names? Yeah, I heard. Sounds real important."

The sarcasm in his voice makes me smile. Just as planned, Darius is getting under his skin.

"I overheard something about Darius getting his own bungalow today. Any idea when that's happening?" he asks.

"I'm not sure."

"I should have thought of this sooner, but if there's a delay, he can take my old one. Not much space for him to share ours."

I smile internally. "I'll let him know."

As we leave the restaurant, Adrian guides me through a gate to the resort's community pool. The water is filled with guests lounging on inflatable pool floats, and all the reclining chairs are occupied with people sunbaking—my mom and Cece Hunter among them.

"Hey, you two. There's a spare daybed beside us." Mom nods to her left.

Adrian glances around, looking for an alternative option, but the pool area is so crowded that the daybed is our only choice. He takes a seat, drawing me onto his lap. I'm inclined to pull away, giving Adrian the impression that I have Darius on my mind, but Mom and Cece are watching us with love hearts in their eyes, and it would crush their souls if they suspected for one-second that something is wrong between me and Adrian.

"So." I settle into his lap, using a hushed voice that only he can hear. "What is so important that you had to take me away from my lunch?"

Adrian draws the sheer curtains of our four-poster daybed shut. When he looks at me, there's tension in his eyes like he's annoyed about something. Please let it be the messy bedsheets I left for him to find. "I don't like how we ended things this morning," he says, low enough to prevent our moms from overhearing.

"Neither do I."

He rubs the back of his neck and sighs. "We have two days left at this resort and I want to keep having fun with you. I'm sorry if I intruded in your personal life."

"It's fine. I want us to have fun too."

"Good. So, I've been thinking..." Adrian pauses to gather his words, his features easing into something softer. He strokes a hand through my hair, curling a finger around a dark lock. The way he touches me sends flutters through my tummy. I'm a total pile of goo for this man and am dying to know what he's about to say, hoping it will be a confession of his feelings for me. "I'm serious about wanting us to be close friends again."

Well, fuck.

That was deflating.

I swear *friends* has become his new favorite word.

"When will we see each other after the wedding?" he asks. "Don't say in another seven years."

"I have a business trip to London next month. My schedule is busy, but I'm sure I can make time for you."

"Perfect. And after that?"

"It will be your turn to fly to me." I poke him playfully in the chest. "I'm high maintenance if you can't already tell. Let's say, theoretically, that I do let you join my inner circle of friends. I expect you to FaceTime me at least five times a day when we're not in the same city. *And* I want hourly texts."

He smiles. "No problem. I do have one request, though. I want to make it a rule that you come home every year for Christmas."

My nose puckers and I lose all sense of humor. "To Sitka? Sorry, but I'm never returning there."

"What about when our sisters have kids? Surely you'll come home for that."

"I'll fly them to New York. I've got enough money."

"Vee, I'm serious." He leans in, holding my gaze. I almost think he's about to kiss me, but there's too much intensity in his eyes and the way he speaks those words. "Come home for Christmas."

"Adrian..." I sigh, shifting my gaze to the pool. "I hate it there."

He places a hand beneath my chin, drawing my face back to him. "Come home to see me. We'll rent an Airbnb so we don't have to live under our parents' roofs."

That proposition is slightly more tempting, but it's hardly sweetening the deal when I think about all the awkward interactions I'll have with my relatives. "What other procedures will you have in place to prevent Christmas from being painful?"

"We'll be together the whole time, so I can save you from any embarrassing family moments."

It's like he's reading my mind. If I shout loud enough in my head, *Stop pretending to be in love with Isabelle*, will he hear me? Why won't Adrian admit he wants to be with me already, instead of dancing around his feelings with this Christmas talk? Seriously, what is it going to take?

"You're overlooking one key point," I say. "You'll be back together with Isabelle by Christmas. I don't want to be a third wheel."

He shrugs. "She'll have me to herself the entire year. I'm sure she'll understand if you're around for one week."

"Oh, really? She'll be fine with your ex-girlfriend bunking with the two of you? I find that hard to believe."

"If she's got an issue, I'll fill her in on the details of our fake relationship. Verena," he emphasizes my name, slipping his hand into mine. "I'm serious. Come on. I want you there at Christmas."

Oxygen evades my lungs as I stare down at our hands. I could get used to this. I want him all day, every day. He notices my reaction to his touch and responds by squeezing my palm. And suddenly, I don't know what's more distracting—that we're sharing this intimate moment, or that I'm considering returning home to Sitka if it means spending Christmas with Adrian.

"What do I have to do to make you say yes?" he asks.

Tell me you love me.

Tell me you never want to be with anyone else but me.

We lose the intimate moment when the daybed curtains slide open and in pops Tory's head. Behind her, Darius, Stacy, and Nia are pulling up a group of tables and chairs, positioning them in front of the bed.

"We ordered lunch," Tory says. "The kitchen staff are bringing our food out here so we can eat with you two by the pool. Unless you want to be alone?"

"No, you can join us." Adrian shifts to the edge of the daybed, pulling me with him.

"Mom, Cece, do you want to sit with us too?" Tory asks them.

"Thank you, darling, but we're about to take off," Cece says, slipping her shoes on and collecting her belongings. Both she and mom head for the pool gate.

"Where are the menus?" I ask as the others take a seat.

"I've already ordered for you," Stacy tells me. "I chose the garden salad because I know you're trying to lose weight."

Darius laughs in disbelief, like he can't believe everything I've told him about Stacy's attitude toward me is true.

"Stacy," Adrian addresses her in a pleasant voice, "how's your weight loss journey going?"

"Excuse me?"

"I was chatting with your husband on the yacht yesterday. He told me you..." Adrian pauses at the fuming reaction on Stacy's face. He raises a hand to his mouth and coughs to hide a laugh. "Forget I said anything."

I lean into Adrian and whisper, "Did you actually speak to Stacy's husband?"

"No. But as if I'm going to let her get away with speaking like that to you. And by the way, she better be making up that bullshit about you wanting to lose weight. You looked amazing in that bikini yesterday. Even better out of it."

Hot flashbacks of Adrian inside me enter my mind. A shiver ripples through me, and from the corner of my eyes, I catch Adrian smile to himself.

"Hello!" Tory waves her arms at us. "Did you two hear anything I said?"

"Sorry, can you repeat it?" I ask, struggling to refocus.

"I said I didn't order Adrian anything because I'm not sure what he wants."

"That's okay," he tells her. "I have to leave soon. I have a lunch date."

"You're calling lunch with Isabelle a date?" Darius asks, hung up on the exact wording I am.

Adrian glares at him. "Date, appointment, meeting—the terms are interchangeable."

"Well, have fun on your *date*." Darius leans back, his biceps flexing as he rests both hands behind his head.

"So, Adrian," Tory interrupts, her voice speedy, as if adamant to change the subject, "I wish you were with us for the dress fitting. Verena looked stunning in her maid of honor gown. You would have loved it."

"She did," Darius agrees. "I can't wait to dance with her at the wedding."

Nia smacks her glass on the table with a little too much excitement. "You two and your Latin dancing. Every time I see you dancing on *Valentine's Day,* I swear you're having a secret love affair."

"Exactly my point from earlier," Stacy says. "Watch out, Adrian."

Even though Adrian holds a straight face, I'm almost certain he groans quietly. It's my turn to cough away laughter. This whole game between me, Darius, and Adrian is going better than expected, especially with the help of Nia and Stacy's comments.

Tory's comments, on the other hand, seem to be in support of Team Adrian. "Darius, do you have anyone special in your life?"

"Yes," he answers with eyes on me. I smile back at him, the two of us sharing a moment of prolonged eye contact that makes Stacy's jaw drop.

"That's so nice," Tory says. "I bet you're happy Verena has found Adrian after all the heartache she went through with her last boyfriend."

"Verena and I grew very close during that period of her life. That's why she asked me to be here with her. I wouldn't fly across the world for just anyone."

"I'm glad she has a good friend in you," Adrian adds with ease. "It's a surprise, though."

"What's a surprise?" Darius asks.

"The way you talk about Verena. She doesn't ever talk about you."

I bite down hard on my tongue to stop myself from laughing. Darius is experiencing Adrian's signature for the first time—the comments that are spoken in a friendly manner but laced with venom. A skill that is only reserved for people he wants to prove a point against, say, shutting down someone who's intruding on his territory.

I love Darius for this jealousy plan so much right now.

A waiter arrives with our meals before any more snide comments can be thrown across the table. Adrian retrieves his phone from his pocket and smiles at the screen while reading a text. It's not any old smile either, but the kind that takes place when receiving a message from the person you're crushing on.

"Who's that?" I ask, trying to disguise the bitterness in my voice.

"Ah... Isabelle. She'll be here in a moment."

The triumph is suddenly kicked out of me. My hands want to clench into fists. Up until this text message, I was sure Adrian would disappear down the beach for an hour to make it look like he was off somewhere with Isabelle. Now, I'm questioning everything again, just like earlier this morning. Maybe he *does* want her back?

"How are things between you and Isabelle?" I ask, quietly enough for only him to hear.

He grins at me. "Really good. Today could be the day that we get back together."

"Oh… great."

"The food is here." Darius interrupts our private conversation once the waiter has placed each of our meals on the table. "Guess this is your cue to leave, Adrian. Don't want to keep that *date* of yours waiting."

Adrian holds his temper and turns to me. "I'll see you later, okay?"

He stands from the daybed, and I think I'm about to punch the mattress, until he leans down and presses his mouth to mine in front of everyone. His *open* mouth, kissing me long and hard. His hands cup my face. His breath is so intoxicating that I can't think straight, only melt into his touch.

None of us say a word as he walks to the restaurant, too stunned to comprehend what just happened. I'm too busy trying to decipher if that kiss was Adrian's way of signaling that he likes me, a means to flex his masculinity in front of Darius, or an effort to make Isabelle jealous if she's watching.

Nia breaks the silence, fanning herself with her hand. "That was hot. I need to find me a man who kisses like that."

Stacy's gaze is bouncing between Darius and the direction Adrian left in, not sure what's going on. Tory and Darius both have their heads down, texting something beneath the table. A few seconds later, my phone buzzes with multiple messages.

Tory: Explain that kiss immediately!!! I thought you guys were only pretending to be a couple?

Darius: You need to have sex with him again so I can live vicariously through you.

Tory: Do you still hate Adrian? Please say no. I think he's in love with you.

I glance in Adrian's direction, hoping to see him one last time before he disappears. He's waiting by the restaurant entrance with hatred in his eyes, staring down Darius. I cover my mouth to hide a laugh. All of my Isabelle doubts leave me once again. I can't believe I started falling for Adrian's tricks.

I'm not pleased when I see Isabelle does actually arrive to have lunch with Adrian. But her forced smile tells me I have nothing to worry about. That is definitely not the face of someone who's about to take back her ex-boyfriend. Adrian's greeting for her is just as awkward. He wraps an arm around her shoulder and they engage in a stiff hug. I'm willing to bet that text message he read beside me wasn't from Isabelle at all. It wouldn't surprise me if there was never *any* text message and he made the whole thing up to get a rise out of me.

I'm even more confident in my theory of Adrian's game when he sits down to dine with Isabelle. He's made sure I have a perfect view of them from my position at the pool. They're dining at an intimate setting for two, sitting face to face, and engaged in deep conversation. Yet there's no laughing or smiling taking place. The interaction looks strained. He probably thinks I'm raging over them sharing a romantic lunch, but it's really quite entertaining to watch. I just hope Isabelle is smart enough to not get hurt at the end of all of this.

After everyone at my table has finished eating, I follow Tory and the bridesmaids to the beach for the wedding ceremony rehearsal. I also help Darius check into his own bungalow. When it's time to attend Phoebe's dress fitting in her parents' bungalow, I'm on autopilot the entire time, silently laughing to myself that I'm one step ahead of Adrian. But I'm not far enough in the lead. I need something beautiful to take the winning prize—that moment where Adrian is so overcome with jealousy at the sight of me and Darius together that he caves in and confesses his feelings.

"All right. You ready for this board game rematch?" Phoebe says once I've finished the alterations on her dress.

"What are you talking about?"

"No one told you?" she asks, smiling at her wedding dress on its coat hanger. "Our families are meeting again for another board game. Everyone says the other night was unfair because you and Adrian got all the easy words to guess."

"Our words weren't easy. We're just in tune with each other."

"That's what I said, but you know how competitive everyone is. So, are you ready to go to your parents' bungalow for the game?"

"We're having a rematch right now?" I ask.

"Yeah, that's the plan."

"Uh... Sure. I guess I can make now work—"

"Actually," Darius interrupts, stepping up behind me, "Verena has to help me check into my new bungalow. She might be a bit late."

"What are you talking about? We already—"

Darius squeezes my shoulder and whispers, "Play along."

"No problem." Phoebe grabs her phone. "I'll let everyone know where you are. We won't start the game without you."

Once we're out of the bungalow, Darius and I head to his new accommodation. His bungalow is small and not anywhere near as fancy as all the other ones I've been in, but it's still beautiful.

"Now are you going to fill me in on what you're up to?" I ask, following him into the bedroom.

Darius stretches out on his bed. "We're waiting."

"For what?"

"You heard Phoebe. Your family is expecting you. She said she'll tell them where you are. Adrian will come looking for you when you don't show up for the board game."

"I'm still not following."

He grins. "You'll understand soon enough."

Chapter Twenty-Two

Five missed calls and three texts from Adrian later.

"Can I call him back already?" I ask, sitting beside Darius on his bed.

"No." Darius takes my phone away from me. "Phoebe told him you're with me. Make him sweat. He'll hate the thought of us together. I can guarantee that any moment now he'll come knocking on my door. We need to commence part two of the plan."

"Which is?"

"I'm taking a shower."

"Right. Because that makes so much sense."

"Trust me." He heads to the bathroom.

As soon as I'm alone, a knock rattles the front door. I jolt upright on the bed, freezing with panic.

The knocking continues, followed by a male voice. "Darius, it's Zac."

I let out a sigh of relief and pull Zac inside with me. He looks terrible. "How did things go with Penny?"

Zac sinks into the couch and covers his face with a

pillow, speaking in muffled tones. "I searched everywhere and couldn't find her. Where's Darius?"

I sit on the couch with him. "In the shower."

"Why aren't you with Adrian?"

"As it turns out, Darius is even more invested in this jealousy thing than I am. He has this plan. I don't fully understand it. Adrian is meant to come find me here."

Zac lowers the pillow from his face. "Now *I'm* jealous. Your life is so... fun."

"I'm actually kind of stressed."

"*You're* stressed? Try being me."

"Sorry." I take Zac's hand in mine, attempting to be comforting. "I know you don't want to hear this, but I care about you, and I hate seeing you so miserable all the time. You're such a good guy and deserve so much more than what Penny gives you. Please, help me understand why you're fighting so hard for her when she doesn't show you the slightest bit of respect."

Zac rubs the heels of his palms into his forehead. "I've been with Penny since high school. She's my closest friend and has seen me through all my ups and downs. I love her. And... she does respect me."

"You're in love with the memory of what you two used to share. Penny is not that person anymore."

"I made a commitment to her when I said *I do*, and I don't back out of things just because times are tough. I need to find her and tell her how much I love her."

My lips press together with concern. I pull Zac into my arms and hug him tight. I wish Adrian would be as open about his feelings as Zac is. In high school, Adrian's way of handling his dislike for me was to distance himself with no explanation. Even the last time we saw each other after graduation, right before our seven years of no contact, he couldn't be honest with me.

I remember that day clearly, fresh out of school and about to embark on my life-changing journey of attending fashion school in Milan. It was nine in the morning, the day of my flight. Mom and Dad had left me home alone to finish packing while they went grocery shopping with Tory. Though the day was filled with excitement, that I'd finally be escaping my hideous roots and creating a new start for myself, I was rushing around the house in a mad panic, scatter-brained as I tried to account for all my belongings. It was as I jogged down the staircase that I noticed something out of place—the shadow of two feet beneath the front door. Yet no one was knocking to announce themselves.

I waited for the visitor to do something, and even started to become creeped out by their presence, until curiosity got the best of me, and I opened the door myself, losing all color when I stood face-to-face with Adrian. He seemed just as shocked to see me, which was strange since he was the one visiting my house. Neither of us said a word. All I could do was glare at the guy who was once my safe place, but as a member of the high school yearbook committee, had the nerve to print *Verena the Vagina* beneath my photo. That was his last hurrah. His way of declaring victory in the war between us.

"Verena... I didn't realize you'd be home. Mom said you were out shopping."

"My family is. What do you want?"

"I was going to leave this on your doorstep but... ah... this is for you."

Adrian held out a plush toy. It took me a moment to recognize the toy as the teddy bear I used to carry everywhere as a child. It was so loved that the stitching in one of its arms was coming undone and patches had been sewn where its fur ran thin. The bear had been a gift from Adrian for my seventh birthday. He'd given it to me because I suffered from nightmares and told me if I hug the bear while I sleep, it will keep all the bad dreams away.

The sight of Adrian holding my favorite childhood toy tore at my heart. Let's be honest, it was my favorite toy *because* Adrian gave it to me. I hadn't thought about the bear in years. Hadn't even realized I'd left it at Adrian's house.

I took the bear from Adrian's hands, wondering if this was some kind of parting truce between us. An ode to the friendship we once shared. Maybe even a *Farewell, some part of me will miss you*. Because, seriously, it wouldn't have been beneath the guy to throw the bear in the trash.

"Thanks," I said, unsure whether the smile I felt pulling at my lips was appropriate. "That was nice of you to think of me."

Adrian cleared his throat, digging his hands into his pockets as his eyes looked everywhere except at me. "I didn't... think of you. It was Mom's idea. She sent me here to give you the bear. She knew how much you loved that thing."

"Oh..." A lump formed in my throat and my gaze dropped to the ground. Now *I* was the one who couldn't stomach looking at him. I'd been mistaken to think the yearbook was Adrian's last strike. This was it right here—him, giving me hope that some small part of him still cared about me.

"Well... good luck in Milan."

He didn't get far down the driveway before I closed the door between us. Tears of frustration trickled down my cheeks. I vowed to myself that was the last time I would let

Adrian hurt me, but I'd been wrong. There was still another punch to the heart waiting for me when I called Cece to thank her for the bear.

"I really appreciate that you gave the bear back to me," I said over the phone to Cece later that morning.

"Bear? Sweetie, I'm not sure what you're talking about."

"The bear Adrian gave me for my seventh birthday. He was here this morning and said you sent him to give me the bear."

"Oh, that bear. Honey, I didn't send Adrian over. He must have found the bear himself. You know, Verena, it's such a shame what happened between you and Adrian. Is there no way the two of you can reconcile your differences?"

My eyes squeezed shut at the revelation of her words, brimming with tears again. "Thanks, Cece. I need to pack. Bye," I blurted, blunt and rude but desperate to end the call before my voice broke.

After all the pain Adrian had put me through, he did something nice for once but without the strength to be honest about his intentions. What made everything all the more painful was that he'd been hoping no one was home. He didn't want to say goodbye to me. Nothing about his behavior made sense. Adrian had mastered the art of being sweet and a jerk at the same time.

And now, seven years later, nothing has changed.

A knock on the front door of Darius' bungalow pulls me from the memory and I spring up to my feet at the sound of Adrian's voice. "Verena? I need to speak with you. Are you in there?"

"Ahh, it's him." I pull Zac into the bathroom with me and flutter my hands in panic.

Darius jumps back with a fright, slipping to the ground

of the shower with a loud *thud*. "What the fuck, guys? I'm naked."

I grab a towel and throw it at him. "Like I care. Adrian is here. Should I answer the door? What do I say to him?"

Zac covers his eyes and faces the wall. "I am officially blind. Verena, is it really necessary for me to be in this bathroom too?"

Darius steps out of the shower with the towel wrapped low around his hips. So low that the heavily defined V shape of his lower abs is on display. "Stay here. I'm answering the door."

"Like that?" I nod at him in his towel. "I can basically see your junk."

"That's the point."

"My eyes are burning," Zac adds.

"Let me fix your hair first." I reach for a brush, but Darius shakes his head.

"No styling." Darius tells me. "I need to look disheveled, like we just had shower sex."

Oh...

OOOHHH...

Now I understand his plan.

Genius.

I said I needed something that would push Adrian to confess his feelings for me, and this might just be it.

As soon as Darius struts out of the bathroom, I huddle up on the bathtub ledge, biting my nails as I listen for Adrian's voice.

The front door opens, but no words are spoken. Not a *Hello* from Darius, nor even a *Can I do something for you?* I'm imagining a stare-off between the two men, and it's beautiful in my mind.

"Can I open my eyes yet?" Zac asks me.

"Shush. I'm trying to listen."

Finally, Adrian speaks with a tight voice, "Is Verena here?"

Darius winks. "She's taking a shower."

Okay, I totally imagined that wink, but I know the guy and I'm ninety-five percent sure the wink happened.

There's another long stretch of silence. I can visualize Adrian's face perfectly as he puts two and two together—strained and bitter, much like when he would have seen the messed-up bed sheets in our bungalow. Oh, I would pay good money to see his reaction firsthand.

"Can you tell Verena that our families are waiting for her."

"Look, man..." There's a patting sound. I will give Darius a pay raise if he's patting Adrian's shoulder. "I don't think she'll make it to your family board game thing. She's kind of busy, if you know what I mean."

The front door closes, and Darius returns to the bathroom. He folds his arms and leans against the door frame, giving me no information other than a devilish grin.

Zac dares to open his eyes. "Well, what happened?"

"Verena, I wish you could have seen the look on Adrian's face. That guy is pissed off. I'm pretty sure he wants to smash my face in."

Chapter Twenty-Three

Darius and I spend the next several hours locked in his bungalow. We don't leave for dinner, and instead order room service like any normal sexed-up couple who can't get enough of each other would do. I'm not going to lie, I was expecting Adrian to admit his feelings for me by now. But so be it. I can keep playing his game. I send the concierge to retrieve my makeup and an outfit for the evening, then spend another hour turning myself into a bronzed goddess.

It's nine o'clock when Darius and I decide to leave our love nest and make an appearance at the cocktail lounge. I'm in a white bandeau top that wraps around my chest and ties behind my neck, accompanied by a sarong skirt with a deep split up my thigh. Along with that, my hair is messy, like I've been thrown around in bed all day. My eyeshadow is smoky and my lips bright red.

When we enter the cocktail lounge, I don't dare search for Adrian. I'm confident he's already here and will be alerted to my arrival when everyone starts whispering and pointing at Darius and me. Spotting Zac alone at the bar, the two of us join him for a round of drinks. As expected, we have a herd of eyes following us.

The young bartender from the first night I was here is serving drinks. She turns around, finding Darius and me waiting to order, and her mouth opens in a perfect circle. "Verena, you're killing me. I love this guy!"

"Everyone does," I say. "Darius, meet Samaya." The two empty glasses in front of Zac tell me Samaya is already well acquainted with him.

"I'll take another whiskey," Zac tells her.

"Still no luck finding Penny?" I ask.

"Obviously not."

"Adrian alert," Darius whispers. "Three o'clock. He's with Isabelle."

"Is he looking at us?" I ask.

"No."

"That bastard."

"What can I get you two to drink?" Samaya asks us. "More shots with dirty names?"

"No," I laugh. "Definitely not."

"We'll take two fishbowls," Darius orders. Samaya pulls out two round glasses the size of my head.

"Those better be for you," I tell Darius. "I can't be getting drunk tonight. I turned into a safety hazard the last time it happened. Besides, you heard Stacy. She's been put on Verena-alcohol-patrol."

Darius lets out a bellowing laugh, the sound so loud and startling that I know I must be missing something. "Verena, you're hilarious."

"What, the Stacy thing?"

Zac looks at him like he's lost his mind. I might have to agree with him on this one.

Darius places a hand on my thigh, so high up that it's

almost touching my ass, and whispers in my ear, "No, you idiot. Not Stacy. I was trying to get Adrian's attention. Pretend we're laughing over some sexy joke."

Zac sips his whiskey. "Verena is terrible at laughing on command."

"He's right," I agree.

Darius leans back from me, allowing Adrian full visibility of my face. "Do it or I'm stealing the hairspray."

Desperate times call for desperate measures. I laugh and pull Darius close, making it look like I'm whispering something dirty into his ear, when all I say is, "The hairspray is sacred in this climate. Please don't steal it."

"Good. Everyone is looking this way. Can't tell if it's because they're starstruck by us, or because Verena Valentine is acting flirty with someone who isn't her boyfriend."

"Drinks are ready." Samaya places two massive bowls of pink alcohol on the bar.

"Seriously," I tell Darius, "I shouldn't be drinking again this week."

Zac gulps down the rest of his whiskey. "I'll drink it if you're not going to. Maybe I'll feel something other than imminent doom for once."

"Drink the cocktail slowly," Darius tells me, which will be close to impossible since I just took a sip and the drink tastes like candy. "We need to come up with tomorrow's plan."

"Tomorrow?" I ask. "I'm too busy thinking about tonight."

Zac steals the fishbowl from my hands and, after a long sip, leans back and starts singing in slurred sentences. *"Tomorrow is dead. Shoot me in the head."*

"You better confiscate that drink from him," Darius tells me.

"Why? I like drunk Zac."

Darius pushes the fishbowl back to me and passes Zac a jug of water instead. "Tomorrow is the men-only golf excursion. We need to prepare for it since I'll be the one doing all the work to make Adrian jealous."

"Oh, right. I read about that in the schedule. Men at golf, ladies at the day spa. Um, okay, how about you make sure Adrian overhears you talking about me?"

"Shit!" Darius smacks a hand to his mouth, staring wide-eyed at something behind me.

"What?"

I spin around to find out what has Darius so shocked. Pain clenches my stomach at the thought of seeing Adrian kiss Isabelle. Instead, Darius points to a waiter talking to a group of people by the entrance of the cocktail lounge. Every other guest seems to notice too and goes quiet. It's the police force. They're here, having a serious discussion with the waiter and my two bodyguards.

"Oh, hey. Coppers." Zac stands on two wobbly feet. "You think they'll want to hear my song too?"

I push him back down on his bar stool, then hide my face behind my hands. "This better not have anything to do with me."

"How could it not?" Darius says. "The cops are heading this way."

I peek through my fingers, realizing he's right. There's a total of five police—men and women—with stern looks upon their faces.

"Verena Valentine?" the tall one in the middle asks as he arrives at the bar. Is it wrong of me to take notice of how good he looks? How good all of them look? Like, wow, cops in Australia are gorgeous.

"That's me. Is everything all right?" I ask.

"Unfortunately not. Knowledge of your presence in Australia has broken out and some of your fans are circling the island. We had word from the resort's security staff that fans have even attempted to trespass tonight."

"Are you serious?" Tory marches up to join the conversation with Phoebe right on her tail. She's about to enter a full-on bridezilla meltdown. "Verena, I thought you told me this wouldn't happen!"

"I took so many precautions to hide my location. I *don't* know how this happened."

I look at my friends, about to ask whether the public noticed their arrival, but Darius gets a word in before me. "No one on the mainland saw us."

The cop nods at Tory and Phoebe. "Who are you two?"

"We're the brides of this goddamn wedding that has now been ruined," Tory answers.

"Honey, calm down," Phoebe reasons, taking hold of Tory's hand.

"How can I when—"

All the lights in the cocktail lounge black out, leaving us in darkness.

"Oh shit!" Tory screams. She's all I can hear over the panic of every guest. "What's going on? It's the rabid fans. They're crashing the wedding."

"Stay calm everyone," the head cop commands over the top of everyone's chaos. "Nobody move. You all have the right to remain sexy!"

Strobe lights switch on as he says that last word. A spotlight shines on the group of police officers, all of them ripping their uniforms off to reveal banging hot bodies in underwear. I knew there was something too good to be true about their appearances. How did I forget about Stacy's strippers tonight?

"Oh shit!" Tory screams again, but this time through laughter.

The waitstaff rush around the lounge, removing all furniture and turning the venue into one massive dance floor. Two female strippers run forward and grab the brides, bringing them to the center of the lounge and placing them on chairs.

"Looks like you're up next," Darius says. I turn just in time to see a male stripper lift me into his arms and whisk me away to be with the rest of the bridal party.

"Darius, no!" I howl, reaching for him and failing. "Zac, don't let them take me!"

They both laugh, enjoying the spectacle of me being the victim of a bunch of strippers. At least Zac is smiling for once. I suppose my humiliation is worth it for that.

The strippers pass a round of shots to each member of the bridal party. Everyone shoots the liquor except Stacy, who I remember is trying to get pregnant. Tory even does two.

I shake my head when a stripper offers me a shot, but Tory pushes the shot glass to my lips. "There are strippers, Verena! You're getting wasted with me tonight! I want to have fun and create sister memories."

"I'm staying clear of alcohol," I yell into her ear so she can hear me over the music. "I don't want to embarrass myself like earlier in the week. And look, I know this isn't the best time, but I've been meaning to tell you something. I'm sorry I didn't come to your engagement party."

"What? I can't hear you," she shouts.

"I said I'm sorry I didn't come to your engagement party."

"Don't worry about it. It's fine."

"It's not fine. I should have put more effort in."

She opens my palm and places the shot glass in it. "You can make it up to me by loosening up tonight."

"Tory..."

"At least do this one shot."

"Ugh, fine. *One.*" I shoot back what I've just realized is pure vodka. It goes straight to my head, and I bend over, coughing and spluttering at the unexpected sharp taste.

"That's it. Woo!" Tory cheers. "Keep drinking."

Through the strobe lights, I catch a collage of images of my sister throwing her head back to swallow another shot. She jumps onto her chair and starts dancing, then bends down and gives Phoebe a sloppy kiss. I can't help but laugh, never having seen Tory like this.

Before I can cheer her on, a male and female stripper start giving me a lap dance. I've got so many boobs and dicks rubbing up against my face that I can't tell which way is up or down. It's between the male stripper's legs that I get a glimpse of Darius and Zac at the bar, the two of them laughing their asses off as they watch me. My eyes search for Adrian, but cock and balls fall back in front of my face, blocking my view. The only thing that would make this situation funnier is if Darius and Zac were right here beside me and we were experiencing this moment together.

I give into Tory's orders, grab another two shots off the passing waiter's tray and shoot them back, then run over to the bar and grab Darius and Zac, tugging them toward the dance floor.

"I'm pretty sure we'll get chlamydia if we get too close to the strippers," Darius objects. "There's a strong chance you already have it."

"I'm married," Zac adds. "I can't dance with strippers."

I pull out my only bargaining chip. "We'll stay away from the strippers. Let's dance and have fun. You need some fun, Zac. And, Darius, you better say *yes* or else I'm firing you."

They both grin, giving in to me. Darius grabs the two fishbowls. "All right, but we're taking these beauties onto the dance floor for the three of us to finish."

I sip on one of the fishbowls as my friends follow me onto the dance floor. We keep clear of the bridal party and strippers and join in with the rest of the crowd, dancing like we're kids again without a care of how ridiculous our moves are. And my God, it's so good to see Zac be carefree for once. Wherever Adrian is, I hope he's watching me have fun without him. I can't wipe the smile off my face, knowing that I am one hundred percent winning at this jealousy game.

It's not long before we finish the fishbowls, then do shot after shot until the term *sloshed* accurately describes us and everyone else in the venue. I stick to my word—getting drunk is a bad idea—but I'm on bride's orders, so this is on Tory if everything ends terribly.

At some point among all the dancing, the music gets drowned out by Nia shouting, "Do it! Do it! Do it!" until her words turn into a chant that everyone cheers. Everyone except me and Darius. Zac is the loudest.

I've been too swept up in my own dancing to take notice of anything else, and it only dawns on me now where I am—in the middle of a circle with Darius, surrounded by people as if we're about to enter a dance-off.

"What's going on?" I ask him.

All of a sudden, Latin music starts playing and people are cheering even louder. "Do it! Do it!"

"Darius, I love you!" Nia's voice is audible over everyone else's. "Do your dance with Verena!"

It takes us a moment, but we catch onto what's happening here and both break out in laughter.

Darius holds his hand out to me. "You wanna dance? He's watching."

My eyes perk up at that proposition, to think that Adrian is out there somewhere in the crowd with that same bitter expression he had when Darius answered the door in his towel. Regardless of that thought, Darius knows I won't turn him down. Any chance I get to dance with him, I take, even if our technique will be messy with all the alcohol in our systems. Latin dancing with each other is our happy place. He introduced it to me years ago when we first met. It's a full artistic expression of sex and passion, yet without any pressure for us to hook up afterward since there's no physical attraction.

I place my hand in Darius'. He pulls me to him so that our bodies are flush with each other, sending the circle around us wild. His forehead rests on mine as his hands slide down the curves of my breasts and hips. Darius slowly sinks down, until he's crouching in front of me and running fingers up my thighs, gazing into my eyes like a man infatuated by his woman. I pull him up by the collar as if I'm about to kiss him, our lips lingering in front of each other, then the beat takes off and the two of us are swaying our hips against each other, our bodies singing the dance of love and sensuality.

It's a surprise that we're able to pull off the routine so well, being this drunk, and that we get cheers every time Darius twirls me around, when he dips me backward, and when he lifts me off the ground.

"So," I say to him during a part of the dance where we're face to face, "you're the secret to all of my success. I'm a social pariah among these people for days, then the moment you turn up, they all start cheering for us to dance."

"Which means you better not fire me." He twirls me out wide again.

I come back into him, laughing, enjoying myself in this blissful daze of intoxication, until my eyes land on Adrian in the distance. My body stops moving at what I see. There's no rhythm left in my soul and certainly no more giggly drunk girl. All I am is a cold and bitter entity with a storm cloud of jealousy hanging over my head. This feeling is worse than anything I've ever felt when catching Adrian and Isabelle together, or whenever he mentions her name in front of me. It's worse than the betrayal when I discovered Jake was cheating on me, or that Adrian had asked me to the school dance as a joke and laughed with all of his friends about it.

There's no sense of tears threatening to appear. It's violence that I feel as I watch Adrian and Jannah standing together on the outskirts of the cocktail lounge, laughing over a drink together.

She's in her bikini again, at this hour of the night, and I have to wonder if the girl even owns a set of proper clothes.

She's laughing, batting her lashes at Adrian, and—

My chest burns with hate when Jannah reaches out to touch Adrian's arm.

What the hell does she think she's doing? What the hell does Adrian think *he's* doing with *her*? These are probably all the same techniques she used on Jake when he was with me.

"Verena, are you all right?" Darius asks.

I'm too angry to answer him. Too pissed off at Adrian for talking to Jannah when he knows how much she hurt me.

"Maybe you've had too much to drink?" Darius says. "Let's sit down for a bit."

He takes my hand, but I pull free of him and push through the circle of guests. As soon as I'm out of the crowd, I march right up to Jannah and rip her filthy hand off Adrian.

Chapter Twenty-Four

"What is *with* you?" I shout at Jannah.

Dozens of eyes in the cocktail lounge snap to the sound of me roaring over the stripper music. In the back of my drunk mind, there's a tiny voice that warns me not to make another scene at Tory's wedding, but anger is writhing in my veins, and I can't stop myself.

"Is it not enough that you already stole one of my boyfriends?" I continue. "Now you have to steal a second? I'll say this only once, Adrian is *mine*! If I see you talking to him one more time, I swear there will be hell to pay. Go back to your own trash and sleep in the mess you made."

I grab Adrian's hand and tug him along with me. I don't know where we're going. Out of the lounge somewhere. Down to the beach, which seems to be my go-to place when I'm drunk and making a fool of myself. My heartbeat pounds in my ears and I'm on the edge of a panic attack because I'm only now realizing how crazy I just acted.

"Verena, calm down," Adrian says.

Fuck! Why am I still holding his hand? I should run away and hide in the ocean.

"Not the ocean again," Adrian says, seeing where we're heading. "I've had too much to drink. I won't be able to pull you out of the water this time."

I come to a stop when we're at the shoreline, clawing my hands through my hair. "I can't believe the nerve of that little homewrecker. She had her hands all over you."

"She did not. We were only talking."

"I saw the way she was looking at you. Why does she have to talk to *you*, of all people? Go and find some other guy. I won't have her do this to me again. I hate her! I hate *you* for talking to her!" I shove Adrian in the chest, but he's so strong that he doesn't even step back.

"I hate *you* for sleeping with me last night!" Adrian raises his voice, and suddenly, we're in a full-on yelling match. "How could you be with me in such an intimate way, then end up spending the night with Darius? Don't even get me started on this afternoon when I came searching for you at his bungalow. Did you have sex with him?"

"You have no right to ask me that question!"

"I have every right after *we* had sex. You know what, I hate *him*. I hate that he showed up last night and how you slept in the same bed as him. I hate how he answered the door in his towel, and that I had to watch everyone cheer you two on while you performed the most intimate dance I've ever seen. Last of all, I hate that I had to resort to flirting with Jannah for you to take any fucking notice of me!"

I'm about to shout back something in my defense but stop short when the last part of his speech registers with my drunken mind. "You were flirting with her on purpose?"

"You seem to have no care factor for when I'm around Isabelle, so I had to play dirty."

I catch onto his meaning quickly.

Adrian played me.

Here I was, thinking I was smarter than him. Thinking that I was winning. Then he pulls the dirtiest trick out of the book and gets *me* to be the one who snaps under the pressure. His tactics are cruel, playing on my Jake insecurities, but I'm more furious at myself for falling for Adrian's game.

"What is *wrong* with you, Adrian? No, you know what?" I start marching through the sand, back to the resort. "I don't have time to listen to some psychoanalysis of what messed up shit goes through your mind. It will take a million years to understand how sick you are in the head. You need help."

Adrian runs after me. Before I have a chance to ward him off, he grabs my waist and spins me around, pulling my body tight to his. In the shadows of the night, I can't distinguish much, but one thing is clear from the intensity in Adrian's eyes. He's livid, yet overcome by desire.

"Did you mean it before, when you said I'm yours?" he asks. "Or was that just in the heat of the moment?"

I glare at him, my chest rising with jagged breaths. "I meant it."

Without wasting another second, Adrian's lips crush down on mine, hot and desperate. I contemplate kicking him in the crotch because I'm so pissed off about Jannah, but the drunken side of me finds this moment too raw and sexy to cause damage to such a valuable appendage.

"Say it again." His voice is husky. "I think it might be the hottest thing to have ever left your mouth."

"You're mine." I kiss him harder, *angrier* this time. I pull him closer to me, so close that my lips probably bruise, but I can't get him close enough. "I hate you so much. You're mine and I'm never letting go."

Adrian growls and picks me up, lowering my back to the sand. "I don't want Isabelle. I don't want anyone except you. I need you."

"Why couldn't you tell me that this morning?"

He kneels above me. "I wanted to, but I didn't know what was happening between you and Darius. Our relationship is so fragile that I was afraid of scaring you off if I said anything about my feelings for you. I needed you to want me."

"I want you so badly."

I anticipate Adrian's weight on top of me, but he pauses, hovering above me on his forearms. "I have to know about Darius. How many times have you slept with him since he arrived last night?"

"Not once." I reach up to kiss him, desperate for us to be touching again, but he pulls back.

"You can be honest with me. I saw the bed. I know you slept in it last night with him. Then there was this afternoon in his bungalow."

"Adrian, Darius is gay."

"*What?*"

"We fell asleep on the floor after he painted my nails last night. I figured out this morning that you were trying to make me jealous with Isabelle, so I thought I'd get even and make the bed look like sex sheets."

Adrian's eyes grow wide as he comprehends everything I said. "Fuck, Verena! I've been out of my mind thinking about his hands on you. Do you have any idea how shit I felt when I saw that bed?"

I shrug, making no big deal of it so we can get back to kissing. "Probably the same way I felt when I saw you on the beach last night with Isabelle."

"I went to Isabelle because I'd just had the most incredible sex with the most incredible girl, and I wanted to sever all ties with my ex."

Yeah, I probably should have trusted that theory when it entered my mind this morning.

"What about today with Darius and you in the shower?" Adrian asks.

"It was all staged. I guess I've been playing dirty too."

He growls and punches the sand. "And you had the nerve to call *me* fucked up and in need of help?"

"Can we just agree that we both need to be medically examined? We're as bad as each other."

"Were you going to tell me any of this if I didn't ask?"

"I don't know."

From the anger on his face, I'm certain Adrian is about to leave me alone on the beach, but he does a complete one-eighty and laughs.

"What's so funny?"

He leans down and kisses me, his mouth pressing me hard into the sand. "You're cruel, you know that?"

My legs wrap around him, and I pull him close. "Am I finally going to get that hate sex?"

"I don't hate you, Verena. Far from it," he whispers against my lips, rocking his hips against mine. I let out an involuntary whimper at the heat that bursts through my groin, which only makes him grind harder. "You sound amazing."

With drunk hands, he fumbles to hoist my sarong up around my hips, then unzips his jeans so we're both rubbing up against each other in our underwear. Without the barrier of his thick jeans, I can feel every bit of his hard cock between my legs. I cling to him as he thrusts over me, the movements teasing my clit and sending ripples of pleasure all the way down to my toes. His breath grows fast as his rhythm accelerates, and I swear he's right there with me, on the verge of exploding if we keep going. But I don't want to come like this.

"Stop. I want to feel you inside me," I murmur against his lips. "Take me back to our bungalow."

"When you talk like that... You make it close to impossible for me to stop." Adrian groans with another thrust, his movements too much for me to take.

My head tilts back. "I'm about to come."

He does the cruelest thing of all and holds still. My hips lift off the ground, attempting to gain friction between my legs, but Adrian pins me to the ground.

"Please," I beg.

There's pain in his eyes as he gazes down at me. "You said I'm yours. Now tell me you're mine, Verena. I need to hear it."

I tug on his collar, bringing his lips to mine. "I'm yours, Adrian. Completely yours. Please, can we go back to our bungalow."

He pulls a condom out of his pocket. "I need you now."

"In public?" Yes, I was begging him to make me come a moment ago, but there was something innocent about it with my clothes still on. If anyone caught us, we could pretend we were only making out. But sex on the beach? This is different. It's so risky, given my status in the public eye. Photos could get leaked.

Adrian tears the condom packet open. "The beach is dark and we're the only ones here. I can't wait."

The moment his dick springs free of his boxer shorts, long and hard, I realize I can't wait either. My groin pulses, aching with the need to have him inside me. Logic tells me to be sensible and wait, but the alcohol says give in to my deepest desires.

I press up onto my knees and kiss Adrian, laughing. "What about the sand? It will get everywhere."

He rolls the condom on then unbuttons his shirt and lays it over the ground, guiding my ass onto it. "Problem solved."

He's rough with me, pulling my sarong up over my hips and ripping my panties from my body. The second I'm naked from the hips down, his dick thrusts hard inside me. A combined moan vibrates through our bodies the moment we're one. Adrian holds still, deep within me as the initial burst of pleasure consumes us, then our pace picks up in speed.

He grits out my name, working hard above me. "Fuck, you make it feel so good."

When Adrian pushes my top up and brings my nipple into his mouth, I can no longer think. I close my eyes and get lost in this moment, my mind swirling with a mixture of euphoria and alcohol.

"Don't you dare close your eyes," Adrian says in that deep bedroom tone that drives me wild. "Watch me while I'm fucking you."

Even though the night is dark, when I gaze down at Adrian's hips, my body shakes with the build of an orgasm as I see his dick disappear into me. In and out. In and out. My fingers run along the grooves of his abs, tingling at the beginning traces of sweat.

Panic takes over and I'm instantly rigid when someone speaks nearby. "The boat leaves early tomorrow for golf."

Adrian pauses, stealing his eyes away from me to examine our company. In the dull moonlight, I catch a vague glance of two men strolling along the beach, thirty feet away from us. They're walking parallel to where we lie near the water, but that doesn't mean we're safe. They could change course any moment and stumble across Adrian and me having sex. The ocean is tranquil; without the crashing of waves, they'll hear us if we're too loud.

"We should stop," Adrian whispers, though his actions speak differently. His cock teases me with another thrust.

My moan is louder than intended, my spine arching at his deepness.

Adrian cups a hand over my mouth and a chuckle leaves his throat. "Do you want them to find us?"

Of course I don't. I also have no control over the sounds Adrian evokes from within me. He's right, we should stop. But I can't bring myself to make that decision, not when he pushes into me again and sends my toes curling. I don't know if it's because I'm drunk, but the thrill of someone catching us suddenly heightens every nerve ending in my body, making me more desperate for Adrian's touch. I rock my hips, encouraging him to continue.

Adrian growls, pumping his dick into me in long, slow strokes. "You like this. Being fucked in public turns you on, doesn't it?"

"I like being fucked in public by *you*. No one else."

"Hey, did you hear that?" one of the men says to the other.

Adrian reaches down to my clit. I clap a hand over my mouth in response, preventing the men from hearing how wild Adrian drives me. He grins with a wicked spark in his eyes, like he knows what he's doing to me. How much he's pushing me. What we're doing is ridiculous and something I'd never allow with a sober mind, but I'm too wrapped up in the moment to care.

"You see anyone else out here?" the other guy asks.

Without warning, Adrian rolls onto his back, bringing

me on top of him. I cry out at the surprise of how deep this new position pushes his dick into me.

"Seriously, is someone out here with us?" the voice calls.

The muscles between my legs throb with need, begging for release. I move up and down, panting as I ride Adrian's dick. Footsteps grow closer. I'm burning up with fear that we're about to get caught, yet at the same time, it's that risk that makes my groin pulse harder. It turns me on that people can hear me fucking Adrian. My clit grows even more sensitive at the thought of them *seeing* me fuck Adrian. I can't stop chasing my orgasm.

Adrian sits up to whisper in my ear. "That's it, Verena. Good girl. Come on my cock."

The sound of him speaking my name in that gravelly tone is my complete undoing. My head tilts back and I'm shaking. The intimate muscles in my core contract around Adrian's erection, and I'm using all my willpower to remain quiet. All I can hear are my heavy breaths as I climax, until Adrian's groans take over.

His dick jerks into me fast and he clenches his teeth, coming inside me with no regard to being quiet. "Yes. Fuck. You're so tight. So... fucking... good."

"What the...?" one of the men says, the sound of his voice closer. "I told you someone is out here. Are they...?" His words trail off in laughter. The silhouette of him and his friend grows more visible.

"Shit," Adrian whispers, pulling out of me and helping me to my feet.

"You couldn't be quiet?" I laugh.

"Impossible." He zips up his fly, grabs our discarded clothes in one hand, and takes my hand in the other. "Run."

Chapter Twenty-Five

Adrian and I stumble into our bungalow well past midnight, covered in sand and laughing from our near miss on the beach. He takes one look at the bedroom, as if contemplating whether to take me to bed for another round, but sees the messy sheets and is no doubt reminded of Darius.

"I still can't believe you did that to the bed," Adrian says through drunken kisses, guiding me backward to the pool area.

"I get it, that bed is a tainted zone. What are you thinking of instead, pool sex?" My fingers unfasten my sarong, but before I get far, Adrian picks me up and carries me to the daybed.

"Water sex only works in the movies."

"Isn't that what they say about beach sex as well? I think we proved them wrong."

He smirks. "Is that a challenge?"

I strip out of my clothes and dive into the water, smoothing my hair back upon resurfacing. "Oh, it's definitely a challenge. And besides, I need to stock up on you tonight since we'll barely see each other tomorrow. You're leaving before sunrise to go on some males-only golf excursion that takes place on a whole other island of the Whitsundays, all while I'll be stuck here with the girls at the day spa. The whole theme of men and women separating tomorrow doesn't even make sense. That's what straight couples do so the bride and groom have time apart. Tory and Phoebe will still be together. And can we talk about how sexist this plan is? Why does everyone assume I'd prefer a day of pampering instead of hot, sweaty golf that I'll be bad at?"

Adrian raises an eyebrow at my rambling speech that I'm sure I slurred several words of. "You are completely wasted."

"Your point?"

He laughs and dives into the water, and I have my world blown again as Adrian fucks me into oblivion.

A text message alert wakes me mid-morning. I don't remember falling asleep, but here I am on the daybed by our pool, naked beneath a beach towel. My head pounds with a hangover and I lose the high from last night when I realize I'm alone, Adrian having already left for the golf trip. I squint at the phone screen, shielding my eyes from blinding sunlight. The message is from Adrian, and I can't bring myself to read it, knowing how honest—not to mention, embarrassingly wild and aggressive—I was with him last night while drunk. But all the possible replies that I'm creating in my head are so much worse. What if it's something shocking like *I can't believe you played me like that,* or *I can't remember a thing from last night*?

What if it's something good like *I miss you*?

I love you.

The unknown makes me look.

Adrian: Morning. How's your head?

Well, that was anticlimactic.

Verena: Not good, but I'll survive. And yours? What time did you leave?

Adrian: 5 a.m. I'm a wreck.

Verena: Do you remember last night?

He doesn't reply instantly, and I start to panic. When his message does arrive, it's blunt and sets off my anxiety even more.

Adrian: Yes. We need to talk.

What kind of response is that? No, *It was amazing*, or any emojis to help me decipher his tone. Our banter is off. It's not like him to be so orderly. If this were a face-to-face conversation, he'd have something smart to say.

I try to form a reply, but everything I type either sounds too desperate or like I'm annoyed. So, I leave our conversation as is, not wanting to embarrass myself further. Adrian never texts back, which has me overthinking the situation even more. I distract myself by messaging Darius in our group chat with Zac.

Verena: The situation with Adrian has changed. He knows about everything. I'd recommend staying clear of him at golf today.

Darius: Good. I can focus on Zac. He's here with me.

Zac: Penny showed up last night. I caught her grinding up against a stripper.

Verena: Ouch. Let me guess, she said it was your fault?

After I've finished texting the boys, I dress for the day and call the lobby, requesting that cleaners change our bedsheets and make the bed look all neat and perfect again, with the hopes that Adrian forgets about my cruel trick.

It's almost midday when I arrive at the resort's day spa,

smelling the hypnotic aromas of lavender and jasmine. The roof is thatched, and potted palm trees are scattered around the venue. Unsurprisingly, I'm not the last one to arrive. Everyone is still puffy-eyed and recovering from their night of drinking and strippers. I guess this is why Stacy organized strippers the night before a pampering session.

The spa offers every treatment under the sun, but what's meant to be a relaxing, rejuvenating day turns out to be the complete opposite for me. During every moment that I lie on the massage table—receiving what should be a heavenly massage with the power to send me to sleep—I can't stop panicking over Adrian and what it will be like when I see him again. When the beautician gives me a facial, the cucumbers keep falling off my eyes because I can't stop cringing over Adrian's blunt text messages. What could he want to talk about? Everything ended great between us last night. Better than great.

After my facial, Tory meets me in the plunge pool. "I know I was the one who encouraged you to drink last night, but I'm being serious, don't touch a drop of alcohol at the wedding tomorrow, no matter what I say. You shouting at Hannah was out of control."

"I'm not apologizing for anything. She's trash, and you told me to drink."

"True," she says. "By the way, where did you end up yesterday afternoon during the board game?"

"Oh, sorry about that. Something came up with Darius."

"Eh. I'm kind of glad you didn't show up. Without you and Adrian, Phoebe and I won. Speaking of which, what is going on between you and Adrian?"

I exhale loudly. "Can we not talk about him? This is meant to be a day of relaxation."

She splashes me in the face. "You're tense. I can feel it. You need to vent to someone. Since I'm the only one here who knows the truth about you and Adrian, you may as well vent to me."

"Fine. I *think* we're together."

"Shut up!" Tory's entire face lights up like I've told her she's won a billion dollars. "Tell me everything. Have you slept with him?"

Steamy memories of Adrian and me enter my mind, and a tiny smile slips past my panic. "Three times."

She covers her mouth, muffling an excited scream. "How was it? I bet it was hot. The sexual tension between you two is insane."

"It was hot. *Really* hot. But..." My smile drops. "We were drunk last night and spilled a bunch of our feelings for each other. Today, he seems distant. He left before I woke and texted me saying we need to talk. Those are the four worst words in the English language."

"That's not true. There are way worse four-word sentences than that." She chews on her bottom lip, deep in thought, then starts listing them off on her fingers. "I fucked your mom. Sorry, I have herpes. Do you like anal? I smell your menstruation—"

"Tory, you are *not* helping."

"Okay, *we need to talk* isn't great, but I mean, what if he wants to talk about good stuff? You guys have had a complicated relationship. Maybe he wants to make sure you're on the same page as him."

With a sigh, I rest the back of my head on the pool ledge and let my body float. "Why wouldn't he say that then, or leave a heart emoji?"

"Try not to overthink this. I'm sure everything will be fine."

"It's impossible not to overthink."

When Tory doesn't respond, I glance over at her, finding a knowing look in her eyes. "What?"

"Nothing."

I splash her. "Tell me."

"You're falling in love with Adrian all over again."

I growl and send her the stink eye before sliding my head under water, desperate to escape this conversation. But hanging out below the surface doesn't hide my problems. I want Adrian's and my teasing banter back. I want him flirting with me. I want him to be a stage five clinger and never let me go.

I blow out all the air in my lungs and resurface in defeat. "I'm totally in love with Adrian."

Tory's face shines brighter than the sun. "I *knew* it! This is amazing! Look, this talk he wants to have, whatever it is, will all be fine. He would never hurt you."

I side-eye her with an unimpressed glare. "You didn't seriously say that, did you?"

She laughs. "You know what I mean. Going forward, he wouldn't hurt you, especially not in the way Jake did."

My phone chimes with a text message, and our eyes flash to it lying on the edge of the plunge pool.

"Is that Adrian?" Tory asks. "I bet it is."

I wipe my hands on a towel, resting both elbows on the pool ledge as I reach for my phone.

Adrian: Sorry, I got caught up in a conversation with your dad. How's the day spa? I can't stop thinking about you.

And *I* can't speak. I can't breathe as I reread his last six words over and over again to reassure myself that he actually sent them. Then I spend another lifetime checking for context. Does he mean he can't stop thinking about me in a good way or bad?

"What does it say?" Tory demands. I show her the screen and she responds with a wolf whistle. "Oh, he sent another one!"

Adrian: Did you mean everything you said last night?

"How do I reply?" I ask while Tory reads the message over my shoulder.

"Say yes!"

"But what if *yes* is a bad answer?"

"Verena, you're an idiot."

Adrian: If you're embarrassed, we can pretend it never happened.

I clutch my phone in panic. Pretend *what* never happened? Me yelling at Jannah in front of everyone? The public sex?

"He's being a gentleman," Tory says, attempting to extinguish my unspoken anxieties. "Say you meant every word from last night. You'll regret it if you don't."

I hate that she's right. Without alcohol in my system, it's scary putting my feelings on the line. A lump rises in my throat—the precursor to the wretched tears that arrive every time I let myself be vulnerable. But I can't weasel my way out of this situation, otherwise I'll never forgive myself.

Verena: I meant every word of it.

A nervous squeak escapes my lips when hitting *send*. No turning back now. My heart is on the line and I'm trusting the one person who has hurt me the most to take care of it.

He replies within an instant.

Adrian: Thank God. I wish I could get out of this golf

day to be with you. I tried to wake you this morning before leaving but you were so out of it.

My heart swells in my chest. I can't stop reading those words. I can't stop smiling at my phone.

Adrian: I miss you. I hope we can find some alone time. There are some things we need to talk about.

I exhale a breath of annoyance. "Why does he keep saying we need to talk?"

"It can't be anything bad. Like I said, maybe he wants to know where you two stand."

"I'll let him know right now where we stand," I say, my thumbs hurrying over the keyboard.

Verena: We don't need to talk about anything. Everything is perfect. I like you so much, Adrian. Time can't move fast enough till I'm with you again.

Adrian: Fuck, you drive me insane <3

Even through a text message, Adrian manages to raise my temperature and make me blush. I reread his message, imagining him saying *fuck* in that deep sex voice of his that I love.

And finally, I get my heart emoji.

"Okay, so what do I do when I see him tonight?"

"Tell him you love him," Tory says.

"Isn't that coming on too heavy?"

"Verena, I've seen the way he looks at you. And let me tell you, that is *the* look. I never saw him look at Isabelle like that. I've never seen him laugh or smile as much as he does when he's with you. Tell him you love him. I'm certain he'll say it straight back."

I'm in a cold body of water, sweating over the thought of confessing my love to Adrian. It might be the most terrifying thought to have ever entered my mind. "You really think so?"

"Stop overthinking it. Get out of here." She pushes me out of the plunge pool. "Go and pretty yourself up for him. It's three o'clock and the men are returning in two hours. I know how long you take to get dressed. And remember, no drinking at the rehearsal dinner tonight."

Chapter Twenty-Six

Even though I look fantastic in my blue dress, push-up bra and five-inch heels, I'm a jittery mess at the cocktail lounge when sundown arrives. I've already demolished one mocktail and am well through my second when the boat of men returns from golf. From where I sit at the bar, I have a perfect view of the jetty and the passengers docking, trailing their way back up to the resort. Through the crowd of men, I spot Dad and my uncles, Darius and Zac, but no Adrian.

Someone takes hold of my hand from behind. I spin around with a smile on my face, hoping Adrian snuck past all the men without me realizing and has come to surprise me, but instead I'm met with the gross surprise of Jake.

"Oh, it's you." I steal my hand from his. Why does he think it's acceptable to touch me each time we see one another?

He's wearing a yellow shirt with a tropical print that I want to burn. His khaki shorts are equally unappealing. I feel like telling him to remove those Ray-Ban sunglasses that rest above his dark hair, because I actually like the brand and don't want to associate it with him.

"Verena." He smiles at me with a doting look in his eyes. "You look lovely. How have you been?"

"Can I help you with something?" I check over my shoulder, adamant to find Adrian. My eyes latch onto Darius and Zac as they walk up the jetty, and I send them telepathic signals to *get over here right now and save my ass*.

It seems to work. Their heads turn to me, both giving an upturned lip the moment they recognize Jake.

"We need to finish that chat we started the other night," Jake tells me.

Is he referring to the first night I kissed Adrian, where Jake ambushed me outside the burlesque dance class? "I wasn't aware we started a chat."

"Do you think we could talk in private? My bungalow is empty."

What the actual fuck? Jake can't be serious.

"You can't be serious?" Darius speaks from behind me. Our telepathy grows stronger every day.

Jake's jaw tightens. "Darius. Zac. Hi. How's it going?"

"Great till we saw you," Zac answers.

"Can you excuse me and Verena? We're in the middle of something."

"No, actually, we can't. I'm pretty sure her boyfriend will say the same thing." Darius nods off to the left, where I find Adrian standing by an alternate entrance to the cocktail lounge, his gaze burning into both Jake and Darius.

I elbow Darius in the ribs and mutter, "What did you say to Adrian for him to be glaring at you? I told you to lay low."

"Oh, I didn't say a word. In case you haven't noticed, the guy's been looking at me like that since the moment I arrived at this resort. He wouldn't come near me all day. Guess he's still hung up on the shower incident."

I place my drink down and stand up from the bar stool, ready to leave my friends and Jake behind, but am frozen in place when Adrian's gaze shifts to me and his harsh expression lights up into the most handsome, swoony grin I've ever seen. I'm a blushing mess as I smile back, unable to take my eyes off him. He's never looked at me like this before, even though Tory claims he's spent the past week giving me *the* look. It's like no one else at this cocktail lounge exists except us. He looks amazing with windswept hair from the boat and is dressed in tan trousers and a white button-down rolled to his elbows.

Our gaze remains locked as Adrian walks up to me, then draws me into a hug so intimate it should be illegal in public. "Vee, how was the pampering session? You all beautified?"

I push up on my toes, greeting him with a kiss. "Couldn't stop thinking about you the entire time. Oh, you haven't met my friend Zac yet. He's here with his wife—" I cut myself off, unsure whether mentioning Penny is the best choice right now, considering what went down between her and the strippers. I make a mental note to discuss this situation with Zac at a more appropriate time.

"What is with you being friends with all these attractive guys?" Adrian jokes, then reaches out to shake Zac's hand.

They exchange a few words before Adrian has his arm around me again and kisses my forehead. Without tearing his eyes from me, Adrian manages to simultaneously greet and dismiss Jake and Darius by only using their names. They get the hint and leave us, taking Zac with them.

"How was golf?" I ask Adrian.

"Boring without you, which got me thinking. Tomorrow will be hectic with the wedding. You'll be so busy with your maid of honor responsibilities. Then I'm flying back to

London first thing the next morning. You and I don't have much time left together."

I hadn't thought of it like that, but he's right. Time is running out, and it hurts to think about.

"So, listen," he continues, "I was wondering if I could get you alone tonight, after the rehearsal dinner? I know it's tradition for the maid of honor to be with the bride the night before the wedding, but Phoebe told me her and Tory want to spend time together."

"Sure. No one will interrupt us in our bungalow—"

"I mean away from this resort. I don't want interruptions from anyone. Will you come to the mainland with me? The owner of the golf course mentioned there's a festival tonight at Airlie Beach."

"Oh…" My excitement drops. "I can't. It's not a good idea for me to leave the resort. You know I'm meant to be lying low. The public aren't supposed to know where I am."

Adrian's fingers intertwine with mine and he pulls me closer, his lips brushing against mine in a teasing manner. He uses his one tool that is my complete undoing—his deep whisper, like he's talking to me between the bedsheets—and I think he must be aware of its effect on me. "Come on. There'll be so many people at the festival that you'll blend in. I don't even plan for us to be among the crowd. The golf course owner told me fireworks go off at midnight and the best view is from the water. What do you say to another round of stand up paddle boarding?"

That last part pulls me out of the hypnotic moment, and I shove him gently in the chest, laughing. "Are you joking? That will be a disaster. And I'm not going swimming at nighttime. Remember how dangerous that was last time? Don't forget jellyfish."

"We won't be getting in the water. We'll be floating on

top of it. Come on, Vee, one night where the two of us aren't on parade for everyone. No acting. No more games." He whispers in my ear, "We're just us."

The way he emphasizes those last words sends shivers all over my body. Tory's advice repeats itself in my mind. *Tell him you love him. I'm certain he'll say it straight back.* I'm beginning to agree more and more with her. Maybe tonight at this festival will be the perfect opportunity.

"All right, I'll come," I say. "But we go straight to paddle boarding. No one can recognize me. And I'll have to let my security know. They'll need to follow us." Adrian gives me a look like he isn't happy about having the added company. "They'll follow at a distance. You won't even notice them."

"Fine, I don't care. As long as I get you to myself."

I smile at those words, my cheeks growing warmer. "One more thing. I'll only agree to this plan if you promise to jump in and save me if I fall off my paddle board."

"Vee," he scoffs, "we'll share a board. Problem solved. I'll keep it sturdy."

"Okay. First, we have to survive this rehearsal dinner. Then we have to find a way to get off this island."

"Problem already solved. I slipped a few fifties to a guy with a speedboat.

"So, you just assumed I would say yes to the festival?"

"Well, yeah. *I like you so much, Adrian.*" He speaks in a high-pitched impersonation of my voice, quoting the text message I sent him earlier in the day.

I push Adrian again, about to tease him back, but he covers my mouth with a kiss, and I feel him smiling against me when he says, "Trust me, I like you so much more."

I'm not sure I hear a single word anyone says during the rehearsal dinner. Throughout the whole event, I keep stealing glances at Adrian, seated away from me and the bridal party. We can't stop smiling at each other, nor can we stop texting each other under the table with cute things like *I miss you* or *I want to kiss you*.

It's nine-thirty when the speeches conclude. Adrian whisks me from the crowd, and we sneak out of the rehearsal dinner like two teenagers climbing out of their bedroom windows to be together. Just like he promised, a speedboat waits for us on an unlit jetty with a driver aboard and my two bodyguards, both of them dressed in casual attire to prevent attracting attention.

What would ordinarily be me performing an awkward leap over the water from jetty to speedboat, turns into pure romance. Adrian scoops me into his arms and jumps aboard, then does that cute thing you see in the movies where the guy holds the girl for a few seconds longer than necessary and they share a moment of prolonged eye contact. The way he looks at me, it's with a tenderness and like I'm his entire world. It might be the happiest I've ever seen him, and it tugs on all of my heartstrings to see him like this with *me*.

Once we're all set on board, the boat silently creeps out of the bayside before speeding toward the mainland. Adrian draws me to the front of the boat for privacy, wrapping his arms around me as we stand at the railing, watching the distant festival lights approach. Neither of us speak a word as we travel toward our destination with the wind whipping through our hair and the scent of salty ocean water filling our lungs. Maybe, like me, Adrian isn't sure what to say and is enjoying this closeness that we've finally found our way back to. We were like this as children too, able to be in each other's company without feeling the need to fill every moment with conversation.

I hug myself when the wind picks up, shivering in the chilly breeze.

"You cold?" Adrian asks. Before I can answer, he opens his jacket and tucks me inside with him.

No acting. No games. We're just us.

I lean into Adrian, dizzy with his scent and never wanting this night to end. My phone chimes, but I don't dare reach for it and end my current bliss of being in this warm Adrian cocoon.

"Are you going to check your phone?" Adrian asks.

"No."

"What if it's something important?"

"What if it's Tory and she's furious because she saw us leave?"

"I'll deal with her."

"I'm inside your jacket with you. Opportunities like this don't come around every day."

He laughs, squeezing me tighter. "Check your phone. The hug won't end. And I promise, there will be plenty of opportunities like this to come."

My heart melts at how cute his words are. I give in and pull my phone out, hearing Adrian cuss when he sees it's a message from Darius.

"I changed my mind. Don't check your phone," he says.

"Did you forget the part where I mentioned Darius is gay?"

"Give me time. I've still got PTSD from thinking he was sleeping with you."

Darius: Where are you and Adrian going at this hour of the night?

"He saw us leaving," I say. "This will just take a second. I have to cover our tracks."

Verena: We're going to a festival on the mainland for a few hours. Don't tell anyone.

Darius: You're going on a date with Adrian!

I grow ten degrees warmer from Darius' words. "*Is* this a date?" I ask, raising the screen and inviting Adrian to read.

His arms wrap tighter around my waist, and I shiver when his deep voice whispers against my ear, "Yes, Vee, I'm taking you on a date."

The speedboat slows down as we reach Airlie Beach. It's a small town, but Adrian wasn't kidding about this festival being crowded. We dock at a jetty and my bodyguards follow us at a distance as we walk hand in hand through the outskirts of the festival. We stay clear of people, but that doesn't stop me from observing the nightlife. The main strip of town is like a street party. Everything is bustling with life, and it's almost impossible to distinguish any face in the sea of people. There's a live band on the beach with large crowds dancing in the sand. Market stalls fill the streets, and restaurants and bars line the esplanade.

Though I'm fine with staying on land, Adrian insists we do stand up paddle boarding like planned. To keep me from interacting with people, he does all the talking when we hire the paddle board.

Before we get onto the water, he pulls out a plastic bag from his pocket. "Give me your phone and anything else you don't want getting wet."

"Can I fit in there?"

"You're only getting wet if I splash you. The bag is for precautions."

"We can give our stuff to my bodyguards." I wave them over and they're with us in an instant. "Do you two mind holding our belongings while we head out on the water?"

They both shake their head, but only one of them says something. "Of course not, Verena. However, I must advise you to rethink this activity. If something happens while you're on the water, we can't protect you. You two will be alone."

"That's kind of the point," Adrian says under his breath.

"We'll be fine." I hand our belongings over.

Adrian steadies the board in the shallow water, then bows forward, welcoming me aboard. "All right, your majesty. Take a seat."

I do an awkward crawl to the front of the board, realizing what a mistake it was to wear this dress. The fabric is too tight for me to sit cross-legged, so I make the executive decision to curl up with my arms around my legs and pray no one takes a photo of my underwear from the front. Adrian steps onboard behind me, standing with the paddle and pushing us off the shoreline. We rock for a few seconds, and I yelp as my arms wobble on either side of me to regain balance.

"So melodramatic." Adrian chuckles, stroking the paddle through the water.

Once I get used to the sensation of floating on the water, the experience isn't that bad. There aren't any waves out here, and instead of a pitch-black night like I anticipated, we're surrounded by floating lanterns. A few other paddle boarders are in sight, but none close by.

When we're far enough away from the shore, Adrian sits behind me, then grabs my body and effortlessly spins me to face him—kind of on par with the sex-flip. Now I'm flashing *him* with my underwear, but what's new?

"Nice out here, huh?" he says.

I gaze at the party life back at shore, the fire lanterns, night markets, and people dancing to the live band. "It's peaceful. We'll have the best view for these fireworks."

Adrian takes my hands in his. There's a moment of silence where we're smiling at each other beneath the moonlight, then he says, "I'm really glad you decided to come here with me tonight."

"So am I."

"Things have been complicated between us, but I want to clear the air about some stuff."

I roll my eyes and laugh, sliding even closer to him so that my legs are in his lap. "We were both immature pricks this week, but that's yesterday's problem. Like we said last night, I'm yours and you're mine."

"I meant about the past."

"Ah, everything makes sense now. *This* is why you lured me out here—so I won't go hostile on you and risk falling into the water while you discuss our childhood."

"Maybe," he says. "No, I don't want to spend a single moment fighting with you."

"Good, so can we agree we don't need to discuss anything? No ex-boyfriends or girlfriends. No childish jealousy games. Nothing from when we were kids. We have a clean slate. There's no need to talk about all the ways we've hurt each other."

"It's bound to come up at some point."

"It doesn't have to. Let's look forward. Not back." I brush my lips over Adrian's to shut him up. I know my tactics have worked when he deepens the kiss.

But then he says, "Come home for Christmas."

"Not this again."

"I know our families can be overbearing, but they adore you."

"Oh, yeah? How exactly? By sharing embarrassing stories and photos of me with all the wedding guests?"

"If you're referring to the welcome dinner slideshow—"

"Of course I'm referring to that. It was terrible, but you weren't there, so you wouldn't know. They included a photo of me with *Verena the Vagina* written across my back."

He brushes a lock of hair behind my ear and frowns. "First of all, your mom apologized for that photo being in the slideshow. Secondly, I know you don't want to talk about the past, but I'm sorry about creating that stupid name."

"So, let's *not* talk about the past or my family."

"Verena, do you know our parents always make a habit to watch your show together with a bowl of popcorn like it's a movie night? They think so highly of you."

I didn't know that. He nods when a surprised look creeps over my face.

"Your parents have been trying to spend time with you all week," he adds. "It's only because I've missed you so much and can't get enough alone time with you that you haven't seen them more. They want you in their life, and not just once every seven years or on a TV screen. And you know those phone calls your mom initiates with me every month? She's always raving about how proud of you she is."

I smile. "You sure know how to be sweet."

"I'm being honest. And hopefully persuasive."

"Okay, I'm not making any promises except that I will *think* about coming home for Christmas."

"I'll find a way to convince you." He grins.

"And *I'm* sure *I* can convince you to be quiet." My lips

find Adrian's. I wriggle closer to him so that I'm sitting right in his lap, straddling him. Again, not the best idea in this dress, but I've moved beyond caring.

He chuckles. "Yeah, this will keep me quiet. For the time being."

"Can we focus on something else, like how amazing this week has been. I'm so glad we found our way back to each other."

"I can't believe we spent so much time apart," he murmurs while kissing me.

"I know."

Adrian's hands and lips on me awaken all the pent-up sexual energy I've acquired today. I want him to take me right now, even if that means we fall off this paddle board doing the deed. But Adrian seems to have other plans because he breaks the kiss to ask me a question.

"What's been your favorite part of this vacation?"

I don't know how he has enough willpower to carry out a proper conversation when all I can think about is feeling him inside me. "My favorite part of this week? Obviously having sex with you."

"Obviously," he laughs. "Mine too. But what else?"

"Maybe this moment right now."

"Really?" His face seems to glow at my words.

"And yours?"

He thinks about the question, trying to fight a mischievous grin.

"What?" I ask.

"Ah... it's nothing. Let me think, my favorite moment..."

That playful look in his eyes is not nothing and is enough to make me start panicking. "Adrian, what?"

"I told you, it's nothing. Something you won't remember."

"I have a superhuman brain and remember every second of my life—from the day of my birth leading all the way up to right now. I especially remember moments involving you."

"You were drunk," he says.

"Fuck. Which night?"

"The first night at the resort. Don't be embarrassed. I loved every second of it." He kisses me again, trying to distract me, but it doesn't work.

"What did I do?" All I can think about is the sex dream.

"It was after I carried you out of the ocean. You didn't have your bungalow key, so I took you back to mine and placed you in my bed. I sat next to you for a minute to make sure you were asleep, but when I got up to leave, you asked me to stay."

My hands fidget in my lap. "What else did I say?"

"It's not what you said, it's what you did. I lay beside you, giving you your space, but you curled up into my arms. You stayed like that the entire night. I snuck out to the couch early the next morning, knowing you'd be furious if you woke up beside me."

"*That* is your favorite moment?"

He smiles. "It's when I realized you didn't hate me as much as you claimed."

Okay, his reasoning is kind of sweet, but I'm still mortified. "Did I do or say anything else?"

He eyes me with suspicion. "You asked that question the following morning. Why?"

"Let's just say I had a dream about you. A very hot dream that made me come in my sleep. Multiple times."

Adrian's lips rise playfully. He presses my hips into his lap, alerting me to the new bulge beneath his fly. "So, I must have been pretty good in the dream?"

"Yeah, but you're better in real life. *So* much better."

He leans forward, lowering my back to the paddle board, the two of us rocking in the water as he kisses me deeply. "I wish I could have you right now."

Something loud cracks in the distance, followed by an explosion of red lights. We both gaze back to the shore, watching as fireworks shimmer through the dark sky. The display continues for a good ten minutes, but we don't see any more fireworks, too consumed with each other's lips.

Chapter Twenty-Seven

Midnight has well and truly passed us when we return the hired paddle board. The fireworks have died down, but the festival is as lively as ever.

"You ready to head back to the resort?" Adrian asks me.

I answer with a nod, but it's a total lie. I'm not ready to end this night. My gaze keeps redirecting itself to the dancers on the beach and all I can think about is how much fun I'd have being one of them. That, plus I haven't said half the things I want to say to Adrian. I still need to find the right moment to tell him I love him, even though Tory would say any moment is the right moment. But I want it to be special, and I want to be one hundred percent sure Adrian will say it in return.

We're halfway back to the speedboat when I come to a firm stop. Adrian's words from earlier at the resort are painfully settling in, that tonight is the last chance we have together. The wedding will be hectic tomorrow, then we're both returning to different countries the following day. I'm not done having fun with him, and I'm not stepping a foot inside the resort until I tell Adrian what he means to me.

Part of the reason I agreed to attend this festival was because of Adrian's promise that we'd be on the water the whole time, *away* from people. It may be the most reckless decision, considering I'm meant to be keeping a low profile, but an impulse rushes over me. My hand slips into Adrian's and I act quickly, tugging him back toward the festival and losing the bodyguards as we're swallowed by the crowd.

"What are you doing?"

"Having fun. Letting loose," I tell him, and he smiles in return.

Adrian follows me through the tight crowd, our shoulders brushing by dancers, the smell of alcohol in the air. To my relief, he was right about no one recognizing me. There are so many people that we blend in seamlessly.

Once we've reached the center of the dance floor, I twirl to face Adrian, swaying with the music and holding his hands. "Dance with me."

For the first time all week, a flicker of self-consciousness tightens his features. "I don't know how to dance."

"There's nothing to learn. Feel the music in your body. Sway to the beat." I step closer and whisper in his ear, "A couple's dance is about sex. It's instinctual. Imagine that *we're* having sex."

A deep, gravely sound escapes Adrian's throat and his eyes turn dark upon me, exactly the way I want them to. He spins me around, his strong arms pressing my back flush to his chest. Adrian's hands explore the curves of my body, his hands trailing to my hips.

"Your mouth says the dirtiest things and I love it." His voice rasps against my ear, sending pulses of heat to my breasts and farther down.

Adrian's body fits to mine as I roll my hips in time with the music, the two of us in sync and grinding up against each other. He spins me out wide, then draws me in close so we're facing each other this time. The heat in his eyes is molten. I can't bring myself to look away. I never want Adrian to stop looking at me like this, like he wants to devour me and take me back to his bed and spend the night doing unspeakable things to my body. Up this close, his breath is hot on my cheeks. His scent is so intoxicating I swear I'm drunk again. His hands slink down my waist, lower, lower, until they curve over my ass. He purrs at the contact, and I lick my lips when feeling how hard he is.

Nothing draws us apart for the rest of the song. No twirling. No solo dancing. We remain locked in place, tangled with each other. His forehead rests on mine and we share breath, gazing into each other's eyes as we sway to the music. When the song comes to an end, there's a moment where we remain in each other's arms before I loosen my grip, only motivated by the thought of returning to the privacy of our bungalow.

"We should go back to the resort," I say, taking Adrian's hand and turning to leave.

I take a step at most before Adrian pulls me back to him, holding my head between his two hands. He searches my eyes, seeming lost for words, then blurts out, "I love you. I'm so crazy about you, Verena. I wanted to tell you earlier—"

My lips are on his before he has a chance to say another word. I keep believing that each new moment with Adrian is the best moment of my life, but this one overrides all others by miles.

Adrian Hunter loves me.

He *loves* me.

Am I living in an alternate reality? Those three words are all I've ever wanted to hear from him.

He kisses me back, just as urgent and unapologetic as I

am, holding me like there's no tomorrow and he can't get me close enough. My body melts into him, my fingers knotting through his dark hair and holding him tight. I could kiss this man forever.

The next song ends, and the next song after that. Our kisses don't slow down. The only time our lips break apart is to take a breath. It only dawns on me now, when the next song begins, that I haven't said *I love you* in return.

"Adrian, I love—"

A flash goes off. I ignore it, the habit ingrained in my behavior. But three more flashes light up our surroundings, followed by people calling my name. Adrian and I step back from each other the moment we hear a distinct, "It's Verena Valentine!"

All around us the dancers have stopped and are holding up their phones, taking photos. Adrian pushes me behind him, shielding my body with his. But it's no use. Fans have formed a circle around us. My typical response to large groups of fans is to *smile and wave, boys*—like the penguins from *Madagascar*—sometimes talk to them, but right now, all that registers is how much attention I'll draw to my sister's inconspicuous wedding when the media discovers I'm in Australia. I've fucked up big.

Adrian acts fast, pulling me through the crowd. The second we're off the beach, he breaks into a sprint, the two of us running through the night markets and farther inland until we've escaped the bulk of the festival and anyone who recognizes me.

"In here." Adrian guides us into the protection of a dark nook between buildings. Panting, he looks me up and down with concern. "Are you all right?"

"I'm so stupid," I say, just as breathless as he is, and kick the wall. "I wanted to enjoy my time with you, but I shouldn't have been so reckless. Shit. Tory will be furious with me."

"No one knows you're staying on Hayman Island. Everything will be all right."

He has a point. It's not ideal that word of my presence in Australia will soon spread, but no real damage has been caused to the wedding. I gaze up at Adrian, smiling as the memory of our heated dancing returns. Before I know it, our limbs are a tangled mess again.

"Verena, you are so beautiful," he says through kisses, pressing me against the brick wall. "You have no idea how much I—"

My fingers creep up beneath his shirt, prickling at the heat of his muscles. I wait for him to finish the sentence, but he doesn't continue. "I have no idea about what?"

"How much I've wanted this." His lips trace down my jaw, igniting an ache between my legs. "I've wanted this for so long."

His words are everything I want to hear, yet at the same time, unintelligible, sending my mind into a spiral of confusion. He's wanted me for so long? Since when exactly—the day we spent together out on the Great Barrier Reef? That's when I felt my feelings return for Adrian. But I wouldn't classify that as a long time. It was only two days ago. Before that, he wanted Isabelle.

I try to shake the thoughts out of my mind. *I've* been the one reinforcing that we don't bring up the past and previous relationships. We're meant to be starting fresh. But now I can't stop thinking about the meaning behind his words.

"How long are we talking about?" I murmur through kisses. "Was it during our day out at the reef when you realized you wanted me?"

He leans back to meet my eyes. "Vee, I've always wanted you. Ever since I can remember."

Always?

I place my hands on his chest, gently pushing space between us while I try to catch my breath and think clearly. "Adrian... I don't understand. What about our childhood? What about Isabelle? You were in love with her at the start of the week."

"I don't want her. I haven't been in love with her for a long time."

"Then why did you suggest we enter the fake relationship?"

"Because..." His face balls up in a grimace. "I'm a complete idiot and panicked when we first saw each other in the lobby. This is what I needed to talk to you about. I wanted to clear the air so there were no secrets left between us. Vee, I have been waiting months for this wedding to arrive, all so I could see you and tell you how much I want you back in my life. I planned to tell you the truth straight away, but you were so furious when we first saw each other. I could see it in your eyes that you still hated me. I lost my nerve and suggested the fake relationship because it's the only thing I could think of to get you near me."

I push more space between us, and by the strained look in Adrian's eyes, I can tell he doesn't like it. But I'm struggling to understand anything he's saying with him this close. "Adrian..." My voice cracks. I'm suddenly furious and shaking all over. My eyes are watering. "I have been in love with you my entire life! I convinced myself for years that I hated you, but deep down I knew it was a lie. When you hurt me so badly that I couldn't bear to see you for seven years, a part of me still loved you. Even when I was with

Jake, you were still locked away in my heart. It's always been you for me."

His face drops with a frown, like he's only learning this information for the first time—which, maybe he is. Maybe he feels as stupid as I do right now. "I'm so sorry. I waited years to see you and ruined everything within minutes of us meeting. That's why I left the welcome dinner early on the first night and you found me venting my anger on the beach. I was so frustrated at myself for ruining my chances with you."

"What about after we slept together?" I ask. "You had to have known I was crazy about you. That was your chance to make me yours. Instead, you acted like the sex was no big deal."

"That's not fair, Verena. You led me to believe you were with Darius. And I told you already, I was afraid of coming on too strong when I had no idea what your feelings for me were. I've resorted to some immature tactics this week and I'm not proud of it, but they've all been a desperate attempt to win you back."

I run both hands through my hair, pulling at my scalp. It's as if my whole life is flashing before my eyes and I'm reliving all of my childhood trauma at once. "What about in high school? I know I said I don't want to talk about the past, but that topic is inescapable now. How can you say you've wanted me for as long as you can remember when you used to hate me so much?"

Adrian takes my jaw in his palms, forcing me to meet his eyes. There's something so desperate in his gaze. So honest yet panicked. A single tear escapes the corner of my eye, and he wipes it away. "Please don't cry, Verena. I never hated you. I've loved you for so long."

My lips tremble. I pull my face free of his hands. "Don't

do that, Adrian. If you loved me, why did you withdraw from me when we were children? There were years where you stopped speaking to me."

"Maybe because I was a dumb kid who didn't know how to express his emotions." I can tell he's trying to remain calm, but his voice rises. "One day you were my best friend, the next I was attracted to you and became all nerves. I couldn't string a proper sentence together around you."

"Don't give me that excuse. You were with half the girls in school. I didn't catch you stuttering around any of them."

"Because none of them were you!"

I wipe my eyes, keeping the tears at bay. "Fine. Why did you start that war between us?"

"Verena, I never started anything."

"You humiliated me in front of all of your friends by pretending to ask me to the school dance!"

"Hold on. Verena, *what?*" The words are sharp, and he's just as frustrated as me now. "I *did* ask you to the dance. A rumor spread throughout school that you liked me, so I built up the courage to ask you out, then you told me to get fucked in front of all of my friends. You want to talk about humiliation, there you go."

"I heard you laughing with your friends about me. Your words are scarred in my mind. *You should have seen the look on her face. What a loser.*"

"Verena, the only reason I said that was because you embarrassed me in front of everyone, right after I'd put myself on the line for you. I'm not saying it's right. I just want you to understand where the comment came from."

Suddenly, the dark nook we're standing in feels too tight, and it's like I can't breathe. I slide halfway down the wall, crouched over with my head in my hands. "I think I'm going to be sick."

"Verena, talk to me."

"I can't. I don't know what to believe anymore. I'm so confused that I don't even know what's real. I need time to comprehend everything." I stand up, not brave enough to look Adrian in the eyes. "I need to be alone right now. I'll find my own way back to the resort."

Adrian takes me by the hands before I have a chance to leave, pulling me in close to him. "Don't leave," he says with a fierceness in his eyes. "This is real, right here and now—me saying I love you. Verena, after all these years, we've finally found our way back to each other. I can't lose you again."

Those are the words that break me, making my tears run freely. "Let me be alone right now, Adrian. Please."

Chapter Twenty-Eight

The sun is almost rising by the time my bodyguards escort me back to the resort. I bang on the front door of Darius' bungalow, begging for him to wake up and let me in. He answers the door like a zombie, with bed hair and eyes only half-open.

"Shit," he says once seeing my teary face, and pulls me into his arms. "What happened?"

"I need a place to sleep."

"Things didn't go well on the date?" he asks. I shake my head, unable to answer the question. "Robe Time?"

"Not even Robe Time will fix this."

Darius welcomes me inside. "Come to the bedroom."

As soon as I enter the front door, I see Zac asleep on the couch. "Trouble with Penny?"

"I think this might be the end of their marriage, but we don't need to talk about them right now."

I crawl into bed with Darius, telling him the whole story of what went down between me and Adrian tonight. If what Adrian says is true, I've been living a lie for most of my life. My perception of reality is warped. I've spent so many years hating the one person I could have been blissfully happy with.

Even if Adrian is telling the truth, that doesn't magically erase years of trauma and anger. This is why I wanted to forget about the past and start with a clean slate. But now, there's no avoiding old scars.

What about Isabelle? How does she fit into all of this? As a pawn? I hope she isn't hurt.

Several hours later, I wake to my phone vibrating off the bedside table and clattering to the ground.

"Are you going to get that?" Darius mutters from beside me with his head buried in a pillow.

I check the screen and swear. Tory is calling.

"What were you thinking?" she scolds as soon as I answer. "There are photos all over the internet of you kissing Adrian at a street festival last night."

"Dammit," my voice croaks, groggy with sleep. "I was hoping the photos wouldn't spread so fast. But don't worry. No one knows I'm on this island. This won't impact the wedding at all."

"Think again. I'm having a breakdown on my wedding day because there is an insane number of fans and photographers that security is holding off from barging into this resort."

"What?" I sit up, suddenly wide awake. "How do they know I'm at this resort?"

"You tell me? Someone must have followed you back here and spread the news."

"Tory, I'm so sorry."

"Verena, this is exactly why I asked you to keep a low profile. My wedding day is not meant to start off like this. I should be enjoying a nice breakfast with my fiancée, not cleaning up your mess."

"Let me take care of this, okay?" I tell her. "You should be relaxing. Don't spend another moment stressing over this."

"How can I relax? Some rabid fan might run through my ceremony."

"Promise me."

She sighs and hangs up. I'm not sure what that means, but I need to fix this immediately. Then figure out what to do about Adrian.

It takes my bodyguards and me over two hours in the lobby to ensure resort security staff are applying the correct procedures to keep this island private. They work all morning to make sure there isn't a single person at the resort who isn't involved with the wedding. On top of that, they've called in extra coast guards to prevent unwanted boats sailing too close to the island.

The morning starts off as an absolute disaster, eating into valuable time that I should be spending in hair and make-up and helping Tory prepare for her big day. Valuable time where I could be figuring out what to do about Adrian. But at least the scandal is dealt with, and I can move on with my day.

It's when I'm traveling back from the lobby, heading across the grass for Tory's bungalow, that an unwanted voice calls for me. "Verena, I've been looking everywhere for you."

Jake is approaching me, so I decide to keep walking. What is up with this guy? He's like a weasel, appearing at all the worst times. "Not now, Jake. I'm too busy."

His footsteps turn into a jog, and the next thing I know,

he's right in front of me, his big head blocking the sun from view. "This will only take a second."

"Fine. Be quick."

"We need to finish the conversation we started."

"How many times do I have to say this? We did *not* start any conversation. I don't care about whatever it is you have to tell me."

"Verena, you're mad with me and I understand, but I need to say this. Seeing you this week... It's made me do a lot of soul searching. I made a massive mistake by cheating on you and will never forgive myself for it. You deserved so much more from a partner. You're such an amazing woman, and I'm so sorry for what I did to you. I will never stop being sorry."

If I were asked to describe my face right now, the saying *a deer in the headlights* is probably most accurate. Either that, or I'm channeling Kevin Hart's shocked face in that famous meme from his stand-up comedy performance.

"Thank... you, I suppose...?"

"There's more." Jake shifts back and forth on his feet, and his palms rub against the fabric of his shorts. Oh God, he's nervous. This can't be good. "I don't know how to best word this, so I'm just going to come out with it. I miss you. No, it's more than that. Verena, I love you. What can I do to fix the way I treated you? I'll do anything. Please give me another chance to be the man you deserve."

I'm staring slack-jawed, not believing my ears. For months after Jake left me, I had dreams of him begging me to take him back. Before Jake blindsided me, I thought he was the man I would marry, and that kind of love doesn't disappear overnight. I cried myself to sleep for weeks, wishing he would knock on my door at three a.m. because he couldn't wait till sunrise to tell me he'd made a mistake.

Now, here he is, giving me everything I wanted, and I can't form a response.

Jake steps right up to me, taking my hands in his. "Verena, we were so perfect together."

"We were," I whisper. It's a miracle I can even talk.

"We can have that again. Please tell me you want this too. Tell me you want *us*."

There's a part of me that feels extremely smug. Jake left me for another girl, and now he's crawling back.

"Verena, talk to me, please."

"I... um... This is a busy day. I can't... um... I have too much to deal with right now. I need time to think."

"Of course, anything you need. I'll be here, waiting for you." Jake places a lingering kiss on my cheek.

My body freezes up as a response. I think I've gone into vampire shock—like that time Edward Cullen realized Bella was pregnant and he became a statue.

The telepathic bond between me and Jake is non-existent because he interprets my vampire shock as being a good thing and presses his lips to mine. The kiss lasts one one-thousand, two one-thousand, three one-thousand, four one-thousand before Jake parts ways with me and walks back in the direction he came.

When I can move again, I'm a shaking mess as I watch him leave. My first reaction is to wipe the gross cheater germs off my lips and rush to the bathroom so I can wash my mouth out with soap, but I don't make it beyond one stride before hearing a blunt, "Wow."

My shoulders raise to my ears and my heart plummets as I register the voice as Adrian's. I turn to face him, desperate to explain myself, but lose all nerve when I see that stark look on his face.

"Should I be offering my congratulations to the happy couple?"

"Adrian, it's not like that. You know it's not. He ambushed me."

"Which explains why you let him kiss you?"

"I froze up. Please, let me explain."

"I'm not sure you have to. *I need time to think?*" Adrian repeats the last words I said to Jake. "Verena, what is there for you to think about? Don't tell me you're considering getting back together with that jerk."

I rub my temples, closing my eyes tight. It's just my luck that the delicate situation between me and Adrian has become even more fragile. "My mind is chaos right now, okay? I've got so many messes to clean up. Everyone is tugging me in different directions. There are a bunch of photographers and crazy fans stalking this island. Excuse me if I can't think straight."

"Let me make this easy for you, then. I love you, Verena. That jerk can't feel even one-millionth of what I feel for you, because if he did, there's no way he would have cheated on you. How you have even the slightest inkling that getting back together with Jake is a good idea is beyond me. I know things are complicated between us right now, but how can *he* be a better option than me?"

"Adrian—"

"I'm not done speaking."

Without giving Adrian any explanation of what I'm about to do, I grab his hand and drag him after me, heading in the direction Jake went in.

"What are you doing?" he asks.

"If you'd given me a chance to talk, I would have told you I hated every moment of Jake's kiss but was too shocked to push him away because I couldn't believe he was asking for me back. Let me make this situation blatantly obvious for you. Stay put and listen."

I release Adrian from my grasp the moment Jake comes back into view. A nervous smile twitches over Jake's lips as he watches me march up to him. It's pathetic that hope lives in his eyes, like he thinks I'm coming to share great news that I broke up with Adrian and want him back.

"Verena, honey..." Jake starts.

He raises a hand to stroke my hair, but I smack it down and speak loud enough for Adrian to hear every word out of my mouth. "How dare you lump me in the same pile as you, assuming that just because you're disgusting enough to cheat on me, I would cheat on my boyfriend with *you*. How dare you consider for even one second that I would think about taking you back. And how dare you do to Hannah what you did to me. I may not like the girl, but even she deserves better than *you*." I poke him in the chest as I say that last word, then storm off, catching Adrian's eyes on me as I pass him. Damn, that felt good.

Adrian is just as speechless as Jake, but the slightest grin spreads across his lips. With Jake out of the picture, at least there's one less mess for me to think about. I'm desperate to solve the tension between me and Adrian, but before I can do that, there's someone I have to talk to first.

Chapter Twenty-Nine

After a well-needed shower in Darius' bungalow, I arrive at the day spa where all the ladies—except the bridal party—sit in rows, either having their hair, makeup, or nails done for the wedding. A certain redhead catches my attention. Isabelle is receiving a manicure. Just the person I'm searching for.

"Hi, Isabelle." I slide into the chair beside her, placing my hands in front of a nail technician. "I like that color. It looks gorgeous with your red hair."

Isabelle blanches the moment she sees me and looks away, swearing under her breath.

"I'm hoping we can chat. I sat here on purpose."

She stares at her nails. "I don't have anything to say to you."

I guess I deserve that. "I'm sorry if I've upset you this week. I've been making some questionable choices. I was wondering... Do you still have feelings for Adrian?"

She spits a laugh, the sound bitter and like she has a mouthful of vinegar. "No. And I know you're not together. At least, you weren't at the start of this week. He told me everything three nights ago when we went for a walk on the beach."

"I'm sorry. I honestly believed the fake relationship was because he wanted you back. I hope you didn't get hurt in all of this, and I'm sorry if you did."

She cuts me off with more sour laughter. "Verena, I don't want him. He's all yours."

"Why the bitterness, then? I don't quite understand your situation."

"That makes two of us. Adrian and I were together for three years. He says he loved me…"

"I'm sure he was telling the truth. You seem very lovely—"

"Don't bullshit a bullshitter. You don't know anything about me."

Her words bring a smile to my face. "I know this isn't the time, but that's one of my favorite sayings."

Isabelle presses her lips together, fighting a smile. "I've always wanted to say it." She instantly straightens her face, as if not wanting to appear too friendly. A few seconds later, she gives in with a sigh and meets my gaze for the first time. "You're hard to hate, Verena Valentine. I've seen you on TV so many times that I feel like I already know you. Despite my anger, Adrian is a good guy. You should be with him."

"I'm still not understanding the situation between you two."

"Let me paint you a visual of what my relationship with Adrian was like. We met through his sister and dated for a while before we moved to London and decided to live together. That's when I discovered his love for your show. Throughout our entire relationship, he never missed an episode. Sometimes I caught him watching repeats. I used to tease him about it and joke that he had a crush on you. Six months ago, he breaks up with me."

"Wait, what? Adrian told me *you* broke up with *him*." And hang on... Six months ago? That's when Jake and I broke up.

"I suppose he tweaked the details for you. It would have made his reason for a fake relationship more believable. Believe me, Adrian was the one who initiated the breakup. I mean, it's not like I didn't see it coming. We were having issues for a long time. Skip forward six months to this wedding and I see Adrian here, supposedly dating you. Then I hear all these stories about how he's known you since you were kids. The two of you were best friends. Not once did he think to mention that to me in our three years? That's why I'm angry. But whatever, I'll get over it. We've met up a few times this week to clarify the situation."

"I know how this must seem to you," I say, feeling terrible for her pain, "but Adrian and I haven't seen each other in seven years. We ended things on bad terms. There was nothing going on between us when you two were together."

"Maybe not physically. And I guess..." She blows a lock of hair out of her face, frustrated. "Okay, yes, I'm just being bitter, because I know Adrian *did* love me on some level, I'll admit that. I'm not suggesting he was using me when we were together. But I also know he's always held you in his heart. He loves you more than he ever loved me. I see it in the way he looks at you. Not once has he ever looked at me that way. I see it in you too."

It's like she's repeating Tory's words.

"As I said," Isabelle continues, "he came clean about everything. It hurts, but I'll be fine. I moved on months ago and have a new boyfriend. Seeing you two together was more a shock than anything."

"Thank you for being honest with me." A jolt of panic shoots through me when I catch a glimpse of the time on her watch. I retrieve my hands from the nail technician and stand up to leave. "I'm *really* late."

"One last thing." Isabelle looks up at me. "I do want Adrian to be happy. You deserve happiness too after the heartbreak of your last relationship. If you're having issues with Adrian, sort them out because a love like this only comes around once in a lifetime... if you're lucky."

"Thanks. I'll see you at the wedding."

It's closing in on midday and I know time is running out for me to get dressed for this wedding, but I have to find Adrian and fix things with him. I head for the exit, stopping short when I notice Jannah enter the day spa, red-eyed and splotchy, and of course, dressed in a bikini. A group of friends are comforting her. Among their chatter I hear mention of Jake. Jannah comes to a halt when she sees me, being the only one out of her friends not death staring me. I'm expecting this interaction to turn ugly, regardless that Jake propositioning me is not my fault. Instead, Jannah nods at me with the hint of a smile.

"I heard you really gave it to that bastard," she says.

"I... What?"

"My friend said she overheard you with Jake, telling him that you deserved better than what he did to you. What *we* did to you. And that I deserve better too."

I shrug, not knowing how else to respond. "Well, it's true."

"That was nice of you to have my back. I don't deserve it but thank you. And I'm sorry. I know that doesn't mean much coming from me. But I'm sorry for destroying your relationship."

"Thanks. It helps a bit."

Part of me wonders why I've placed so much hate on Jannah over this past week. Yes, she had an affair with my boyfriend, but if Jake's behavior today shows me anything, it's that once a cheater, always a cheater, and that he probably had more to do with seducing Jannah than the other way around. I can't even blame her for talking to Adrian during the night of the strippers because that was *his* doing, plotting to use her to make me jealous. I'm not saying she's innocent, but that maybe Jannah is really just a Hannah, who I give zero shits about.

"If it makes you feel any better," she says, wiping her nose. "I dumped Jake's sorry ass the moment my friend told me about him propositioning you. He's packing his bags as we speak and won't be at the wedding."

I'm about to dive into a speech about how terrible Jake is and that it will be a relief not to have him around for the remainder of this vacation, but I pause, coming up with something better. "You know what, I have more important things to worry about than Jake, and so do you."

"Vera!" someone calls in the distance. I don't take much notice since that isn't my name, until I realize the voice belongs to Stacy and she's looking at me, furious as she hurries through the day spa in a dressing gown and a head full of hair rollers. "Where have you been? Tory needs you for bridal photos. Oh goodness, your hair and makeup aren't done."

She clutches a hand around my wrist, her nails digging into my skin as she drags me out of the day spa at such high speed that I don't have a chance to duck beneath overhanging palm leaves on the walkway.

"Ouch! Stacy, let go of me!"

"That's not an option. You are so late. This wedding will probably be delayed because *you* can't stick to a schedule."

She keeps tugging me, but I yank free of her grasp, wincing at the scratch marks on my wrist.

Stacy throws her arms in the air with a growl. "Vera, I don't have time for another one of your tantrums. Your sister is about to get married. I need you to pull yourself together and support her."

"It's *Verena*! My name is Verena. Why do you have such an issue pronouncing it? Or better yet, why do you have such an issue with me? You've been rude to me this entire week. It's like you resent me for being the maid of honor or something."

"Of course I resent you!"

My mouth opens and shuts, surprised at the honesty. "Why? What have I ever done to you?"

"I'm Tory's best friend, and yet she chose *you* to be her maid of honor. You want to know why? It's because she misses her sister and is trying to rekindle a relationship with you. But you're too busy making out with Adrian in front of all the cameras to care."

"I didn't do that on purpose. And of course I care."

"My point is, you should be more present in your sister's life. And not just hers, but your whole family's. They adore you—"

"Stacy," I groan. "You don't know anything about my family life."

"I do, actually. Tory tells me things. And yeah, I was there during the embarrassing welcome dinner slideshow presentation your parents gave. It wasn't great. But I've also spent this entire week listening to them rave about how incredible you are. They all love you so much, Tory especially, and you don't even see it."

Stacy's words leave me speechless. I want to defend myself, but there's no fight left in me.

I want to create sister memories.

Tory's words from the night of the strippers echo in my mind. Then there's everything Adrian said last night about my family. I've been so adamant to run away from my past, hating certain behaviors of my family, like how my mom's first reaction when seeing me this week was to share embarrassing stories with her sisters about my childhood. But... perhaps I can't blame her for that when those are the only memories she has. I haven't given her the chance to create new memories of me as an adult and the woman I am today.

"You're right, Stacy." The words come out quiet, but I mean every one of them. "I don't deserve to be maid of honor. I've let Tory down in so many ways. I'm sorry if it's been difficult for you to stand by and watch."

Stacy is lost for words too, probably having expected me to make a rebuttal. She gives a stoic nod and says, "Let's make things right, and stop wasting more time by standing here talking."

"Agreed."

The two of us continue toward Tory's bungalow in silence. I hate putting Adrian on hold again, but right now, the priority is this wedding and being the sister Tory needs.

As we arrive at Tory's bungalow, Stacy's hand pauses on the door handle before we step inside, and she gives me a tiny smile. "Listen, *Verena*, I'm sorry too. I haven't been the nicest person to you this week."

"Thank you. Now let's get Tory married."

Chapter Thirty

A stylist in Tory's bungalow does my hair and make-up in record time. Darius is here too, organizing everyone's outfit and ensuring no wardrobe malfunctions arise.

I slip into my dress—a baby pink strapless gown that is boring compared to my standards, but that's the point, to direct all eyes to where they belong, on the two brides. For Tory, I designed the real masterpiece: a dress full of diamonds that clings to her body, sparkling in the light like she's stepped out of the ocean. A sheer ivory fabric sits on top, intended to billow in the wind and sweep out behind her.

"You ready to wear this beauty one last time?" Darius asks Tory, unzipping the protective bag her dress is stored in.

"You'll be worth fifty-thousand dollars. Literally," I tell her, helping Darius retrieve the dress.

Mom and the bridesmaids gather around Tory as Darius and I bring her the gown. My sister's face lights up when she sees it, able to wear the dress for real this time, instead of staring at pictures of it each time she fantasized about walking down the aisle. The smile on Tory's face brings tears to my eyes.

Mom and I assist Tory when stepping into her dress, while Stacy and Nia tend to her shoes. "Thanks, Darius," I say. "I've got it from here. Can you check on Phoebe to make sure there aren't any issues with her outfit?"

"Of course. Tory, you look like an angel."

Darius squeezes my hand before exiting the bungalow. We probably won't see each other until tomorrow. Though he's been added to the guest list, my guess is he'll be tending to the Zac and Penny situation.

"It's true. You look amazing," I tell Tory, lacing up the back of her dress. "You're the most stunning bride I've ever seen."

Mom wraps an arm around both of us, teary-eyed and with smudges in her makeup. "Oh, my beautiful daughters."

"Mom!" I warn, repositioning her a step back. "Don't you dare cry on Tory's dress."

She wipes her tears away, laughing. "Sorry. It's just that I've dreamed of this moment for so long. It's every mother's dream to dress her daughter on their wedding day. And it's so rare to have you girls together with me."

I rub Mom's shoulder, remembering everything Adrian and Stacy told me about my family. "You're right. We don't see each other enough. I'm going to make more of an effort to be around from now on."

She blinks through tears. "What do you mean?"

"I'm coming home every Christmas."

"You are?" Tory gasps at the same time as Mom's face crumples into a mess of sobs.

I draw Mom away from Tory, pulling her into a hug. "I'll let you cry on my dress, but not the bride's."

"Do you really mean it, Verena?" she sniffles. "You're coming home every year?"

"Yes. I'm sorry that I stayed away for so long."

"Oh, Verena, your father is going to be so happy when I tell him."

"And Tory, I'm sorry for going to the mainland last night and causing a scene. All the security dramas have been taken care of. Today will be amazing for you and Phoebe, I promise."

"Thank you." Tory twirls in front of a full-length mirror with the biggest smile on her face. "Verena, you've outdone yourself with this dress. I love it. Thank you so much."

A phone alarm beeps, signaling that it's time to leave for the ceremony, and everyone squeaks with excitement.

At three o'clock, I arrive with Tory and her half of the bridal party at the beach ceremony. It's the perfect day for a wedding. Beautiful warm weather and no unwanted fans or photographers sailing nearby. The wedding arch is decorated in pink and cream roses, and petals are scattered over the sand. When I hear Minnie Riperton's *Lovin' You*, I know it's the bridesmaids' cue to walk down the aisle. Nia goes first, followed by Stacy, then it's my turn. I leave Tory with a kiss on the cheek and tell her I'll see her at the other end.

Phoebe is the first person I see when I begin walking, standing with a nervous smile beside the celebrant. She looks perfect in her black gown. I designed it to have a sweetheart neckline with sleeves that drape off her shoulders, and a full-length skirt that opens at the front to reveal tight pant legs.

With the wedding well on the way, the only thing left for me to worry about is Adrian. I search for the man I love, locking eyes with him sitting in the front row, and damn, does he look suave in his fitted suit. But his expression is impossible to pinpoint. There are so many emotions in Adrian's eyes. Joy for his sister. Longing for me. But most of all, what I see is uncertainty over our relationship.

I direct my smile at him, attempting to give a signal that we're good. But I've been smiling since the moment I arrived at this aisle, and he doesn't get the hint. All he does is gulp at the sight of me.

"Please stand for the arrival of the second bride," the celebrant says as I take my place at the front with Phoebe and the rest of the bridal party.

My dad comes into sight, escorting the most beautiful woman I've ever seen in my life down the aisle. Everyone gasps at how exquisite Tory looks, but I'm sure she doesn't hear a sound. She doesn't glance sideways at the guests to acknowledge them. I can read the look in her eyes and the smile on her face perfectly. For my little sister, no one exists in this moment except Phoebe waiting for her at the end of the aisle.

My attention switches to Phoebe. Tears pool in her eyes as she smiles at her bride. The electricity between them is unmissable. The world revolves around them and nothing else. A sense of longing washes over me, and I know—part of me has known my entire life, regardless of the seven-year separation—that I want to experience this exact moment with Adrian at our own wedding.

As Tory arrives at the end of the aisle, my dad hands her to Phoebe, and the two brides greet each other with a kiss.

"Easy," the celebrant laughs, "we're not up to that part of the ceremony yet."

Giggles travel throughout each row of guests, and everyone takes their seats as the ceremony commences. I'm consumed with awe over how magnificent my sister and her soon-to-be wife are, holding hands and smiling as they gaze into each other's eyes.

I look at Adrian when the celebrant begins with a speech about love. His eyes are already on me with that same sense of uncertainty in them. They're almost pained, and the very sight of them tears at my heart. This is exactly why I'd hoped to speak with him before the ceremony. Who knows what's going through his mind? We can't talk now, but I'm desperate to send him a message.

I smile and mouth the words, *I love you.*

He blinks back a moment of confusion, perhaps even disbelief, then his lips rise into the most heart-warming grin. I'm sure if anyone were paying attention to us, they would see that same spellbinding connection in our eyes that Tory and Phoebe share. It takes everything in me not to run to Adrian and feel his lips upon mine. For now, though, I practice patience and listen to the celebrant.

After the ceremony, everyone gathers on the beach to offer congratulations to the happy couple and take photos. I do my maid of honor job of holding flowers and puffing up dresses, but the moment I'm not needed, I sink into the background and slip away to find Adrian. Our eyes meet across the crowd and we both break into massive grins.

"Get into my arms now!" he calls.

My pace turns into a run, the two of us laughing as I race over the sand and launch myself onto him, our lips fitting together perfectly. Adrian squeezes me tight, lifting me off my feet and spinning me around.

"Get a room, you two," Mom tells us. "Anyone would think you were the ones who just got hitched."

Adrian places me down, stroking hands through my hair as his gaze devours the sight of me. "So, you love me too, huh?"

"I one hundred percent love you. I just needed time to clear my head and comprehend everything. And I'm so sorry that you saw Jake kiss me. Adrian, there wasn't ever one second where I was considering taking him back. It's been you all along. I've been crazy about you this entire week—"

"I know. You don't have to explain."

"But I want to. There are so many things I need to tell you, like that I want to make this work between us. I want to be your girlfriend. Your *real* girlfriend. I want to be with you for the rest of my life—"

Adrian's lips return to mine, hushing my frantic words. His kisses are sweet and delicate, and I'll never get enough of them. "I want all of those things too, Verena."

When he pulls back to take a breath, something crucial returns to my mind. "So... Isabelle and I had a little chat this morning," I tease. "I had no idea you're such a fan of my show. She said you've watched some episodes multiple times."

I expect Adrian to play with me and give a smart response. Instead, his voice lowers with shame. "It was the only way to stay connected with you."

"You never thought to ask Tory for my number?"

"Would you have honestly spoken to me if I called?"

"Fair point."

He squeezes my hands, his eyes pleading with me. "I

don't know what else Isabelle said to you, but you have to know that I wasn't leading her on during our relationship. We were happy together for a while. You were just... always somewhere at the back of my mind. I couldn't let you go."

"She said that too."

"I'm sorry for lying to you about wanting her back."

"Don't be. We wouldn't be here if it weren't for your scheming ways."

Adrian kisses me again. "Now that I have you, I'm not letting go. I won't ever mess this up."

"What if I mess up?"

"Not gonna happen."

I peer up at him, remembering one more question that has been lingering in my mind. "There's something else Isabelle said that sparked my attention. You two broke up six months ago in August. Is it a coincidence that your breakup occurred on the same month that my breakup hit the media?"

This may be the first time I've seen Adrian blush. He rubs his lips together, then says, "Isabelle and I weren't happy at that stage. I was going to end things with her anyway, but when I heard you were no longer in a relationship... Knowing that I would have an entire week with you, single, at this wedding, it gave me the push I needed. Can you blame me?"

I shake my head and smile. "I'm glad you were fighting for us."

Someone calls my name, and the two of us turn in the direction of the voice, finding Stacy waving me toward her. "The professional bridal party photos are about to begin."

I glance around the beach, realizing the majority of guests have cleared from the area and are relocating to the cliffside restaurant for cocktail hour.

"I guess you're needed," Adrian tells me.

"I'll miss you."

His lips brush against my ear, whispering in that deep, raspy voice that always gives me chills. "Just think about our night together when we're alone after the wedding. That's what I'll be doing to pass the time."

Adrian walks backward, heading to the restaurant as he grins at me. It's an art form he's mastered—having the skill to send me from one extreme of the emotional scale to the other in only a few seconds. One moment, I'm sentimental. Then the next, hot and struggling to breathe because I'm so caught up in images of Adrian above me. *Inside* me.

I'm serious when I say this wedding can't pass fast enough.

Chapter Thirty-One

The wedding reception speeds by in a blur, mostly because I can't stop thinking about all the things I want Adrian to do to me once we're alone. I continue with my maid of honor duties, like saying a speech and helping Tory with her dress when she needs the restroom. Adrian and I partner up during the first dance, which I enjoy every moment of, being in his arms.

When the bouquet toss arrives, both brides throw their flowers into the sea of single women. I catch Tory's bouquet, and everyone cheers, Dad being the loudest, whistling with two fingers in his mouth. Across the other side of the venue, I lock eyes with Adrian, and I'm a blushing mess when he winks at me and nods.

As for Phoebe's bouquet, I'm not sure if this is the universe's way of joking around with me, but Hannah catches it. In her bikini.

So... I guess that answers my weeklong question. Hannah *doesn't* own anything other than her swimwear.

Guests continue partying in the restaurant well after

we've farewelled Tory and Phoebe and sent them to the resort's honeymoon suite, but all Adrian and I have to do is look at each other to know the wedding is over for us and we can finally be alone.

As soon as we step into our bungalow, everything falls silent between us. Our eyes linger on each other and we both ease into knowing grins.

"That dress looks really good on you," Adrian says with a husky voice.

"You better not ruin this one by throwing me in the pool."

"No, I plan to ruin it in other ways."

And just like that, I'm burning up inside, accompanied by a longing ache at the peak of my thighs.

Adrian steps up to me, running soft fingers over my arms as he murmurs, "Is it true what you said at the festival, that you've loved me your whole life?"

"Yes," I breathe, feeling goosebumps rise over my skin at his touch.

"I can't believe it's taken me twenty-five years to learn that." He scoops me into his arms, kissing me the entire way as he carries me to the bedroom—the bedroom with neat sheets once again, waiting for us to dishevel them on our last night here.

With an elbow, he flicks the lights off, and suddenly, everything feels more intense between us. It's like the world has disappeared, leaving only me and Adrian in existence. I can hear every breath he makes and feel every muscle of his strong arms around me.

"First time we're using this bed." Adrian lowers me onto the mattress, hovering over me on two hands.

My legs find their place around him. Sparks of desire

shoot through my body as the hard bulge in his trousers rocks against my crotch.

"I'm in no rush to fall asleep, Vee. I plan on enjoying you for the entire night."

Nothing can deter us. No secrets. No visitors knocking on the door. It's him and me and a whole night ahead of us.

Adrian removes my heels, adorning my legs with kisses as his lips travel up my thighs, sending my breath faster. I fist the bedsheets as his mouth teases between my legs, brushing over my underwear but never giving me what I'm aching for.

My fingers race to the buttons of his shirt, hurrying to undo them. I push the fabric down his shoulders, gulping back desire as the moonlight traces the contours of his firm torso. Adrian's muscles are glorious above me, flexing with every movement, making me frantic to feel him inside me.

"I need to get this dress off you," he rasps, pulling me onto his lap.

My legs fall to either side of him in a straddle. I rub up against his dick, working a desperate groan out of him while his hands fumble at the back of my dress to undo my zipper.

"The hook and eye is stuck," he says, making me laugh.

"How do you know what a hook and eye is?"

"You've mentioned it on your show."

Before I have a chance to say anything else, he rips the dress off me in one clean motion and tosses it to the ground. It's a good thing I wasn't fond of that design.

"You know," I giggle, "I could have turned around for you to get a better understanding of the hook and eye."

"Too slow." He unlatches my bra and slides my panties down. A deep growling sound escapes his throat at the sight of my naked body. "Verena..." His voice comes out in a guttural tone. "Let me get a condom."

I grab his wrist before he can climb off the bed. "Have you been tested?"

"Yes, I'm clean."

"No condom, then. I'm on the pill. I got tested after the cheating scandal and haven't been with anyone since."

His eyes turn sinister with need, as if he loves what I'm suggesting. "Are you sure you don't want to use one?"

My lips brush along his jaw, up to his ear. A shiver ripples through him at the sensation of my hot breath on his skin. "You coming inside me without a condom has always been one of my fantasies," I whisper. "I'm desperate for you to mark me as your own."

With a hiss, he has me on my back and is unbuckling his trousers. "Vee, you're going to regret saying that. I won't last a second inside you now."

I laugh, pushing down his boxers, my eyes widening as I marvel over the view of his hard length. Adrian wastes no time climbing over me again, and the two of us share a sigh of ecstasy as he pushes deep inside me.

"Fuck," he groans. The way he says that word makes me more desperate.

My legs circle tighter around him, pulling him closer. "Deeper," I beg. "Adrian, *please*."

His breath grows shallow as he pushes harder into me, then he leans back to watch his fingers slide over my ribs and cup my breasts before kissing me again. "You feel incredible. You're so beautiful. And you're all mine."

"Say that again." I'll never get tired of hearing it.

"You're all mine, Verena." Each time he enters me feels deeper than the last. "And I'm yours. I love you."

My head rolls back and I grip the sheets, his words shattering my world. He's the one that said he won't last long, but I'm right on the edge, struggling to not let go.

"You're not coming yet. I'm nowhere near done with you." He flips me over onto my knees, positioning my hands on the headboard.

The delicate muscles in my core tighten around his cock when he pushes into my wetness from behind. I've never found this position appealing with other guys. For me, it felt degrading. There was always an emotional disconnect as soon as we weren't facing each other. But Adrian's chest meets my spine, and he turns my face to his, worshiping me with kisses. I'm engulfed in flames when his right hand cups my breast, his thumb flicking over my nipple. His other hand lowers between my thighs, stroking that sweet spot on me.

The pleasure climbs in me again, and I clench the muscles in my groin, squeezing them tight until I'm gasping Adrian's name as I come.

"That's it. Let me hear you," Adrian growls. "Come on my cock." He juts into me faster, his own deep sounds escalating and his hands clutching me tighter. Adrian thrusts deep into me one last time, his breath deliciously hot on my cheek, then his muscles relax and he falls onto the bed, bringing me into a hug.

Both of our chests rise up and down with jagged breathing. "That was quite the workout," I laugh.

"I told you earlier in the week, sex is about exerting yourself, otherwise you're not doing it right."

I have *so* not been doing it right before Adrian. My head tilts up to him and I flash him an impish smile. "I don't know if I'm exerted enough. I might need round two already."

"Are you challenging me again? Because if so, I promise you'll be sorry by the morning."

My teeth sink into my lower lip, and I grin.

"All right. Challenge accepted." Adrian carries me to the shower, and we do it all over again.

I wake in Adrian's arms with his lips trailing kisses along my neck. "Good morning," he whispers in that deep, crackly voice I love. "Have a good sleep?"

"I'm not sure we did sleep."

"We got about two hours. Ready to go again?"

"Three rounds weren't enough for you?"

Adrian rolls me beneath him, the two of us already naked between the white sheets. "No number of rounds will ever be enough with you. I need to take every chance I can get. We're saying goodbye to each other in a few hours."

The harsh reality of our time coming to an end kicks in like a slap in the face. I don't want to think about it, and instead, let Adrian slide back inside me. The way we fit together is different this time. He makes love to me. We cling to each other as if we can stop time moving forward and prevent the inevitable of us boarding separate flights. When we finish, there's no banter. We lay in each other's arms, soaking up every detail of each other's body until we're forced to prepare for our departure.

I run the shower, waiting in the doorway for the water to heat. Adrian remains in bed, propped up on one forearm as he admires me, yet there's something smug about his gaze.

"What?" I ask.

He nods at my hips. "I didn't realize I was so rough with you last night. I'm... sorry?"

I look down at myself, seeing the early traces of bruising. My cheeks grow warm at the hot memories of him holding me tight while he came inside me. "That's what four rounds of Adrian Hunter does to a girl."

He rolls onto his back and laughs. "Get in the shower before I make it five."

Chapter Thirty-Two

The dreaded moment has arrived. Adrian checks out of the resort and the two of us say our goodbyes at the jetty. I hold him tight, disregarding the impatient captain who was meant to depart with this boat of guests ten minutes ago. My stomach clenches, sick with the reality that this week has come to an end and Adrian is about to leave the resort, get on a plane, and fly thousands of miles away from me.

"I don't want you to leave." My eyes scrunch shut to avoid tears. They fall down my cheeks, anyway. "Pack me in your suitcase with you."

Adrian pulls back to meet my face, frowning at my tears. He wipes them away with his thumbs and kisses my lips. "This is only goodbye for a little while. We'll see each other soon. Remember your rules—we FaceTime five times a day and send hourly texts."

His attempts to make me laugh don't work. "FaceTime isn't the same. And what if they sit you next to some beautiful woman on the plane?"

"I don't look at women the same way I look at you.

Everything is perfect between us, okay? Promise me you know that."

"But... What if I wake up and this has all been a dream? What if this isn't real and you hate me again?"

"Impossible. I've never hated you."

I hold Adrian tighter, soaking up his scent and hoping it clings to me long after he's gone. I take a mental note of how his arms feel around me and the warmth radiating from his body.

"We haven't had time to discuss our relationship," I say. "Are we one of those long-distance couples? How is this all going to work?"

"Verena," he hushes, leaning back to meet my eyes again. "Stop worrying. We'll talk about this on the phone. Everything will sort itself out. Please don't panic."

"How are you so calm about all of this?"

"I'm not. I'm just trying to be the strong one. Nothing will ruin what we have. Promise me you know that."

I nod when words fail me. Adrian pulls me into one last kiss, then he's gone, and my vision is blurred as I watch the boat take him away from me.

Instead of packing for my own departure, I spend a good hour back in my bungalow, sprawled out on the bed and feeling sorry for myself. How is it possible that a few hours ago Adrian and I were in this exact spot, making love, and now he's gone? I decide I hate the invention of time, and that whoever created it should be burned at the stake.

At midday, Darius and Zac come knocking at my bungalow. As soon as they answer the door, they see how miserable I am. I see how miserable Zac is. His eyes are red from crying. Without a word, Zac and I step into a hug to commiserate each other.

"It's over with Penny, for real," he mumbles into my neck. "She's filing for divorce."

"I'm sorry."

"No, you're not."

"Okay, I'm not. You deserve so much better. Someone who is crazy in love with you and makes you happy. Penny hasn't fit the criteria in a long time. But I am sorry for the pain you're going through. I'll be here every step of the way to help you."

He holds me closer. "Thank you."

As soon as Zac steps back, Darius ruffles my hair and drapes an arm around my shoulders. "Cheer up, kid. Let's get some lunch. I'm dying to hear all about how good Adrian is in bed."

I wipe my eyes and follow them to the restaurant. When we arrive at the buffet, Darius goes against Zac's and my wishes and makes a plate for each of us, even though we insist we're too sad to eat. Barely a minute after we sit down and I pick at my food, Tory and Phoebe take the other two seats at our table, glowing with the love and happiness of newlyweds.

"Here's the happy couple," Darius says. "How does it feel to be married?"

"Amazing." Phoebe smiles, kissing Tory's cheek.

Tory is too busy eyeing me to respond. "So, now that I can focus on something other than the wedding, how did things go between you and Adrian? Are you officially together?"

"Wait, what?" Phoebe asks. "What do you mean *officially*?"

I let Tory and Darius catch her up on the situation as I drown in my sorrows with memories of the most blissful night with Adrian.

When their explanation finishes, I add, "We had an amazing week together and a perfect night last night. He says we'll work things out, but I don't see how. He lives in London and I'm in New York. I've tried long-distance before, and it doesn't work. I want to be with him. Right now and always. We've wasted too many years apart."

"Why don't you go to him?" Zac asks. I'm surprised he's able to focus on anything other than the divorce. But that's Zac for you, always the believer in grand gestures of love. He put his heart on the line for Penny by bringing her to Australia, and it pains me that this time his grand gesture failed.

"Adrian's plane is taking off right about now. I won't make it to him in time. Even if I do, then what? He'll still have to board it, and I'm flying back to New York this afternoon."

"No, I don't mean go to him right now. I mean, go to London. You're the boss of your own company. Surely you can take time off to figure out your relationship with Adrian."

I stab a piece of carrot with my knife. "It was a stretch enough taking this week off. I panicked and called Darius out here, who was meant to be handling the office. Without him holding down the fort, we'll probably be returning to a shitstorm at work. I need to be back in New York."

"Oh, listen to you," Darius tsks. "You're a workaholic. I'll fix the shitstorm. You need to focus on your relationship."

"But—"

"Verena," Zac croaks, his voice thick with grief. "So what if your business suffers—which it won't—but I'm just saying. Adrian should be your priority. If you're so adamant that you're going to lose him, go after what is yours and claim it."

Phoebe waves her phone. "I just looked up flights. There's one seat available on a flight at six p.m. tonight. Should I book it? Quick, it could be gone any second."

"No need," Darius says. "You obviously didn't hear, but Verena has a private jet waiting for her."

Phoebe laughs. "Of course she does."

I gaze around the table at all four of them, finding them staring back at me in anticipation. The pressure is heavy upon me to make this spur-of-the-moment decision. Am I being too rash? I promised Adrian I wouldn't panic, and now panicking is exactly what I'm doing. These long-distance relationships always start off manageable, then spiral out of control.

"Vee, what will it be?" Darius asks, pulling me from deep within my cataclysmic thoughts.

I flinch over the nickname Darius just used. *Adrian's* name for me. Adrian and I have already destroyed things between us once. It's a miracle we found our way back to each other. Something breaks inside me, thinking that the day might arrive where we truly are unfixable. That Adrian will never call me *Vee* again.

I spring to my feet. "Darius, call the pilot. Tell him we're making a detour to London."

A playful look sits on Darius' face, making me wonder whether he called me *Vee* to get this exact response. "We? No, Verena, I've already scarred Adrian enough. Your reunion will be much hotter without me and Zac. We'll make a booking on another plane and let you have your alone time with him."

I bend down and plant ten fast kisses on his cheek.

"What would I do without you? And Zac, thank you for suggesting this plan." I wrap him in a bear hug.

Darius taps my ass. "Go and pack a suitcase—only *one*, I'll take care of the rest—and then get your ass out of here. I don't want to hear a word from you until you've sorted everything out with Adrian."

"I'll text you his address," Phoebe says.

"Thank you, all of you. And no one tell Adrian about this. I want to surprise him," I say, smooshing Tory and Phoebe with a hug before dashing to my bungalow.

It's dark when a private car service drops me in front of Adrian's London apartment. I have texts from him when his flight landed hours ago, filled with heart emojis and sweet words, telling me he's exhausted from travel and will call me when he wakes. Considering how I've been in transit for over twenty-four hours, I should be tired too, but I'm too buzzed with the anticipation of seeing Adrian for fatigue to affect me.

He lives in a block of apartments covered in snow. And here I am, freezing my ass off as I cling to a sheer blanket from my jet, dressed in summer gear beneath, because that's all I packed when leaving New York. Not the sexiest look, but it will do. At least I'm not Hannah right now, strutting around in a bikini.

With my arms clutched around myself, I walk up the driveway to Adrian's apartment building. The door opens before I reach it and a man in a trench coat rushes out, wheeling a suitcase behind him. We both pause the moment we make eye-contact.

"Adrian. Fancy seeing you here."

He breaks into a soft laugh, shaking with disbelief. "Vee, what on earth are you doing at my front door?"

"Coming to be with you. Please tell me you're not going somewhere." I nod at his luggage.

"Actually, I am. I arrived here hours ago but realized I'd flown to the wrong city. This isn't home. I've booked a flight to New York that leaves in three hours. You see, there's a girl I'm crazy about and the last time I saw her there was a sadness in her eyes that broke my heart. I need to get to her before she panics and does something foolish like break up with me before we've even started."

Tears pool in my eyes as I laugh. Adrian abandons his luggage and strides up to me, pressing his lips to mine. My head swirls from the intoxicating scent of his breath. His warmth spreads into me, and I know I'm home. Being in his arms is the only thing in this world that feels right.

"You must be cold." Adrian unbuttons his coat and wraps me inside it with him. "See, I told you there'd be more opportunities to cuddle up inside my jacket with me."

"I bet you didn't think my craziness extended this far—showing up in London out of the blue."

He chuckles. "I didn't see this one coming, but then again, I never know what I'm going to get from you."

"I'm willing to do whatever it takes to make us work, even if that means uprooting my life and moving to London."

"Too bad. I've already asked my boss to transfer me to the New York office. I'm hiring an agent to put my apartment on the market too. Our life is in America."

"You always have to one up me with the scheming, don't you?"

Adrian shakes his head. "There is no scheming this time. Only us and the truth. I'll get an apartment in New

York. We can start fresh and be together, like it was always meant to be."

"What part of you getting your own apartment is meant to sound appealing?" I tease.

"I didn't want to assume anything."

"Well, assume away. We'll buy a place together. It will be ours. We'll get married like they always said we would as kids. We'll never spend a night apart for the rest of our lives."

He kisses me again, the two of us laughing against each other's lips as snow floats down on us. The next words out of his mouth are spoken as a whisper, and he's the happiest I've ever seen him. "You are mine and I am yours, Verena Valentine."

"Always."

WANT TO READ MORE?

Sign up to my newsletter at www.skylasummers.com and receive a free copy of Chapter 18 (the first **sex scene**) from Adrian's perspective. Download the chapter from the "Bonus Content" page on my website.

FAKE DATING ZAC DELAVIN

Book 2 in the Celebrity Fake Dating Series

Fake Dating Zac Delavin is **dual POV** and steamier than book 1. It features a **grumpy/sunshine** romance with a Broadway musical setting. Follow Zac's journey as he heals from the heartbreak of his divorce and falls in love while fake dating his Broadway musical co-star. The first chapter is at the back of this book!

FAKE DATING DAXTON HAWK

Book 3 in the Celebrity Fake Dating Series

An anonymous pen pals romance

Come join my Facebook group **Skyla Summers Reader Group**. I'm also active on Instagram @authorskylasummers and TikTok @skylasummersauthor

REVIEWS AND SPREADING THE WORD

Book reviews are invaluable to an author's success. If you enjoyed this book, leaving a written review and star rating on the *Fake Dating Adrian Hunter* Amazon and Goodreads page will be much appreciated. Spreading the word via any social media platforms you may have is also greatly appreciated.

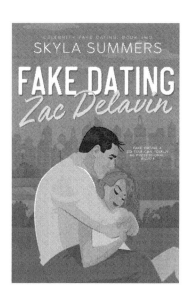

Mina has dreamed of being a Broadway star for as long as she can remember, but never did she suspect her debut would involve starring alongside the famous and handsome Zac Delavin—who is also the world's biggest jerk. Despite having a celebrity crush on Zac, Mina can't stand to be around him. But when they sing together, their on-stage chemistry is undeniable, and after leaked rehearsal footage turns viral, the public goes crazy for their relationship, believing they are in love.

Stuck in the middle of a bitter divorce resulting in huge financial loss, Zac has let his happiness slide. All his money problems will be solved if this musical is a success, and there's only one way to assure that it is: hype up the show and everyone's excitement for it by fake dating Mina. Pretending to be Mina's boyfriend can't be that difficult, not

Afterword

when she's so gorgeous and bubbly and, despite their personality clash, is the only person who makes him smile. No, the issue will be keeping his hands off Mina, because once they kiss during rehearsals, Zac is obsessed with getting her into bed.

FAKE DATING ZAC DELAVIN
Chapter 1

Mina

It's three in the afternoon when I decide to call a spade a spade: Zac Delavin has stood me up.

I'm sitting alone like a loser at Bertolo's Café in Brooklyn, with the waitstaff constantly asking me if I'm ready to order food, and me constantly saying, "I'm waiting for someone." I kept my hopes high that Zac would show up, until a minute ago when an elderly waitress gave me a sympathetic smile and said, "I don't think they're coming, sweetie."

I drink the last of my coffee, which, in hindsight, was a terrible choice of beverage for my jittery nerves. Even on my best days, with the amount of energy I have, I shouldn't be a coffee drinker.

The coffee doesn't taste great but I can see why Zac suggested we meet here. The cafe is fancy with alfresco dining that is sheltered from the sidewalk with a lattice covered in ivy. Besides me, there are three other customers here. I get it—as a celebrity who's received a lot of mixed press due to his divorce, Zac wants to meet someplace secluded where people and photographers don't swarm him. What I don't get is how he can be so rude as to stand up his future colleague. We haven't been introduced yet, and this is not a great way to start our professional relationship.

Giving Zac one last chance, I open my phone to check if he has canceled. An empty email inbox stares back at me, like all the other fifty times I've checked in the last thirty minutes. As with all those fifty times, I open our email chain to see if I've misread the date and time of our meeting.

From: Mina Midnight
Hey Zac!
This is Mina Midnight :) :) :) I'm SOOOO excited that we'll be working together!!! You are the epitome of musical theater. I cried tears of joy for an entire day when I got the call that I'd been cast as the lead female vocalist in The Velvet Cigar. This is the first lead role I've ever had, so I am going to bring my all and slay. And you as the male lead is just perfection! We're going to be amazing on stage together!

I'd love to meet you before rehearsals for the musical begin so we can get to know each other and discuss our characters. My schedule is flexible so let me know if/when you have time to meet. I can give you my phone number if it's easier to communicate that way.

Sending you my most exhilarated regards,
Mina.
Gah!!! I'm so excited!!! :)

Next, I read Zac's scroungy reply, which came a week later.

From: Zac Delavin
Monday, 2:30. Bertolo's Café in Brooklyn.
Sent from my iPhone

That's literally all he said. No friendly banter or phone number exchange. I feel like a fool for how much excitement I expressed in my email to him. I can deal with Zac's lack of enthusiasm for emojis and exclamation marks, but at least give me the curtesy of a *Hi Mina*. Then there's the super professional and elite *Sent from my iPhone*. Come on, seriously? Zac couldn't spare the two seconds it takes to delete the automated text and replace it with his name?

Calling it quits to this meeting that has flopped, I thread my arm through my purse strap and stand from my table. Pissed off, I shove my phone into my purse, not looking where I'm walking, and yelp as I smack straight into something.

Some*body*.

That somebody clutches my shoulders, steadying me from falling to the ground. When I look up at their face, of course the person is Zac Delavin. It's only natural that I embarrass myself in front of my soon-to-be colleague who is... damn... way more attractive in real life than on screen. He's more handsome than when I saw him on tour in my home country of Australia, where I stupidly bought a five hundred dollar front-row ticket to see him play Raoul in *The Phantom of the Opera* because I was a die-hard fan of his.

Zac is far more attractive than the day I performed for him during that ridiculous masterclass he hosted for fourth-year students at the Sydney Conservatorium. I swear, I will *never* get that masterclass out of my mind. Zac didn't offer me the time of day while I sang a solo. His focus had been on his phone the entire time.

But unlike those two occasions when I saw Zac in the flesh, this is the closest I've stood to him. Close enough to see each individual strand of black hair, the hazel flecks in his blue eyes, and the strength in his clean-shaven jaw. I can even smell the hypnotic scent of his woody cologne. This close up, my fangirl ways are returning, making me forget how much I don't like him and how terrible his punctuality is. More importantly, his good looks are distracting me from the one rule I made for myself upon landing this job: be professional around Zac Delavin.

I step back from his grasp to clear my thoughts. There's no greeting or smile on his behalf. No sign of recognition. Standing in front of each other right now, I'm positive he has no clue we've met before. Which, I mean, fair enough. It was over three years ago that I sang for him during the masterclass and it's not like we even spoke. He actually walked out of the room mid-way through my performance, which I've spent years trying to understand and being offended over. But I at least thought he'd recognize me from the casting photos that all production members in *The Velvet Cigar* received.

"Sorry." Even that one word out of Zac's mouth is dismissive. He straightens his suit jacket while scanning the café, not bothering to meet my eyes as he apologizes for bumping into me—if you call this an apology.

With several Tony awards under his belt and having played the lead in multiple film adaptations of musicals, Zac is arguably the most famous male vocalist in the musical theater industry. It's clear that the fame has gone to his head. Note to self: when *The Velvet Cigar* becomes a big hit and I'm famous, don't turn out to be like Zac Delavin.

"I'm late for meeting someone," he says with the tone of a goodbye.

"Yeah. Me."

Zac's gaze shoots to me, narrowing in confusion. "Mina?"

"Yep."

He studies me for another long moment, his eyes lingering on my pink hair. The pastel color is a new addition to my appearance. *Cotton-Candy*, the box dye calls it. My roommate and I dyed my hair on a whim when I got the good news about landing this gig. I'll give Zac the benefit of the doubt and assume that's why he doesn't recognize me.

"Should we get this over with?" he asks.

Wow. He certainly has a way with words. I could scold him for being thirty minutes late. I have the greatest urge to walk out on him for the inconvenience he's caused me, but this musical is the most important thing in the world to me.

Since the age of ten, I've dreamed of being the lead in a hit Broadway musical. After graduating with a Bachelor of Musical Theater three years ago, I moved to New York with a hunger to make my dream a reality. And for the past three years, I have been a chorus girl with no other purpose than to look pretty in the background. It doesn't pay the rent. Waitressing does. The biggest role I've ever landed was the side character, Rumpleteazer, in *Cats*, which is still an accomplishment, but come on, it's *Cats*. That is the most memed musical in history. *The Velvet Cigar* is a breakthrough for me.

To be honest, I'm not even sure how I got picked for this

role. I'm talented enough, I know that, but I'm a nobody in this industry. So, yeah, I want to tell Zac off for being disrespectful of my time, but I can't let my dislike for his behavior interfere with my career's success. Instead, I push down my pride and let my excitement bubble to the surface again as we take our seats opposite each other at the table.

The elderly waitress returns with a grin. "*He's* who you were waiting for?"

I look around the café, realizing everyone is staring at us. There aren't many people, considering Zac's arrival now brings the customer tally to five, but all the staff are peeking at us too.

"Can I have your autograph?" the waitress asks Zac. "My daughter loves you."

Without saying a word or even responding with a smile, he grabs a pen out of his pocket and scribbles on a napkin.

I order a cheesecake, which makes me feel ridiculous when Zac only asks for water. As soon as the waitress leaves us, Zac says, "Get used to the staring. Once a public announcement is made about *The Velvet Cigar* cast, you won't be able to go anywhere without people watching you and taking your photo. And trust me, fame is not all it's cracked up to be. You'll wish you had your privacy back, especially when details about your personal life are leaked."

Ever the mood-killer, he is.

When I first accepted my role in *The Velvet Cigar*, my agent warned me about the influx of publicity I would receive. Honestly, I'm excited about the fame. I've waited so long for this moment in my career, and I'm not shying away from it. Unlike most musicals, *The Velvet Cigar* started off as a book. Its fandom is huge, on par with *Twilight*. People are so obsessed with the romance between the characters that the book was adapted into a movie. I remember lining up for the second book's midnight release when I was seventeen. Now, the first book is becoming a musical, and I can't believe *I'm* cast as the female lead.

Ignoring Zac's negativity, I give in to my excitement, my voice climbing a full octave. "Being cast as Seraphina is the best thing that has ever happened to me."

Zac's phone *pings*.

Without excusing himself, he retrieves his phone and busies himself reading a message. His brows crease and he groans.

"Is everything all right?" I ask.

"Divorce lawyers. I'm sure you've heard all about my divorce," Zac mutters, still preoccupied with his phone. "My private life seems to be anything but private."

Yes, I am aware. For the past year, all I've seen of Zac in the media are photos of him looking hungover, and not because he's been out partying all night. Gossip sites say he's barely left his apartment and hasn't been working because he had a mental breakdown when his wife filed for divorce. I would like to have sympathy for him, but I've heard rumors he cheated on her, and that's where I draw the line.

"Look, I can only stay for twenty minutes," Zac says while texting. "What did you want to talk about?"

Jesus Christ. "The musical. Obviously."

"I'm listening."

Coming into this meeting, I had been nervous, given Zac's reputation, but psyched myself up, knowing I'm good with people. Ever since I was young, my mother has always told me I have charm and charisma. From the number of friends I have, I know my mother speaks true. But this meeting is going far worse than I had imagined. I didn't ask to meet with Zac so I could talk *at* him while he reads emails from his lawyer. We're co-stars and are supposed to be in this journey together.

"Listen, Zac." I try to be forceful with my tone, but it's an act that physically hurts and makes my insides shrivel up. I *hate* confrontation. "This musical is important to me. A job like this may be common for you but this is my chance at a breakthrough in the industry. I'd appreciate it if you could—"

My words are cut off by Zac's phone ringing. He answers the call, and a moment later he's growling into the speaker. "No. This divorce is costing me so much damn money. I want it over with *now*."

Wow, his temper went from zero to one hundred in a matter of seconds. I sit silently across from Zac like I don't exist, listening to him discuss what assets his wife will get in the divorce. It may be petty, but I thrum my fingernails on the table to give him the hint that I'm waiting.

He doesn't even notice.

After five minutes, when it's clear Zac has no intention of ending the phone conversation anytime soon, I stand from the table and head for the exit.

Zac doesn't call my name. He doesn't follow me. I can feel the blood boiling beneath my skin. What an insufferable human Zac Delavin is. And I have to work with him for the next several months of my life.

When I reach the street in front of the cafe, I come to a halt at an even worse realization. Not only do I have to work with him, but our characters in the musical are lovers. Once rehearsals begin, I'll have to spend every day *kissing* Zac Delavin.

Zac

"It's good to see you're getting back on track," Darius says, helping me box the few belongings Penny left in our apartment before she moved out.

Barely any furniture remains. It was *so* generous of her to clear this place out and leave only our wedding photos, wedding china, and all our wedding gifts, as if she thought I'd want the memorabilia. All of it is going in the trash as soon as I get it in boxes. Our nine-year marriage is something I wish I could forget about.

I shove everything from the fireplace mantel into a box. Glass photo frames shatter in the process, so I rattle the box to assure extra breakage. "I'd hardly say I'm getting back on track. This divorce is sending me broke."

"Yeah, but you're about to be working again. You didn't shave for a few months, wear anything other than a tracksuit, and barely left this apartment, so I'd say you're doing well for yourself."

Considering Darius looks like a male model with his dark hair always groomed to perfection and his wardrobe consisting only of designer suits, I know it's been a struggle for him to watch me in this slump.

On the outside, it may appear like I'm making progress. Seven months ago, Penny and I returned from the vacation in Australia that was supposed to save our marriage but had the opposite effect. And for seven months, I've been bitter and twisted inside. I'd still be doing all those things Darius mentioned if it weren't for this divorce forcing me off my ass with the need to earn money again.

Though I have die-hard fans, my public reputation has suffered tremendously since the divorce hit the media. People think *I'm* the one who cheated. My career has suffered because I've been too miserable to accept any jobs. And then when I did try to get a job, no one wanted to work with me, believing my current mental health and reputation makes me a wild card. I'm lucky to have secured the male lead in *The Velvet Cigar*, and it's only because I'm friends with one of the producers and convinced him of my dedication to the role.

"How long until your divorce is official?" Darius asks.

"Thirty-one days."

Soft laughter trickles in from the kitchen. I tilt my head to the side, peering through the doorway, and groan. Verena is sitting on the edge of my kitchen counter with her fiancé Adrian wedged between her legs, the two of them laughing between kisses.

"Stop it," Verena giggles, swatting Adrian's hands away when he grabs her ass. "Our friends are in the next room."

Adrian smirks, stroking a lock of brown hair behind Verena's ear. "They can't hear us. But fine, I'll behave. And just so you know, as soon as we get home, I'm spending the entire night fucking you."

"No complaints here." She gives him one final kiss, then slides off the counter and pours four glasses of wine.

I glance away the moment I realize they're returning to me and Darius in the living room. I should have looked away long before, not only to give them privacy, but to prevent this shit feeling of jealousy growing in my chest.

Verena and Adrian enter the room with the distance of a five-foot pole between them, pretending they're not desperate to touch each other. They put on this act for me. Darius confirmed it months ago. As Verena's personal assistant, he is constantly around her and Adrian, and he says they never stop kissing. They have no shame. So I know this whole act of not touching each other is for my benefit, to spare me the memory of being in love.

But the way they look at each other is all the reminder I need. Verena could be far across the room from Adrian, and I still catch him looking at her like he's counting down the seconds till he can be alone with her. And Verena... She's always smiling. Always stealing glances at him.

Don't get me wrong, I'm happy for Verena. She and Darius are my closest friends. I've known Adrian for seven months now—since the cursed Australian getaway we all went on—and I'm happy for him, too. He's a great guy. I just wish I could have what he and Verena have. I *did* have it once, with Penny. She was so kind and loving. My high school sweetheart. I don't understand how a person like that can turn so manipulative. You think you know someone, but you don't. I can't see how I'll ever trust another woman with my heart after Penny's cheating.

Verena passes me and Darius a wine, joining us with the packing. "It's such a shame you're moving out of this apartment. The city views are amazing."

Yeah, it's a shame. I did love this place once. I love living on the Upper East Side. And Verena is right, the glass walls are its prize feature, offering stunning city views. But I can't stay here. Not when everything about this apartment reminds me of Penny and costs the price of a kidney.

When I look at my surroundings, I'm reminded of the life I worked so hard to give Penny, but that she never appreciated any of it. I get angry whenever I walk into the bedroom, because all I can think about is how toxic Penny was and that she gaslighted me into believing *I* was the problem in our marriage. The woman who I once thought would be my forever is now nothing to me except a multimillion-dollar divorce fee. I was young and stupid when I got married and didn't sign a prenup.

"I need a new home. Some place that's mine and isn't tainted by Penny," I tell Verena while shoving more crap into boxes. "This divorce is costing me all my happiness and so much fucking money."

Verena swirls her wine. "New beginnings are good. But I'll lend you money if you're struggling. Say the amount and it will be in your bank account tomorrow."

I could say any amount and she would come through on the offer. Verena is a fashion designer with her own reality show. She's on Kardashian level of fame, with bodyguards and private jets.

"I'm not taking your money." My life savings will be flushed down the toilet and I'll be living paycheck to paycheck—a very different lifestyle from what I'm used to, but I'll survive. "Can we just... change the subject?"

"The offer is there if you need it."

Adrian assembles a box and passes it to Verena. "So, now that you're returning to semi-normality, you should join me and Darius in the gym."

I should. I used to work out a lot. But I have no motivation anymore. These days, I don't want to do anything. "I'll pass."

"Man, come on. Working out will do yourself some good. You've lost muscle definition. It will be good for your head too."

I *have* lost muscle definition. But when you're as big as I was and you lose muscle, you still have a ton of it.

"Not right now," I tell him. "I've got too much to deal with."

"Zac's right," Verena says to the other two in her

supportive voice. "He's making small changes. One step at a time is all he needs to focus on."

For fuck's sake. My friends are great, and God knows I haven't been the easiest person to be friends with in the last few months, but the pity in Verena's voice is one thing I can't handle.

"Rehearsals for *The Velvet Cigar* start in three weeks. We rehearse for six weeks. The show will open in late September." My subject change isn't the least bit subtle and an equally bad topic to mention. I cringe, thinking about how my meeting with Mina went yesterday afternoon.

"What's that look for?" Adrian asks, taping a box shut.

"I met with my co-star yesterday and—"

Darius cuts me off. "The hot one you asked for?"

"Hot one?" Verena gasps. "What hot one? Is Darius referring to a guy or girl?"

I glare at Darius, annoyed at him for steering the topic in this direction. "My female co-star. And I never said she was hot. Darius made that judgment when he asked to see a photo of her."

Verena raises a questioning brow at him. "Since when do you think women are hot?"

He holds both hands up by his chest, surrendering. "Hey, just because I'm into men doesn't mean I can't gauge a girl's attractiveness." Very few people know Darius is gay. Only his closest friends. "Verena, she is sex on legs. Zac, you need to sleep with her."

"Dammit, Darius," I groan. "Do you have any idea how unprofessional that would be? Not to mention, I'm getting divorced."

"Which means your cock needs someone to play with it."

"Verena, make him stop."

She laughs, placing more of my belongings in a box. "I kind of agree with Darius."

"Same," Adrian says. "When was the last time you had good sex? No, scratch the good part. Sex in general."

The depressing thing is I don't know the answer to either of those questions. "Mina is not my type. And she's young. Twenty-four, I think. There's like a six-year age gap between us."

"Six years is nothing," Verena says. "Let me see a photo of her."

"I'm not in the mood for this conversation."

"Show me a photo, then I'll drop the topic."

Knowing how persistent she is, I choose my battles and give in, opening my emails on my phone. I bring up a photo of Mina on the casting list and pass it to Verena.

Her eyes light up and a suggestive smile spreads across her lips. "Not your type, huh? Zac, this girl is everyone's type. I'm questioning my own sexuality looking at her. And you asked for her?"

I roll my eyes. "It's not like that. My producer friend showed me the top selections for the female lead. When I saw Mina was on the list, I told them to choose her. I heard her sing a few years back and her voice has stuck in my mind ever since. She's incredible."

Verena's smile grows wider. "Well, Mina is gorgeous. And you're going to kiss her."

"My God, it's like talking to a schoolgirl with you. Obviously I have to kiss her for the musical. But that had nothing to do with the decision. And besides, there is no chemistry between us. I didn't leave the greatest impression on her. I actually think working with Mina is going to be a challenge."

"Message her and make amends," Adrian says, winking at Verena.

They smile at each other, no doubt remembering how they were on no-speaking terms for seven years before they fixed their relationship during our vacation to Australia. The vacation where Penny asked for a divorce. Ugh... *everything* reminds me of her. To make matters worse, I have to return to Australia in a few months, to the exact island in the Whitsundays where my marriage ended, because Verena and Adrian decided it's the perfect location for them to tie the knot.

Darius tilts his head back to finish his wine, then rests the glass on the fireplace mantel. "Can we back up a minute and get to important details? Zac, you said you'll be kissing Mina."

"As actors," I explain.

"What kind of kissing are we talking about?"

Acknowledgments

I am so grateful for my husband's support of my passion for writing. Without him, this book wouldn't be in your hands.

To my good friend Karen who has been with me every step of the way during writing this book, thank you for all of your encouragement, for listening to me rant almost every day about my imposter syndrome, and for being such a great friend.

Thank you to my critique partners, beta readers, and ARC reviewers. Thank you to my editor who went above and beyond her job.

I want to thank myself. To quote Snoop Dogg: "I want to thank me for believing in me. I want to thank me for doing all this hard work. I wanna thank me for having no days off. I wanna thank me for never quitting."

Lastly, I would like to thank *you* for reading this book. I would be no where without my readers. If you enjoyed this book and would like to support me as an author, please spread the word of this novel.

About the Author

Skyla Summers is an Australian author who lives with her husband and daughter in the sunny state of Queensland. Like many others, she fell in love with reading as a teen girl when discovering the likes of Edward Cullen and was convinced that book boyfriends were better than the real deal. When she was in her early 20s, she began her career as a music teacher in a small country town where she felt isolated from society, and it was here where she found her passion for writing. Before long, writing became her whole world, and she realized her true joy in life came from storytelling and making characters fall in love. Skyla loves hearing from her readers. If you enjoy her work, you can message her at www.skylasummers.com or find her on social media at the links below.

tiktok.com/@skylasummersauthor
instagram.com/authorskylasummers

Printed in Poland
by Amazon Fulfillment
Poland Sp. z o.o., Wrocław